The Three Books of

THE JASPARD FAMILY
CHRONICLE

The General
The Fortunate Adventure
The Bristol Cousins

THE GENERAL

D. A. Ponsonby

London

WHITE LION PUBLISHERS LIMITED

D.A. Ponsonby
THE GENERAL

© Copyright, D.A. Ponsonby, 1950

First published in the United Kingdom by
Hutchinson & Co. (Publishers) Ltd., as the
first part of *Family of Jaspard*, 1950

First published in this White Lion edition, 1971

ISBN 85617 660 5

Published by
White Lion Publishers Limited
91/93 Baker Street
London W1
and printed in Spain
by Euredit

CHAPTER I

IN THE GREY ROOM

Two problems persistently, if intermittently, fretted the minds of those of the Jaspard brothers and sisters who came between Delia, the eldest, and Jacky and Dorothy, still in the nursery.

The one that allowed the greatest scope for speculation was the identity of the mother of Barney and Fan, a pair who, though they were politely called cousins to the world, were well known both there and at home to have the same father as the legitimate Jaspards.

Barney and Fan themselves chose to believe their mother had been a Court beauty, possibly even allied to Royalty; at the very least a fine lady in the land. Though Fan's astonishing beauty, her clear skin, her aristocratic features might support this theory, it was somewhat let down by Barney's blunt nose and wide mouth, which hinted a more ordinary heritage. All of beauty that he had lay in his dark eyes, oddly flecked with green, large and nearly as thickly lashed as his sister's.

The other problem was a less disreputable one, but seemed as little likely to be solved, since the only person who could so easily have allayed the curiosity of her brothers and sisters did not choose to do so.

Ten or eleven years ago Delia Jaspard had been a lively, happy girl; now she was a crabbed, humourless woman. Though still three years short of thirty, she already appeared to twenty-two-year-old Creswell, no less than to the others, as a middle-aged spinster without thought or hope of matrimony.

Delia had missed, even in girlhood, the Jaspard good looks, and though content would probably have rounded her face to matronly comeliness, instead it was thin and sallow; and the long, well-bred Jaspard nose appeared, with the graved lines running to the mouth, bony and high-ridged. The only clue her juniors had to this metamorphosis—a change as it seemed to them as much against nature as if a butterfly were to turn into a chrysalis—was a remembrance, not very distinct, that a certain tutor, a Mr. Sylvester, teaching the nine- and ten-year-old Barney and Stephen had disappeared abruptly from the family circle, and thereafter Delia came no more to the schoolroom to listen to the boys' lessons or, in their playtime, to romp with them and their little sisters, Kitty and Fan.

But, after all, other tutors besides Mr. Sylvester had come and gone. And it might have been only chance that Delia, at a certain time, had elected to be grown-up and disdain the childish pastimes of the school-room. In all reason—so thought the young and untried Jaspards—even had there been a tenderness between Delia and the tutor, no disappoint-ment at seventeen years old could have so lasting an effect, so that it was as if her heart and mind, instead of her eyes, had beheld the Medusa's head, and they alone been petrified from that hour forward.

Barbara, the next in age to Delia, a mere year younger, should have been able to enlighten the others at least as to whether or not there had been a disastrous love-affair in Delia's life; but she had married almost immediately afterwards, and gone to live far away in Northumberland.

On the very few occasions when her brothers and sisters saw her, it was never in such circumstances as made it possible for any of them to broach a subject which—as they had learned from addressing their mother on the same matter—was one forbidden to be spoken of.

As for Creswell's being of any help, he had been away at school during Mr. Sylvester's time, and could be expected to know even less of him or of Delia than his younger brothers.

On this January morning in the year 1720, Delia, with Stephen, Barney, Kitty and Fan, was sitting in the big room on the second floor, known on account of its hangings as the Grey Room; and which had been given over to the younger members of the family in this brand-new house in Hanover Square, whither Mr. Jaspard had recently removed from a less fashionable quarter further eastward. Building was not yet finished in the Square, and through the closed window came the faint tapping of hammer on stone and the subdued call of men's voices.

Delia, without raising her eyes from the embroidered firescreen she was working, and in tones as sour as old milk, was saying to Barney:

"You have always known you are different from the others. Why should you grumble then, because you cannot go to the University or upon a Continental tour?"

The young man whom she addressed and who was leaning against the wall close to the window, scowled more darkly, but did not answer.

The difference she had spoken of was not confined only to the matter under discussion: it was to be seen also in his dress. His suit, though it was of fine cloth, was dark in shade where Stephen's was light; the skirts of his coat stuck out less arrogantly, and the lace at his neck and shirt-cuffs was not so plenteous; the stockings rolled over the knees of his breeches were of fine wool and not of silk.

The reason for this lack of ostentation was, as who should know better than himself, because his clothes had been chosen for him with a view to their suitability for one who was not a gentleman at large, but a secretary or even a clerk.

But it was by his own choice that he wore his natural hair powdered and fastened behind with a narrow black ribbon, instead of having a shaven poll and a tie-wig as had his brothers. Mr. Jaspard would have spared him seven guineas for that adornment, had he wished it.

Stephen, who had been sketching on a scrap of paper in a casual and unconcentrating fashion, now threw down his pencil and sighed with purposeful loudness. He was not one to quarrel, but his eldest sister exasperated him as no one else could do with her deliberately tormenting remarks, her constant peevish ill-humour. It was not chance but malice that directed her to taunt Barney about his birth; it pleased her to flick at his extreme sensitiveness on that point.

"At all events," he said, after a short but noticeable silence, and by way of consoling Barney: "I am going only for eight months, and merely to Paris, Hanover and The Hague. Creswell's tour did not bring him home for the better part of two years, and he was half over Italy too, which is where I should like to go above all places."

"Eight months are better than none," answered Barney sulkily, "and when they are over you will step into a place at Court Creswell has made ready for you." He went on quickly, lest Delia should interrupt him with an obvious retort: "I should not mind so much if I could be secretary to another gentleman as I have been to Mr. Osborn these two years. But to be sent to live in lodgings and be a paltry clerk in the Office of Trade and Plantations, that is too much."

"Then what about me?" The shrillness of Fan's tone was in disagreeable contrast to her perfect face. "At least you have something to do. You will meet people, and when you are not working you will be far more independent than when you were Mr. Osborn's secretary and lived here. How would you like to be me, who just sits at home, and does not even go to the dances and routs which Kitty attends?"

"Neither Papa nor Mamma can *force* people to invite you to their houses." Delia's clipped words fell clear and with intent to wound.

"Delia! You go too far!" Stephen jumped up and eyed his sister rebukingly.

"It is true," she answered with her usual sinister calmness. "The sooner Fan learns she cannot expect to be received everywhere, the better it will be for her."

"You know very well I am asked," burst out Fan indignantly. "At least, quite often. It is the General who will not let me go."

It was many years now since Barney had nicknamed Mr. Jaspard the General. The name was suited to him, as he was the giver of all orders in that household, and when the children had been younger had so regimented them that he expected upon his return from any outing (provided this did not take place, as it frequently did, late at night) that his family should be in two lines by the door, bowing and curtseying to him. Even now, Jacky and Dorothy were hastily summoned by a footman if the carriage was known to be approaching.

But his martial severity was not the prime reason for Barney dubbing him with a name convenient to be used in the schoolroom. He was, officially and for form's sake, supposed to call his father by the title of Uncle. This, since he could just remember a time when Mr. Jaspard was Papa to him, he refused to do. He addressed his father to his face invariably as "sir", and in conversation referred to him either as the General or Mr. Jaspard, according to his company.

The nickname had been adopted by all Mr. Jaspard's elder children, with the exception of Delia, who would not condescend even to that level of amiability. But whatever Delia's crankiness, one and all of the Jaspards knew they need keep no guard upon their tongues when speaking of their father in her presence. She could be counted upon to repeat nothing they said, however rebellious or disrespectful. For Delia hated her father. The others, though unable to love him, tolerated his despotism and admired him for his handsomeness of person and his exquisiteness in dress. Even his known life of gallantry had taken on something of the aura of the legendary feats of a classical hero: not perhaps to be emulated, but too remote and stately to be condemned.

The General was certainly whimsical in his treatment of Fan. It was true she received invitations along with Kitty, except from a few eminently aristocratic and respectable hostesses who did not choose to be deceived by the professed avuncular relationship, and who cared not a whit should they irritate the Hon. Robert Jaspard. But he, for his part, would not permit Fan to go much in public. For one thing he considered it proper to draw a definite line between his natural children and his heirs legal; for another, Fan was too pretty, and he had not decided yet to whom he should marry her. Kitty, though a year younger, must be disposed of first.

Had Mrs. Jaspard had her way, Fan would not have gone even to the few parties for which her father allowed her to accept invitations.

"Assemblies are wasted upon Kitty in any event," went on Fan. "She does not care what she wears, and her hair is untidy five minutes after she has come from her maid. Look at her now, with her fingers in it, and she has ink on her thumb."

As she spoke, Fan preened herself. Her hand went caressingly to her well-groomed, rich black hair; she adjusted a ringlet on her shoulder and gave herself a little shake, like a bird that has just done smoothing its plumage, while her large, thickly-lashed eyes of a blue that was in arresting contrast to the darkness of her hair and their own lashes looked round the company as if to say: You see how Kitty is not to be compared with me.

Fan, indeed, unlike her brother, was not restricted in her dress, only in her entertainments. But then, she was neither secretary nor clerk and—whenever it might be that the General pleased it—she must become the wife of some gentleman worthy to take even an illegitimate Jaspard to his bed and board.

Kitty, who all this time had been bent over a book as far away from the others as she could get, looked up and glared at her half-sister. She was certainly untidy. The corsage of her dress was crooked, the billowing material over her hoop twisted into untidy ruches, not neatly and straightly laid as were her sisters'; her hair appeared as if she had recently risen from bed, and ink had wandered to more parts of her person than Fan had remarked upon.

"I wouldn't be you," she said, "thinking only of a ribbon or a lace every day of my life. I like reading, and why should I not? Though, to be sure, it is hard enough to get a moment in this house to do so."

She had a pretty, soft voice, but now there was a defensive note in it. This was because all the family, even sympathetic Stephen who wrote poetry when nobody was by, viewed with varying degrees of disfavour her propensity for books. The term "bluestocking" had not been invented yet by nearly forty years, but if it had Kitty would have embraced the title proudly.

"Read in your bedroom," said Fan. "Why should we stop talking for you?"

"It is too cold, and you know the General won't let a fire be lit before four o'clock."

The quarrelsomeness of the girls' tones had nothing to do with the subject of which they were speaking. For a fortnight now they had been declared enemies, and neither reading nor vanity in dress was concerned.

A young Lieutenant of Foot Guards, Mr. Carlton Stafford, had been paying his attentions to Kitty, whom he had first met at one of those assemblies to which Fan had not been invited. He had little money in his own hand, but since he was great-nephew and heir to an elderly Viscount, Mr. Jaspard had permitted and encouraged his subsequent calls. During one of these, and upon an occasion when Mr. and Mrs. Jaspard chanced to be from home, Fan had contrived to appear upon the scene. With Fan that was enough. Her lovely face and person were not her only weapons: she had in plenty those indefinable wiles which subjugate a man. Complete victory, however, could not be said to be hers. Kitty's lack of neatness may have become more apparen to Mr. Stafford, and her pretty but not markedly beautiful features faded into insignificance; but the solid fact remained that she was the daughter of the Hon. Robert Jaspard, who might expect to become Earl of Manvington at his elder brother's death, and would bring to her marriage a dowry of £4,000. Fan, however fascinating, had the drawback of her birth, which was not to be got over, and for all the cautious and impecunious Mr. Stafford knew, she would not be granted a dowry more than her wedding clothes. So he continued to call in Hanover Square, ostensibly to see Kitty and really in the hopes of furthering a discreet flirtation with Fan.

Now Delia glanced at the tall grandfather clock with the three gleaming balls upon its case-head, and began gathering up her silks. Everyone in the room knew that it must be exactly half past eleven. One could set one's watch by Delia's movements. Her days, as uneventful as a prisoner's, were as rigorously, if more variously, parcelled out. She had a certain hour for reading, whether the news-sheet or some book heavy in content, perhaps sermons or an historical memoir of the late reign; another hour for needlework; one for walking; needlework again; one for driving out with her mother; and so on through the day. This was the hour for her morning walk. With a footman behind her, she would go down Prince's Street, and so in a few yards reach the fields adjoining Hyde Park; or, by way of a change, go across the Tyburn Road and into the open country north of it. Always she returned home exactly three quarters of an hour after she had set out. It happened that sometimes she wished to do some shopping, and then her airing might be extended by a half-hour. On those occasions she usually requested Kitty to accompany her.

"I hope you will come with me," she now said to her younger sister, in tones a shade more agreeable than she had yet used. "I wish to match a ribbon for Mamma's new evening cloak."

"Oh—I cannot this morning," answered Kitty in the hurried voice of one who expects to be persuaded against her will. "Miss Dale said she hoped to call towards noon."

"I see. Miss Dale naturally comes before your sister. Her friendship for you does *you* no good, let me tell you. It might be as well for you to have a friend three years older than yourself if she did not encourage you in this nonsense of poring over useless and uninformative books——"

"One reads to please the senses as well as to be informed," retorted Kitty grandly.

"Fiddle-de-dee! Poetry is of no use to a woman. If you had your nose in a cookery book, that would be another matter."

"Why? I certainly hope I shall never have to cook for myself."

"A good housewife should at least know how those things are done."

"I am sure Mamma doesn't. Anyway, it is not only poetry I read, and many of my books are informative. For instance, only yesterday I was reading how the Isle of Dogs got its name, and I'm sure you couldn't tell me that."

"It is hardly important, and I cannot waste time arguing with you."

"No, indeed, you will be one minute late in starting out if you don't hurry," put in Fan pertly.

"But it is *interesting*," said Kitty plaintively.

Delia ignored them both. As she went out of the room she said, with a glance at Stephen: "If it were not for another reason, I should not be the only one in the family who would discourage Miss Dale's visits to you, Kitty." The door closed behind her.

Colour came into Stephen's fair, handsome face. He said: "I have to go out. I—I have promised to meet a friend. It is deuced unfortunate. Pray give Miss Dale my compliments, Kitty, and tell her I am sorry I could not be at home. Though, to be sure, it is you she is coming to see."

It was to the accompaniment of laughter from Barney and Fan that, in obvious confusion, he left the room.

"The only friend he has promised to meet is himself, I'll be bound," said Barney. "That's one thing I don't envy him, at all events. Now don't take offence, Kitty. I am sure your wonderful Miss Dale is a model of propriety, brains and virtue, but to have her for a wife—Heaven spare me!"

"She is not pretty," conceded Kitty, though in a severe tone which reproved him.

"And her figure!" interrupted Fan. "She has no more, it's truth, than Barney here." She laughed vulgarly.

Kitty blushed with distress. "She can read both Latin and Greek."

"The most necessary accomplishments for a wife," said Fan witheringly. "On those recommendations I shall die an old maid, sure."

"Pretty faces become wrinkled, and then you've nothing left," said Kitty with the air of a grandmother.

"Well," said Barney judiciously, "it is no matter what Miss Dale's qualifications or disqualifications for wifehood may be. Since the General has decided upon her for Stephen's wife, he must have her, and that is all there is to it."

"She is rich," said Fan who, having no money she could call her own, was particularly interested in the possession of wealth.

"True. Stephen thinks now that he does not care about that. He is romantic like you, Kitty, and believes in love, beauty, innocence and such sweet things. But once in his hands Miss Dale's money will mean something; and like many another he may find his romance to boot—not though, I should wager, in Miss Dale herself." Barney's long lashes lifted suddenly in a way he had when he was pleased or amused. It gave quick, live charm to his ordinary face.

"She is my friend. You are not to speak that way. She is a nice person. Far nicer than you. Stephen will be very—very fortunate." Kitty was nearly in tears. Taking up her book, she ran out of the room.

Barney and Fan, the illegal members of the family, were left alone.

It might be supposed that their position as intruders would have given them a bond of deep affection. Certainly they usually took each other's part in any squabble; but their love went little deeper than this. Fan had no room in her heart for anyone but herself; and to Barney, who had lived till recently in a boys' world, all sisters were remote from his immediate interests. Besides, he was often jealous of Fan for her physical perfection. Being kept all but penniless in a well-to-do family, he had learned young to watch the world, and had seen that beauty of person is a key to power second only to wealth. If people are charmed by you, they will open doors to positions leading to fame and honour; and if, by the way, rich women can be made to love you, the path is considerably smoothed . . .

Fan said peevishly: "I do not see why you are so aggrieved at going to lodgings. I only wish I had the chance to leave this house."

"Do you indeed? To a suitable marriage, as seeing it from your point of view, I agree with you. But to a lodging-house, with a slatternly landlady, and but a skinny brace of fowls to my dinner, or salmon such as apprentices won't eat, day in, day out, is that a change for the better? Whatever may be said for the disadvantages of Hanover Square, at least I eat and drink as a gentleman should."

She pondered this. "I should not care about those things if I could only be free of everyone here. I could make my way in the world if I had but the chance, I know I could. Yet here I am, at eighteen years old, kept in the schoolroom like a puking miss because, forsooth! Kitty must be married first."

"Yet when a suitor does appear, you spoil her chances for your own vanity's sake."

Fan raised her full skirt an inch or two and swung into view a finely shaped ankle. She put her head on one side. "Mr. Stafford? I must practise my charms lest they grow rusty. It is little opportunity I have, in all conscience."

"You would flirt with anyone."

"Only anyone worth flirting with," she corrected.

"That is why you made such sheep's eyes at Mr. Folkes when he called for a charity subscription, I suppose?"

"I was merely polite to him." She smirked. "He is very well-to-do. I heard all about him from dear Gertrude Dale, who of course agreed with the General that a charity to assist bastard children was not worthy of any support. Though she veiled her terms, and referred to the babes as pledges of sin." Here Fan giggled. Her illegitimacy—a subject upon which Barney had long ago enlightened her—was no shame to her. Only its inconveniences did she deplore.

But Barney's long lips tightened. Then he said angrily: "I have no doubt the General told him a man should bring up his own children, however begotten."

"I believe he did. . . . Mr. Folkes is a dear man. And though he is quite old—how old would you say he is, Barney?"

"Forty, perhaps. Not more."

"No. He hardly looks so much. And if he is rather old, he has as straight a figure as the General, which everyone so admires and—and he is a very personable man."

"So you seemed to find him, I noticed."

"And *he* found *me* personable—at the very least." Her discordant little titter rang out.

Barney never encouraged his sister in her vanity. He merely said: "The General and he parted on bad terms, I believe?"

"Yes, indeed. He was furious with Mr. Folkes for presuming to come to him for his charity. Mr. Folkes, though he is wealthy, made his money in trade, or, to be exact, his father did; so you will understand he was hardly fit to speak to a Jaspard, let alone call at his house. *I* don't mind that money should come from trade," she added.

"Is he married?" asked Barney, giving her a quizzing look.

She made a face at him. "Yes, he is. But he and his wife do not agree. He pays her a good annuity, and she has returned to live with her mother. There are no children."

"You appear very well informed on Mr. Folkes's private life."

"I had it from Miss Dale. A friend of her uncle does business with him, and she happened to know."

"Too bad," grinned Barney. "A wife is not easily removed, even one he is not well with."

Fan did not answer. She seemed to be turning something over in her mind. Suddenly her beauty was lit with vivaciousness. Even Barney, who knew her so well, was startled by the shining of her huge blue eyes and the lovely mobility of her vivid red, unpainted lips.

"Barney!" she cried, "I shall run away from here, and keep house for you. Think what fun that would be!"

No answering enthusiasm disturbed her brother's face. "Indeed you will not. And who would be to pay for your lodgings, pray?"

"Not you, I suppose?" She blinked her eyes at him as though he, like all men, was to be charmed by her. "I would cost very little, Barney dear, and you would be better looked to than by a landlady who cares nothing for you."

"It is news to me if you are gifted with housekeeping qualities. And let me remind you that my salary, by the time I have paid for my own lodgings, will allow me the barest amount for clothes and necessaries, to say nothing of any amusement. No, I do not feel inclined to support you, Fan."

"Always money!" she cried petulantly. "If I had but some money . . ." Again pensiveness overtook her, and her face settled to the lines of a perfectly modelled statue. Presently she said: "Barney, if —if I should get some money, and ran away, you would not refuse to take me in?"

"Is it of Mr. Folkes you are thinking?" he asked with something of a sneer.

Her eyelashes flickered. "No, to be sure. But if I did—I have an idea, one you could not guess—you would let me live with you, Barney?"

"Whether I let you or not would hardly matter. If you were to run away, the first place they would look for you would be at my lodgings, and so you would very speedily be carried back to shame and bread-and-water."

"You will see. I shall not wait here growing old, while Kitty is looked at and discarded by all the eligible suitors in town. I will not. I do not see why the General should care, and Madam for certain will be glad to be rid of me."

It was by the title of "Madam" that Barney and Fan spoke always of Mrs. Jaspard, just as they used it to her face. As small children they had been daunted by her chilling manner from calling her Aunt, as their father had directed them to do.

"But the General would care," said Barney. "I am not pretending it would be on account of love, or even affection, for you. Simply, he likes to direct the lives of all his family, and does not choose that they should go their own ways."

"I know," said Fan. "But here is one of his children who does not mean to have her life arranged to suit his wishes. *I* shall prove myself a chip of the old block, and out-General him."

She looked at her brother challengingly, and he saw that behind the laughter in her eyes there was an obstinate determination. For a moment her feminine loveliness seemed to fade, and he was looking instead into the hard, uncompromising blue eyes of his father.

"What are you going to do?" he asked curiously.

"A good general," answered Fan, "does not divulge his plan of battle." She crossed to the spinet, and playing to herself, began to sing softly the old song, *Lilli Burero.*

Barney, watching her, was shaken by envy. She would, because of her great beauty, get everything she wanted out of life. . . . And he would, too. Somehow, some way, in spite of all the drawbacks. He swore this to himself, standing there in the Grey Room, with its newly-painted stucco walls, its jumbled pieces of furniture, each there because it was required nowhere else in the house. With the notes of *Lilli Burero* twisting in his mind, he made his oath.

As though she had heard his thoughts, Fan stopped singing abruptly, and swinging round, said: "Barney, what do you want out of life?"

"Amusement, pleasure, love," he answered without hesitation.

She shook her head. "You really mean money. Everything else follows after." Her voice was solemn, as of one who believes he is speaking great wisdom.

"Yes," agreed Barney, "I mean money."

"I, too. And I think I shall get it first." She went on with her singing.

CHAPTER II

ARRIVAL OF BARNEY AND FAN

As she heard the opening and closing of the front door, Mrs. Jaspard, who was seated at a small bureau in her ground-floor boudoir contemplating a list of names, glanced out of the window. Her view, dimmed though it was by gauze curtains, showed the cobbles of the Square, a corner of palings round the green in the centre, three waiting sedanchairs with their attendants, and the new bright brick of the houses opposite. But she noticed none of these. Her gaze was following the demure figure of her daughter Delia, in her sober hoop of dark blue, surmounted by a cape a few shades lighter which matched the bunching of her dress behind; and attending upon her, a few steps in the rear, a footman wearing the family livery of olive-green and silver.

It must be twenty to twelve, she reflected, and a long time to dinner yet. . . . The sight of Delia now seldom roused in her any cogitation much deeper than that. Long ago she had trained herself not to continue feeling pity or anguish for Delia. That past was past; and it was pleasant to have a daughter at home, one that would never leave her.

B

Barbara was married so young. Soon Kitty would be betrothed, and in her turn Dorothy too. Here she caught herself wishing that Fan, no daughter of hers, might also be more speedily disposed of than at present appeared probable. Yes, there was always Delia. What would she do without her, to do some small shopping errand, to pen invitations and acceptances? This list for the dinner-party was ready now. Delia could write the notes after dinner.

She was deliberating in her mind the disposition of her guests when the door opened very slowly and after a pause and some scuffling a little girl, seeming but a capped head and a pair of hands appearing out of a stiff bell-shaped blue dress, walked in. Behind her, half pushing her, came a boy about a year older.

"I saw Papa go out a half-hour back," he announced, jerking his eyebrows significantly, "and Dorothy would come too."

"You ought to be in the nursery. What is Miss Finch thinking of to allow you down?"

But Mrs. Jaspard spoke perfunctorily. She was a frail, rather tired-looking woman whose manner and voice alike were indefinite. Beauty still lingered in her cheek-bones and the pretty shape of her mouth, but round her eyes lay many fine lines, and about the column of her neck the flesh was loosening its tight, smooth hold. To these, her two youngest children, she was still supremely lovely. Where Miss Finch was plain, and clothed in material not unlike the nursery curtains, Mamma with her pink cheeks beneath grey hair and her dress and embroidered petticoat of bright and rustling satin was a queen.

"Miss Finch has a headache and went to lie down. Besides, it is the holidays, Mamma."

"Has a headache. 'Tis the holidays," cooed Dorothy in as proud a tone as though she originated the remarks instead of merely echoing them.

"Mamma! I can stand on my head. Look!" Jacky turned himself rapidly the wrong way up and waved uncertain legs in the air.

"Mercy! mind!" cried his mother.

Dorothy jigged about, clapping her hands.

"It's easy," came a muffled voice from Jacky.

"Careful, child, the vase!"

Mrs. Jaspard, startled into activity, spoke too late, and as she reached the small table that was in danger, Jacky's legs, out of his control, descended swiftly. One foot caught the edge, and the Chinese vase which had been decorating its centre slid to crash in pieces on the floor.

"Oh-h!" moaned Jacky. His face turned very red, and puckered up as though he were about to cry.

"Now what will your father say? He valued that vase."

"D-don't tell him it was I, Mamma."

"Broken! broken!" said Dorothy solemnly, and stopped dancing.

"If he asks me, dear, I must. You would not have one of the servants turned away for a fault he did not do."

Jacky pondered this. "I don't know. I should think any of our servants would not mind going to another master who did not get so angry as Papa does."

"You don't understand what you are saying," said Mrs. Jaspard, resorting to a favourite comment when her children were in need of explanations she did not feel capable of giving them. "Pick up the pieces, dear."

As he stooped to obey, Jacky asked hopefully: "Do you think Papa will notice the vase is no longer there? He might not, you know."

"I think that is unlikely," answered his mother somewhat drily.

"Mamma! What do you think?" Jacky, with the leaping inconsequence of his six years, was happily upon another subject. "Mr. Osborn gave me a whole guinea this morning, a whole gold guinea."

"Nobody gave me a guinea," said Dorothy, but without sadness.

"I hope you thanked him nicely," answered Mrs. Jaspard absently. Then her son's words sank more fully into her mind. "He gave you a guinea?" she asked in surprise.

"Yes. He came this morning to say good-bye before he goes to Holland. He is going to live in a place called The Hague. Did you know, Mamma? That is why he does not want Barney to be his sect'ry any more. He must have a sect'ry who is a Dutchman. I wonder if he gave Barney a guinea. Do you think he did, Mamma?"

"I am sure I don't know, child. What have you done with your guinea? You had best give it to me to keep for you, or you will lose it."

"Oh no, Mamma! It is safe in my money-box. I have not opened my money-box since before Christmas. I expect I have perhaps nearly four guineas in there now, Mamma. Do you think I have? In small bits of money."

He began to recite such coins as he could remember putting in during the last few weeks, and so intent was he upon his recollections, and his mother in prompting him while she played with the little girl, that none of them heard the return of Mr. Jaspard.

He came unawares into the room, where Jacky still knelt on the carpet, talking loudly, and with his hands full of the broken pieces of porcelain.

Robert Jaspard was one of those men who is best described as having a presence. He was of fine, erect build, and though now about fifty years old was still exceedingly handsome. His head was covered with a brown full-bottomed wig, and beneath this his dark blue eyes, set higher at the temples than by the nose, gleamed with nothing of age in them. His clothes were as fine as his person. The apparently negligently-tied cravat had ends of valuable Mechlin lace, and this was repeated in the long ruffles at his wrists; the dark-green coat was plentifully decorated with gold lace at the edging and the seams, and his glossy breeches made of the finest black velvet procurable.

At sight of this splendid figure who represented for him all of awe and grandeur that he knew, Jacky's words were cut off as if he had been smitten dumb. Scrambling to his feet, he made an awkward bow, with hands still burdened and spilling out the tell-tale shard. Dorothy, with a very set face, made a curtsey. Mrs. Jaspard said nervously:

"I was just talking to the children. Run along upstairs now, dears."

Mr. Jaspard could not possibly fail to observe that the Chinese vase was broken. "How did that happen?" he asked.

Though his voice was stern, it was unhurried. For, contrary to the general opinion, Robert Jaspard very seldom lost his temper. Perhaps it was only his wife who knew that his wrath was always perfectly under control, and that he ruled his family through apparent anger, because that seemed to him the most effective method. He was not, as Stephen had once remarked, concerned to be loved: only to be obeyed.

Jacky's answer to his father's question was to burst into tears. He knew that this was by far the most unhelpful line of conduct he could adopt, but, as so often before, he was quite unable to prevent himself.

"So you did it?" remarked Mr. Jaspard.

In sympathy Dorothy also began to roar.

"Have the girl removed," he commanded his wife. "Jack, I dislike cowards. You will suffer double punishment for crying without any cause."

Mrs. Jaspard picked up the wailing Dorothy and went out of the room. She knew from past experience that no interference of hers could alleviate her child's punishment, and she preferred not to see it administered.

Even before the door closed on her, Mr. Jaspard had seized Jacky and laid him across a chair; he removed one of his own shoes, and with the sole of it decisively hit the boy half a dozen times.

When he had done, he shook his ruffles out over his hands and said: "You will learn, Jack, that it never pays to be afraid. Not when you are a little boy. Still less when you are a man. I trust you will profit by this lesson, and if you are a grateful son you will later thank me for teaching it to you. Also, this room is not for you to play in, and if you had not played here the vase would not have been broken. You were telling your mother about your money, I believe, when I came in. . . . Answer, boy, answer!"

Jacky with great difficulty gulped down his tears, and rubbing at his sore flesh muttered: "Y-yes, sir."

"How much have you?"

"I don't know, sir. I haven't opened my box for a long time."

"Bring it to me after breakfast to-morrow."

"Y-yes, sir." After a long pause Jacky said, still more tremulously: "Are you—going to take all my money away, sir?"

"You shall see. Now——"

"I was saving up to—to buy a blue bridle for my pony," he blurted out.

"Go to your nursery," said Mr. Jaspard in a bored voice, "and on the way tell your mother that I wish to see her."

"Yes, sir."

The little boy went out of the room, hot with resentment against his father. Not for his beating. Not even for the probable loss of his money and therefore the coveted blue bridle. But because of that last message that his mother was to go to the boudoir. Always his father asked for her after he had been punished, and he knew that it was solely to prevent him from having the delight of her consolation, which would have made up for a great part of any punishment.

.   .   .   .   .

The Hon. Robert Jaspard had married Melissa Creswell because he fell in love with her. It happened conveniently that she was of impeccable blood and brought with her a dowry sufficient to satisfy any reasonable man. Once this propitious fact was known, Robert Jaspard's father raised no objections to the match, and probably well knew that his headstrong second son would not, even though arranged marriages were more usual than those entered into for reasons of emotion alone, be amenable to accepting a lady chosen for him by his parents.

Melissa, being very young and perfectly heart-free, responded immediately to his ardour, and indeed saw every reason to congratulate herself on being the affianced bride of the exceptionally handsome and elegant Robert Jaspard who, though a younger son, had been so fortunate as to inherit property and a considerable sum of money from his maternal grandmother, whose favourite he was.

So all augured well for the marriage. And for a year or two the pair were as blissful as any couple who have love, health, means and beauty.

Looking back, Melissa believed that it was at the birth of her second daughter her husband's attitude towards her had begun to change. He had set his heart on a son. Delia's birth was a disappointment, but one that he could bear. With Barbara's arrival he probably foresaw his wife following in the footsteps of his sister-in-law, who had already ·borne his brother, now since their father's death the Earl of Manvington, four daughters—and she was to bear him two more, and never a son. However it was, Robert Jaspard began to neglect his wife, and was frequently out till the early hours of the morning. The coming of their third child, also a girl, who was born dead, did nothing to mend matters, and by the time the heir, Creswell, appeared, he was too set in his licentious ways to wish to change them. It must be said that he continued to treat his wife with every courtesy, and gave her all she required, except his devotion. She, poor woman, having the habit of being in love with him, suffered greatly.

Another child, who was to die of smallpox when he was four, followed Creswell within the year; two years later came Stephen, and when he was three, Kitty. Since Kitty she had lost three other children in infancy before Jacky or Dorothy were born.

It was while Kitty was yet an infant that her mother made the irreparable mistake of trying to combat her husband with a feeble replica of one of his own weapons.

Being a very pretty woman, though a foolish, brainless one, she could any time in the past ten years have found gentlemen ready to console her. Perhaps it was because she knew her youth was waning and that if ever she wished to hear again a man's tender love-words she had better lay hold of the passing opportunity, that she encouraged the passion of a certain Captain Hamilton. This gentleman professed himself ardently in love with her, and told her as often as she would listen, not only that she was beautiful and the queen of his heart, but that she was shamefully ill-used by her husband. Such words are soft ointment to a nature chafed with jealousy and resentment. After a few applications she could as little resist it as Robert Jaspard could resist calling his sedan-chair of an evening and whispering to the men directions that his wife, leaning by an open window on the floor above, never succeeded in overhearing.

Robert Jaspard soon learned of the constant visits of Captain Hamilton, and though he believed it proper that he himself should do as he chose, he did not intend extending a like latitude to his wife. In short, he forbade the Captain the house. The lover was undaunted by this order, and suggested to his dear one by a letter, delivered when Jaspard had been seen to go out, that he should arrange a place of assignation. But to this bold plan Mrs. Jaspard would not agree. If she were discovered—and it seemed certain to her that she would be—not only would she have to face her husband's justifiable and terrible wrath, but also the disapprobation of all her world.

The servants being paid by Mr. Jaspard, and in perpetual fear of his severity, were unlikely to disregard his orders for the sake of their mistress. Nor indeed would Mrs. Jaspard's pride allow her to ask them to do so. She hit upon another plan. Sending a note to Hamilton's club, she told him to be on her front doorstep at precisely noon the following day. He was not to knock, and if the door did not open within two minutes he must go away again.

There was a porter constantly on duty in the hall, and at noon on the day appointed Mrs. Jaspard came down the stairs and bade the man carry some urgent order to the cook. The moment he had disappeared, she opened the street door and let in her admirer.

So far so good. But to get him out again required a similar ruse. It was not easy to be for ever sending the porter on a valid errand, and this with the fear of her husband's unexpected appearance always hovering. Yet the lovers did contrive to meet thus three times before one of the servants betrayed them to the master of the house. He returned early and surprised his wife and Hamilton together. It is true in no criminal or even indecorous circumstances, but nevertheless alone in her boudoir, and had he not already forbidden the gentleman to call? His dealings with Hamilton were brief, but of long-standing consequence for the young officer. He was ordered out of the house peremptorily, and probably considered himself lucky not to be run through with a sword then and there. More was to follow. A word to high authority in the right place (and Robert Jaspard had friends at Court in a very literal sense), and Hamilton found himself appointed for a term of five years to the bodyguard of a Governor of a distant and unhealthy island. He was in no position to refuse the post, as it was intimated to him that if he did not take it up he would be requested to resign his captain's commission. This, as Robert Jaspard very well knew, he could not afford to do.

The consequences of her folly were for Mrs. Jsapard of even longer duration.

He said very little to her at the time, for it was not his way to bluster with words. As all his children early discovered, he believed in punishment, not reproach.

Even so, it was nothing but bad luck for Mrs. Jaspard that only that week—naturally quite unknown to her—her husband had been exercised in his mind as to what he should do with his two illegitimate children. Harsh, and as it seemed without much kindness in his make-up, he was nevertheless a man with a sense of duty, and when the mother of his children proposed placing them upon the parish that she might be free to take up an advantageous offer of marriage, he could not believe it right that his own flesh and blood should be raised as paupers.

What he would have done with them, or what measures he would have taken had this rod not been to his hand to bring home to his wife the enormity of her crime, in not only receiving a lover, but flouting his orders under the very eyes of his servants and demeaning herself to the tricks of a kitchen wench to gain admittance for her gallant, there is no need to speculate.

As it was, two days later he sent a footman to summon Mrs. Jaspard to the ground-floor withdrawing-room, and there the astonished lady saw her husband with a boy of perhaps three years old standing by his side and, more extraordinary still, propped up at one end of the settee an infant wrapped in a shawl. It occurred to her afterwards that the woman she had seen leaving the house as she came downstairs, and whom she had supposed to be some sewing-woman, must have carried the baby in.

"Who are—these children, sir?" she said; and a slow suspicion made her heart beat faster and her breath come unevenly.

"Two new additions for our nursery, my love. The boy is just of an age to companion our son Stephen, and the little girl—it is a little girl, madam—may be a playmate for Kitty."

"In my nursery! These children! That—that common, horrid little boy! No, never, I say!" Her voice pitched higher.

Truth to tell, the boy was not a prepossessing child. The most noticeable thing about him was a scabby sore on the side of his long mouth. For the rest, he had a round face with hard red cheeks, and his eyes, though large and dark, were expressionless as glass as he stared hard at this angry lady who had just come into the room.

"Hush, my dear," said her husband with an assumed air of concern, "he is of an age to understand you. Besides, madam, it is of my son you speak thus slightingly."

She made a sound that was both a sigh and a groan. In it was heartbreak, anger and despair.

Mr. Jaspard went on as though he had not heard her: "He will grow a fine boy yet. He has a little cold at his mouth, that is all. And, see, what bonnier baby could you want than my daughter Frances?"

The infant, who was playing happily with a coral, was indeed a pleasure for anyone—except poor Mrs. Jaspard—to look at. Her pink and white colouring was clear and lovely, her dark hair clean and curly, her eyes, blue as sapphires, were set a little slanted in her head and so betrayed her as undoubtedly the daughter of the man looking down at her.

"Oh, the boy is called Barnabas," continued Mr. Jaspard. "He was born on St. Barnabas' Day, and his mother is religious in her way. Though I think she could not have been aware of the significance of the name. She did not, so far as I could judge, see him as a son of consolation. Indeed, she was less pleased at his appearance than a mother has a right to be." He laughed lightly, as though he had made a pleasant witticism. "Bow to your stepmamma, my dear."

The child put his leg forward and performed the little ceremony in the concentrating manner of one who has recently learned his lesson.

"Well done. Now go to her for a kiss." He pushed him forward.

Mrs. Jaspard, disgust contorting her face, retreated a few steps. Barnabas stood, apparently not the least disconcerted, midway between the two grown people, and continued to stare like a little reptile at the lady.

"Whose—children are these, sir?" Mrs. Jaspard managed to find voice to ask.

"Mine. That is enough."

"Is—is their mother dead?"

"No. She has the chance of marriage—and a deal better one than ever she had any reason to expect. A deuced pretty woman, though. But naturally she cannot take her two brats with her. Oh, you may rest easy about her. She knows their father has the children, to be sure, but she don't care a whistle for them—not now that this chance has come to her. What is more, she don't know my real name. I appeared always at her house in the character of Mr.—but no matter what. Never Jaspard, I assure you. But for my paternal care the children would be on the parish. And there I might have left 'em—or boarded 'em out with some suitable woman—had you not shown me, madam"—his voice became suddenly severe—"you have not domestic cares enough to keep you out of mischief. I can afford to raise them with ours, and here they are."

Mrs. Jaspard had gone very white as her husband laid his cards on the table, and she understood why these children were being forced upon her.

"I refuse," she said. "I absolutely refuse."

"Do you, my dear?" His eyes narrowed, giving his face in spite of his light eyes, an oddly Chinese cast. "This is my house, and I am master in it. If you endeavour to thwart me in this, I shall suggest to your mother that it is expedient you visit with her indefinitely. There is bound to be talk. . . ." He shrugged his shoulders and made a gesture with his long white hands.

His threat subdued her. She could not, as he knew, face the ignominy and loneliness of a woman who has left her husband's house as a result of her own indiscretion—and that interpretation of the affair he would put about, she had no doubt at all. That it was publicly known he was not a faithful husband would not help her. There is one morality for men; for women quite another. Once again he had defeated her.

After some further parley, Mr. Jaspard, with an air of graciousness, conceded that the children should not acknowledge him as father, but should appear to the world as his nephew and niece. This was not so much consolation to Mrs. Jaspard as it might have been, since her husband was unshakably determined his bastards should bear his own name, and obviously it was easy for anyone who cared to take the trouble to discover that the late Earl of Manvington had had only two sons, and the legal issue of Robert Jaspard's brother was accounted for. But it was a gesture towards convention which slightly allayed her humiliation.

In the meantime, the baby, tired of her coral, had begun to whimper; and the boy, leaving off his staring, had gone to her and was poking her in the chest by way of restoring her to good humour.

Mr. Jaspard called him over. "Barney," he said, "who am I?"

The child stood in front of him, his hands behind his back. "My papa, sir."

"No," said Mr. Jaspard, "I am your uncle. Your *uncle*, do you understand? This is to remind you, and so that you will not make the same mistake a second time." His hand went out and slapped him smartly across the face.

Barnabas let out a roar. When his snivelling had a little abated, and he was commanded very severely to stop, Mr. Jaspard again asked:

"Who am I, sir?"

"My—my uncle, sir," gasped the tear-stained Barney.

"Good boy. Now kiss your new aunt, and then I am going to ring the bell for someone to take you and your little sister to make the acquaintance of your—er—of your cousins. . . . Kiss the boy, if you please, Melissa."

"No," she said, though the word was hardly audible.

"Do as I tell you."

She bent forward slowly, and if she had been asked to kiss a toad her face could not have shown greater distaste and reluctance.

Barnabas felt her cold lips unmoving against his hot, wet cheek before she crossed the room, at another command from her husband, to do the same to the baby.

That was the only time in their lives she made even a pretence of kissing either Barney or Fan.

Her frigid manner never relaxed through all the years of their childhood. Only because Mr. Jaspard insisted upon it, did they come down from the nursery with the little legitimate Jaspards in that evening hour when their mother liked to have her children round her. Of the two it came more hardly to Fan to be excluded from the inner circle of love and fire-warmth, for she could not remember, as Barney did, that the lady in rustling satin who had kisses and caresses for their companions, inexplicably hated himself and his sister. Fan, wayward even as a baby, had loudly demanded her share of love, and being denied it, had crept, sobbing, back to Barney, who in these playtimes' sat always a little apart on a small stool, staring at the spade-shaped horn-book he had carried down from the nursery.

As soon as she was old enough to understand, Barney explained to her that Mr. Jaspard was really their father and that he had stolen them away from their own mother, who was beautiful as a Princess; and that they were forbidden to call him Papa lest by that means their mother should discover them. The result of this rather unfortunate and quite illogical information was that Fan, wishing to be found by her Princess-mother, went up to Mr. Jaspard and addressed him stoutly as Papa. She never did it again. Mr. Jaspard was only slightly less gentle with naughty little girls than with their brothers.

Barney, while he sat looking at his horn-book, did not see its cross or its line of letters. He was weaving tales about his mother (the reality of whom he had by now quite forgotten), seeing her as a being far more beautiful, far more loving, than Mrs. Jaspard. He never entirely lost the influence of these early images, which was the reason why even now, as a young man, he was convinced of her beauty and her nobility.

It would be a mistake, however, to suppose that Barney's and Fan's childhood had been passed in wistful sadness. Only in those hours with Mrs. Jaspard was their plight brought home to them; and as she was, in a social sense, a busy woman, they were by no means of regular occurrence. And their half-brothers and sisters accepted them with the unquestioning simplicity of childhood. If they early realized these two were treated differently from themselves, it seemed to them perfectly natural that their Mamma should not care so deeply for children not her own. For a long time that was explanation enough, and when at length they understood the reason their mother had for disliking them, the interlopers had established themselves as an integral part of the family.

Barney, indeed, was a closer brother to Stephen than the latter's own full brother, Creswell, two years older and absorbed in his own life as a Gentleman-in-Waiting at the Court of St. James. Kitty did not feel quite the same about Fan; but then, Fan in her vanity and self-sufficiency, derided her bookish, ink-stained half-sister.

CHAPTER III

STEPHEN IS JILTED

THE following morning, soon after breakfast, Barney was crossing the landing on his way to the back-stairs, which was a means of egress he frequently adopted to avoid the risk of meeting his father. It was not that he had, at least upon this occasion, any nefarious intent; but Mr. Jaspard was inclined to question any member of the family as to what he was about, and as this was Barney's last free day before becoming a clerk at the Office of Trade and Plantations he was not in a humour to be impeded.

On his way to the back-staircase he had to pass the nursery. The door was wide open, and as this was unusual he glanced inside. What he saw caused him to pause. Miss Finch, the governess, was standing in profile to him staring towards the mantelpiece; her hand, clasping a handkerchief, was at her mouth, and she was crying. She made no sound, but the tears fell fast from her eyes and her shoulders quivered. Beyond her, in a tiny chair, Dorothy sat, completely absorbed in sticking a needle trailing a long scarlet thread in and out of a square of cloth. Of Jacky there was no sign.

Barney's first impulse was to go quickly on and pretend he had seen nothing. Miss Finch, though she had been in the house several months, he hardly knew, and indeed might have passed her in the street without recognizing her. The nursery lived a secluded separate life from the rest of the family. However, he remembered that in the summer, when he had been unwell and everyone had gone out to Bartholomew Fair, she had been very kind to him; had read him the news-sheet, and given him some sweet-smelling lotion for his headache.

He moved into the doorway. "Is anything the matter?" he asked, rather stupidly in the circumstances.

Miss Finch started, but she made no effort to conceal her grief.

"I forgot the door was open," she said blankly.

Barney came in and shut it.

"Can—I do anything?" he asked awkwardly.

"It is very kind of you, Mr. Barnabas." She blew her nose and gained control of herself. "Thank you. I am afraid there is not." She glanced at Dorothy, who continued to pay attention only to her sewing. "They will think I took the money. But I didn't."

"What money?" asked Barney, puzzled.

"Have you not heard? From Jacky's money-box. He broke a vase downstairs yesterday, and Mr. Jaspard told him he must bring him his money-box after breakfast to-day. When he went to get it, he found it had been broken open."

"But why should anyone think you would have had anything to do with it? A child's money-box! How ridiculous!"

"Oh, there would be four or five guineas in it. Presents he had at Christmas, and a guinea from Mr. Osborn yesterday. It is not so silly, sir. Nobody comes into this room except the girl who does the fire and keeps it clean. I am sure she is honest, and they will believe her so. She has been in Mr. Jaspard's family five years."

"And you only six months or so. I see. But I think you do Mr. and Mrs. Jaspard an injustice. They would not condemn you without proof."

"No. No, I know they wouldn't. I was crying because—because—— Oh, Mr. Barnabas, I don't know what I should do if I was sent away from here without a character, indeed I don't. I have no one to help me to another place. No one. And—and I have no money at all."

Barney was embarrassed and could think of nothing to say. She went on talking. A little hurriedly, like one who does not know when the opportunity to speak may come her way again. And as she told him her slight tale—of how she had got her first position with Lady Manley through the influence of her godmother and had come to Mrs. Jaspard from her ladyship with an excellent character; of the death of her godmother, and how her father, a naval officer, was dead too, and her mother very delicate—while she told him her commonplace history, Barney found himself, for the first time, noticing her. Till this moment she had been merely Miss Finch the governess, not a person with an individuality of her own. Her eyes were red-rimmed from her tears, and her nose red, too, and pinched; but he observed that she must be much younger than he had supposed, probably no more than a year older than himself: crying had broken down her mature defences.

Her face was a pretty oval shape, and her eyes, for all the disadvantages at present imposed upon them, showed green as leaves in summer. She had a ridge of freckles across her nose; apart from this blemish, her skin was very white. It was a pity her hair was so nearly red, a shade generally agreed to be unfortunate, but if the sun were shining on it, it might take on golden tones. She would look her best in the sunlight, with her green eyes and her bright hair. . . . Her clothes, to be sure, were drab and without taste, but that was because she was a subordinate and poor. In one of Fan's or Kitty's dresses how might she not appear? True, her figure was not as robust as he himself liked to see, but that was a matter of taste. Many men might think it trim enough if it were encased in low-cut silk instead of decorous cloth. In the circumstances, however, it remained undesirable. Miss Finch was not attractive because she lacked the opportunity to be so and also, he suspected, because nobody had ever told her that she was. . . . Miss Finch. A stiff, remote name.

"What is your name—if I may ask?"

This unexpected query following upon an apparently sympathetic nod as she spoke of her mother's frailty, not only surprised, but abashed, Miss Finch. It is not flattering to find that the member of a household in which you have lived for six months does not know wha, you are called.

"Er—Finch. Miss Finch."

"Yes, yes. I meant your first name. I am sorry if you think I am presumptuous. It is simply that I can see a person more wholly if I know what they are called in their own family. Do you not feel the same?"

"I never thought about it, sir. My name is—Carola."

"Carola. That is an unusual version."

"Yes. My father named me after a ship he was in at the time of my birth. It was his first command, and I was his first child. He was—very proud of us both."

"You have brothers and sisters?"

"No. I had two brothers, but they died as infants."

"Yes, to be sure. You said you were alone."

Miss Finch's manner, that in the last few minutes had been natural and young, changed suddenly. She said with some stiffness:

"I must apologize, sir, for wearying you with my troubles. It has been very kind of you to be so patient."

"Not at all," he answered, and regretted the words because, though he had not meant them so, they sounded condescending. He added: "Please do not worry about the money. Mr. Jaspard can have no reason to suspect you."

"No," she said doubtfully. "I dare say I am stupid and hysterical."

He wished he could say he would go to the General and tell him that of course Miss Finch had nothing whatever to do with Jacky's loss. But even Miss Finch, he knew, would not suppose that anyone could dictate to the master of the house what views he was to hold. So he said, merely: "Don't be unhappy about it. You shall see."

Moved by curiosity as to how she would receive it rather than by any emotion, as he spoke he laid his hand upon Miss Finch's and pressed it.

Her chin went a little up, and she moved herself and her hand away with a dignity that made him feel snubbed. He watched her, as she bent over Dorothy, her back to him. He was unreasonably angry, and his mind pounded out two questions. Such questions as he did not often allow himself to ask, but sometimes they, or similar ones, took him unawares, slashing the light of his normal life with ugly dark streaks. *Does she know I'm a bastard, and does she despise me for it? If Stephen or Creswell had held her hand, would she have drawn it away so readily?*

Without saying another word to her, and thus by his mannerlessness putting her in her place as a servant, he left the room.

Now he thought no more of going down the back-staircase. It might be interesting to see what was happening in the front of the house if the General was on the trail of a robber of money-boxes.

The curving stairs, flanked by the intricately wrought iron balusters, widened out into the hall. In front of him, across the black and white tiles, was the street door and the porter sitting on his small red cushion in a niche. To the left lay the library and Mrs. Jaspard's boudoir; to the right an anteroom for unimportant visitors, and the Blue Drawing Room which was used when the great reception-room on the first floor was not required. Beyond this the dining-room, a breakfast parlour and the baize door to the kitchen premises.

The door of the Blue Drawing Room was ajar, and from within came the sound of voices. Barney hesitated only a moment, then laid his hat which he had been carrying under his arm on one of the stiff-backed chairs carved with the Jaspard crest, and went in. There were several people in the room, but the General was not one of them. Mrs. Jaspard was seated on a settee near the fire; next to her, her hands for once idle, Delia. Opposite sat Miss Dale, with Kitty beside her. Apart, talking by the window, stood Stephen and Creswell.

Creswell's visits home were erratic, being ordered by what free time he might find from his duties at the Palace. He had lodgings in St. James's and came to see his parents usually once or twice in the week. But it was not common for him to be here at this hour of the morning.

Of all the family, Creswell came nearest to the handsomeness and dignity of his father. His face, taken feature by feature, was not as good-looking as Stephen's, but as to physique, where Stephen was slight and long, Creswell had with his height breadth and muscle. He was gayer, too, than his brother, whose cheerfulness, while it seldom failed him, was of a quieter and more philosophical colour.

Creswell had had many advantages since childhood. Though the General had been strict with him as with his other children, yet his position as eldest son had allowed him a certain laxity in his behaviour that was not permitted to his younger brothers. If his debts were paid with grumblings, rebukes and admonitions, yet they were paid; which was a favour greater than Stephen or Barney could hope for. It was, in short, allowable for the heir to cut a figure, to be a fine fellow in the world. In consequence of this preferential treatment and the knowledge of his own importance in the family, Creswell, quite unconsciously, was inclined to adopt towards his brothers and sisters a princely condescension. They, as certain as himself of his superiority, accepted it without protest.

Barney would probably not have stayed—at least not beyond asking some question about the stolen money—if Mrs. Jaspard had not been present. Often it gave him malicious pleasure to remain in a room with her because he knew that she always wished him out of it. Thoughts of the money-box were soon swept from his mind when Miss Dale, as he bowed to her, said:

"I am an early visitor, you see, but Creswell kindly brought me the news of Stephen's ship on his way, and insisted on bringing me with him."

"What news of Stephen's ship?"

"Oh, he hasn't heard," said Kitty. "A message came just after you had gone from breakfast that if the wind holds favourable the *Queen Anne* will sail to-night instead of to-morrow. So Stephen and Mr. Osborn must set off directly. Creswell has come up to say good-bye, and Miss Dale, too."

"Oh, I see." Barney frowned. It had been an added sore point that Stephen was making this journey he, Barney, longed to make in the company of Mr. Osborne, who had no hindrance from travelling as bear-leader for eight months before settling down to a government position at The Hague. Barney, having worked for him for two years while Stephen was enjoying himself at Oxford, felt that he might have done more than he had to persuade Mr. Jaspard to let him go too.

"Please close the door, Barnabas." Mrs. Jaspard spoke in chilling reproof. She always called him by his full name, and Frances by hers.

"It was open when I came in, madam," he answered, unnecessarily loudly. "I supposed you wished it so."

The slight shaking of Mrs. Jaspard's head and the little sigh that came from between her lips intimated that of course Barnabas was a boor, and one could not expect of him anything but boorishness.

For the next few minutes Barney found himself held in a conversation with, or, to be more exact, a monologue from Miss Dale. Though he did not much care for her, he was bound to admit that she never treated him as one in any degree inferior to either Stephen or Creswell. It was possible, certainly, that she did not know the open secret of his birth, but he felt that in any case Miss Dale would not allow it to make any difference. She was a young woman who rather too obviously practised toleration. Whatever the faults of any person or system under discussion, she would judiciously weigh them, peer at them closely, head first on one side, then on the other, before passing an opinion. Kitty, if she were by, always watched her raptly. Just now Miss Dale was discoursing not, as a less tactful person might have done, on the most interesting sights of Paris, Hanover and The Hague, or even of remedies for seasickness, but upon, of all subjects, the stupid brutality of the pillory. It appeared that she and Creswell had passed by an unfortunate in one of these machines on their way to Hanover Square. Miss Dale, though she had never studied law, had no hesitation in laying it down, and her criticism of the English penal system was not complimentary either to its compilers or those whose duty it was to put it into practice. . . . Barney began to think of Carola Finch set up in a pillory for stealing Jacky's money. . . .

Delia let Miss Dale's words fall by her like rain. As on a wet day one sometimes becomes aware of the long slow sighing of the rain, hitherto unheeded, so she sometimes heard half sentences which came to her as words rather than as sense, before she was withdrawn again into the insensibility of her lonely calculations. An unexpected episode such as this comparatively early morning gathering was such a boon to Delia as no one else could have understood. It was eating away one of those futile hours she had mapped out in order to get as speedily as might be through her jejune days. Now the hour of embroidery could be superseded by reading the news-sheet. Then she could choose whether she should do her embroidery or walk. It might be more agreeable not to go out for a change. The wind had been cold yesterday, and she was so tired of the environs of Hanover Square. It was better in the summer when they went to Gartonby, their country house in Hampshire. The walks were more varied and there were the dogs. . . .

Oh the bitter tedium of her days! So slow they went, so long, so utterly uninteresting! Only planning them, working them out to the last minute, made them bearable. How different from what might have been! Might have been. Three common words that can carry the tragedy of a lifetime, of generations. Another woman, not this Delia who still walked in the flesh, but a breathing, lively woman, the mother of children, mistress of a house, she might have been. Ten years now, and an endless avenue of so-called life stretching still before her. Papa, that cruel, proud, wicked man! Yes, she could murder him if it could give her back— In pain her mind started away. Had anyone been noticing her they would have seen her demure clasped fingers tighten till the skin glistened and the knuckles lost their blood; and the lines running from the corners of her mouth deepen in the muddy colourlessness of her face. But it was seldom anyone more than glanced at Delia. . . .

C

Over by the window, Stephen, the topic of his own affairs having been exhausted, was saying: "And what news from St. James's? Have you had any other adventures since the Schulenburg dropped some of her false hair at the Drawing Room?"

Creswell laughed. "That in the main is the extent of our adventures. By such small things are we amused. What a Court! Without a Queen, and no pretty princesses to cheer the eye. Only our plump monarch who can scarce speak English, and the long maypole of a Schulenburg and the fat Kilmansegg. 'Pon my soul! if the General would but let me, I'd go on the Prince's side to-morrow. But the old man thinks a bird in the hand . . . *I* say, when the Prince does come to the throne, where shall I be then?"

"Yes. But the General owes the King a good deal. He could not like to see you a turncoat."

"I suppose not. A fig to politics! There *is* one piece of news may make you laugh. Old Comberley's got him a girl."

"A girl!"

No wonder Stephen was astonished. Lord Comberley, who had the King's ear more than any courtier, was an austere middle-aged man who had the reputation, odd indeed so the young bloods thought, of neither drinking nor whoring.

"Yes, I believe he is still waters. These righteous fellows so often are. It is all holding up hands in horror in public, and when the door's locked upon them in their homes, God alone knows what excesses they are up to. Let me see honest, open vice any day."

"But not Comberley?"

"Comberley himself." Creswell tapped his brother on the chest with a long white finger. "He has a girl living in his house in Cleveland Court, that is a fact. What is more, my dear Stephen, a girl as desirable as a houri, as beautiful as a poet's vision. Her hair is gold as a princess's in a fairy tale, and she wears black to set it off as though she were a widow instead of a miss. Perhaps fifteen years old. Damme! I find I can't blame the old man."

"You must be mistaken. She——"

"No, no, listen," interrupted Creswell. "You would say she must be a visitor, with her mother or other female relative. But that is not so. Penge, who is sharing my waiting now, had his man make inquiries, and there is only the girl there with Comberley, and an elderly gentle-woman she brought with her. What is more, Penge, greatly daring, asked his lordship who was his charming visitor. I wish you could have seen Comberley's face. You know those queer, hooded eyelids of his, he drooped them down till he looked like some ancient eagle, and he said in his stiffest voice: 'Sir, she is none of your concern'."

"I can hardly believe it."

"I'll tell you something else." Creswell looked mischievous and his slanting eyes were bright as Puck's. "Penge has laid me a wager, and a vastly big one, too, that I will not make love to the girl. Oh, I do not need to go all lengths, but a willing kiss I must have, to win."

"You haven't taken it on?" Stephen sounded like the elder brother chiding the younger instead of the other way about.

Creswell twice nodded his head slowly.

"You are crazy! If you offend Comberley you are finished at Court. You know he can make the King do as he pleases. If you think the kiss of a trull is worth that." Stephen's voice was angry.

"I can't resist a gamble, and that's a fact. No less than 500 guineas Penge has wagered me. Like you, he thinks I have too much at stake to dare. But that's not the whole of it. I wish it was." The liveliness went out of his face. "I want to kiss the girl. I want it as much as I've ever wanted anything. Oh, she may be a trull, Stephen, but— but I'm a fool over her. I lie awake at night and think of her, of the turn of her nose and the way her breasts rise. I dream—no, I could not tell you my dreams. . . . The risk is not so very great," he went on, as Stephen continued to wear an air of elderly disapproval. "Why should his lordship ever know? 'Tis not likely *she* will tell him. Damme! I needn't be vain to suppose she might find a buss from a lusty young fellow like myself something agreeable after desiccated old Comberley, who is a bare ten years younger than the General."

"And will it be only a kiss?" asked Stephen, raising his eyebrows.

Creswell laughed slightly shamefacedly. "As to that, I take the first fence before I think of the second. I swear you to secrecy on all this, I need hardly say, Stephen."

"I'll hold my tongue. But I still think you a fool. Penge is trusting of his 500 guineas, to be sure, for I suppose you cannot kiss the girl under his nose; he must take your word for it."

"Penge knows me for a man of honour. But he can look through the window or the keyhole for all I care."

"And how do you hope to find the opportunity to be alone with this charmer? How indeed have you managed to see her at all if Comberley keeps her so close?"

"We have a scheme afoot already. We see her—the only times we have seen her—in her chair in Pall Mall. Every afternoon she goes to Pinelli for singing lessons, and the old dame follows behind." Creswell broke off. Barney, who had freed himself from Miss Dale, was approaching.

"Good day to you, young fellow. You are not plying your pen yet at the Trade and Plantations?" His manner was a mixture of cordiality and patronage.

"I start to-morrow." Barney's tone was short.

"If there is anything I can do for you. A word to Chetwynd perhaps. . . ." He spoke perfunctorily.

"Mr. Chetwynd is hardly likely to be concerned in any way with the newest clerk in the Office," answered Barney coldly.

"To be sure, to be sure. But you will not remain the newest clerk in the Office. . . . You know how he came by his post? He bribed the Kilmansegg. Several hundred guineas down and a pension of two hundred so long as he holds it. *And* those fine diamond ear-rings that she wears. As suited to her ugly head as they would be in the ears of my spaniel. But you see Chetwynd is a man to be in with." He looked at his watch. "How the time does go on! I must go. I have to be in waiting an hour after noon. Good-bye to you, Stephen, and *bon voyage*. You have those letters of introduction I wrote for you?" He grinned at Barney. "Not the sort of introductions the General will supply him with."

The brothers embraced; while Barney felt again resentment and the acute disappointment of a child that he could not share with Stephen the gaiety and the adventure of a continental tour. That Stephen was supposed to be going primarily for educational and artistic instruction was not an aspect that occurred to him. Creswell now made his farewells all round, and took his departure.

Presently Miss Dale said, addressing herself to Mrs. Jaspard: "I must get back to Mamma in half an hour. May I please, madam, have your permission to see Stephen privately for a few minutes? There is something rather important that I think he would not wish me to say in public."

At this bold, even unmaidenly, request—which was indeed perfectly characteristic of Miss Dale, who never made any bones about what she wanted—Stephen felt himself blushing. It was fortunate, he thought, that Fan was not in the room; certainly she would have tittered loudly. Even Mrs. Jaspard, accustomed as she was to Miss Dale's forthrightness, looked somewhat confused. Kitty on the other hand was thinking: How sensible and courageous she is! If she wants to see Stephen alone, why should she not say so?

"Er—yes, by all means," said Mrs. Jaspard. "Since you are affianced there can be no harm in it. Stephen, take Gertrude to the ante-room. If you will give yourself the trouble," she added to her future daughter-in-law.

Without a smile Stephen went to the door and held it open for her.

"I do not like her manners," remarked Mrs. Jaspard after the pair had gone. "We shall have to try and mend them. It comes of having no father, and a mother and an uncle she can twist round her little finger."

In the ante-room Stephen, still grave, faced Miss Dale. "Please sit down," he said. "What is it you want to say to me?"

"At least, sir, you make no pretence of wanting a lover's fond farewell to his mistress. No, I prefer to stand, thank you. What I have to say will not take long . . . You showed uncomplimentary dismay at my request to see you alone. Yet would not many affianced couples be glad of a chance to bid a tender and private farewell? It is a long, long time before I shall see you again, Stephen."

Stephen had never seen her coy before, and he was horrified. "I—I beg your pardon, madam," and the easy colour swept again into his face. "I am very honoured indeed." He made two uncertain steps towards her.

As Kitty had admitted, Gertrude Dale was not pretty. She was tall, nearly as tall as Stephen, and angular rather than rounded. Her features were not in themselves ill-formed, though her nose was long, and the line of her jaw from ear to chin too long also; her complexion was at all times over-rosy, as though she had been sitting near to a warm fire. But her hazel eyes, if one took the trouble to notice them, were very fine, and her mouth a pleasing shape and size.

"God bless my soul!" she now exclaimed in her loud, clear voice. "The man thinks I meant it. Away with you, sir! I want none of your kisses. Away, ere I scream for help!"

It was the idea of the redoubtable Gertrude screaming for help in any situation that made Stephen smile. Not relief that he did not, after all, have to bestow a kiss; because, unreasonably, he was a little piqued that she showed herself quite unwilling to receive it from him.

"You tease me," he said. "How was I to know? I have a good mind to punish you by doing it whether you will or no, and a fig for your screams!"

"Come now, we must be serious. You are going away to-day for— eight months, is it not?"

"Yes, I shall be back in the early autumn."

"I wanted to tell you before you go away that I do not intend to marry you. . . . Wait, don't speak yet. I suppose you are one of those people who feel they must make some polite remonstrance. But, to be sure, there is no need for that. This marriage was arranged between your father and my uncle, my guardian. I do not know whether you were consulted, but I was not, beyond being told that if I had a positive dislike to the idea, my uncle would not press it. I had no such dislike. We had known each other since we were children, and I am sure, Stephen, you will make an admirable husband—but not for me. I have been thinking things over. I do not want to marry. That is to say, only if I should fall in love. I am free, I thank God, of this idea that marriage is the only tolerable life for a woman. I intend to be very happy without it.

"I did not tell you of my decision sooner, as I thought it might make things difficult for you with Mr. Jaspard. I know when he has set his heart on a thing, he is much put about when it fails. Say nothing to him before you leave. After you have gone I will get my uncle to inform him I have changed my mind. Rant as your General may, there is nothing he can do to *me*, and you will be safely out of reach of his recriminations and his threats.

"That is all. And now I wish you a very good voyage, and pray do try and *learn* something while you are abroad. I envy you your tour in all conscience."

"Don't go for a minute," said Stephen, as she moved towards the door. He had been overwhelmed by her talk as by floodwater, and was still, as it were, spluttering, and trying to open his eyes upon the new scenes to which it had carried him. "But, Miss Dale, if you are doing this for my sake, I assure you——"

"For *your* sake! The vanity of it! I assure you it is for my own sake, and that only." She sounded really angry.

"I meant only," said Stephen humbly and miserably, "that perhaps you thought because I had not—not been very warm or—or kissed you that—that I did not—not want you to be my wife. That is not true, Miss Dale. I was much honoured, and——"

"Oh, let us be done with this being honoured and so forth. Why were you honoured? Over my money-bags perhaps. That is what your father has his eye on, at all events."

"Miss Dale—Gertrude—I never——" He stopped, unable to decide what to say. She broke in too quickly for him.

"No, you never yourself gave my money a thought, did you? You fell in love with my pretty face, my dainty form. Oh, yes. For the love of Heaven, sir!" and here Miss Dale stamped her foot, "let us be honest together. Our marriage was arranged. I was to give money and get a husband—an addition to female life my uncle, till I talked him out of it, considered indispensable. You were to receive the money to take for your wife a shockingly outspoken, book-brained woman with an unattractive exterior."

Stephen began to laugh. There was nothing else he could do.

"It is true," said Miss Dale challengingly. "Deny it if you can."

When he could speak he said: "In the first place—and I am *not* being merely polite—I should not have dreamed of describing you in those terms. Also, as you earlier said, it was entirely my father's idea, and you have surely visited in our family long enough to know that one must dislike a thing very much indeed to ride counter to his wishes. Personally, I am not strong-minded enough. Finally, if it *were* true, all the same I believe you would be very refreshing to be married to. I should know where I was with you, that's certain."

"You would." For a moment an odd tenderness crossed her face. "I like you, Stephen," she said. "I dare say we would not have done too badly. But I prefer it this way, and if it were not for your damnable politeness you would admit that you do, too." She was smiling again. "I like swearing occasionally. Ah me! I should have been a man. Once more, good-bye."

For some minutes after she had left him, Stephen remained in the ante-room, staring at the feeble and inhospitable fire which was considered adequate for the needs of Mr. Jaspard's toadying callers. He had not wanted to marry Gertrude Dale, but for all that he was not pleased he had been jilted by her. In spite of her dowry, he had held the typically masculine view that Miss Dale had reason to be grateful for her side of the bargain. It seemed she did not think so. It was with a still sore vanity that, instead of rejoining the others, he went upstairs to his bedroom.

On the way he overtook Jacky. The little boy's face was scarlet with joy. In his hands he carried, the reins trailing and tripping him, a pony's bright blue bridle. Mr. Jaspard, in one of his infrequent moods of benevolence, had taken his youngest son out and bought it for him.

Though these manifestations of generosity, when they occurred, astounded his children, they might have reflected that if the General had not another side to his character than that which he usually chose to display at home, he would hardly have been the irresistible lover, the sought-after man-about-town that he was.

CHAPTER IV

FAN PLANS AN ELOPEMENT

Miss Finch's fears were baseless, as Barney had told her, and though she had the ordeal of ten minutes' close questioning by Mr. Jaspard, she was not dismissed from her post. The affair of the rifled money-box blew over. It was not remembered again until the day Fan disappeared, which she did less than two weeks after Barney had left home.

Barney liked his new life as little as he had expected to. His lodgings, though good of their kind, were naturally not as comfortable as Hanover Square, and his fare and the attention he received fell far behind the style of life to which he had been accustomed. Even the independence which Fan had envied him proved rather a possibility than a reality. He had often had arduous days with Mr. Osborn, but to compensate for these there had been many free mornings or afternoons according to Mr. Osborn's inclination to go out and leave his affairs. At the Office of Trade and Plantations he was bound long hours, and when these were over had not cash enough in his pockets to enjoy the pleasures of the town. The work itself did not worry him: the letters he wrote were different only in substance from those he had written for Mr. Osborn, and the other clerical business well within his ability.

It was the drudgery, the being fettered to a desk; when Stephen was on his way to Hanover, and Creswell both in and between his duties leading the right life for a gentleman. Always richly dressed, in the company of Royalty or attending assemblies where thronged beautiful women; at other times in coffee-houses and clubs where he gamed and jested. Could he, Barney, but have gone to Court . . . His colleagues at the Office, though estimable young men enough, he saw as inferior to any who would be received in the Jaspard house. Some came of good families, but they were younger sons of younger sons; poor men, and none the company where Barney saw himself at home.

He had been commanded to dine every Sunday in Hanover Square. Coming in the first time since he had ceased to live there, he thought he noticed a shade of difference in the manner of the porter who opened the door to him, the footman who took from him his hat, his coat and his cane. It was nothing he could define: less deference by a muscle-twitch, the porter's bow not so obsequious, his coat removed with not quite the slow ceremony of former times. Or perhaps he imagined it. Yet the servants knew he was not facing the world with the same advantages as the sons of the house.

Before he went upstairs he had occasion to go through the baize door to the only house of office the mansion possessed, which was situated at the foot of the cellar steps. (It should, perhaps, be added that, for convenience and comfort, every principal bedroom had its commode).

As he was returning, he heard the flurry of skirts and saw Fan disappearing in haste into the ante-room. He was about to hail her when Mr. Jaspard came out of the library on the other side of the hall.

"Oh, there you are, Barney. Good day to ye."

Barney bowed. "Good day, sir."

Splendid as always, in a brocade coat and lavishly-embroidered, long waistcoat negligently held together by only the two central buttons, Mr. Jaspard overawed him and made him feel, in his unlaced dark red velvet coat, like a lackey before a master rather than a son (or a nephew) before his father (or his uncle).

"Have you been to church?"

"Er—no, sir."

"Pray, why not? Have I not brought you up to worship your Maker in public at least once in the week?"

"Yes, sir." Barney racked his brains to think of an acceptable excuse. None that the General would so consider was forthcoming. "I was tired, sir. I rose late."

"Tired? At your age! And what were you doing the night before to make you so tired, eh?"

Barney's resentment got the better of him. In point of fact he had spent an unexciting evening in a middling type of coffee-house with one of the young men from the Office, and had been in bed before midnight. But why should he be questioned thus, a grown man and earning his own bread? He was made bold by the swiftly following recollection that the General could hardly punish him now. He was beyond the age to be beaten, such money as he had was his own, and he could no longer be confined on a diet of bread and water. Should he be turned out of Hanover Square, he would not care. Even so, the audacity of his reply amazed him when the words were out.

"I think, sir, I may be allowed to call my evenings my own when I toil all day."

Mr. Jaspard drew from the pocket of his waistcoat a jewelled spyglass, and through this looked at Barney as though he were some objectionable and dirty puppy which had presumed to come across his path. Barney's hands clenched. He thought: I won't quail to him, I won't.

"So!" said Mr. Jaspard, returning his spy-glass to its place and shaking out his long lace cuff as he did so. "So! We grow defiant, do we? Well, a young colt will kick his heels, I dare say. But don't come running to me the first time you fall foul of a fence. And what's more, sir, whatever you may do six days out of seven, on Sundays you shall go to church."

"Yes, sir," said Barney, at the same time wondering how he could best avoid this weekly imposition.

Fortunately Mr. Jaspard did not pursue the subject.

"Be careful of the women," he said nonchalantly. "Loss of health is never made up for by the enjoyment of a minute. That is all I say. Be careful. . . . Come upstairs; my Lord Manvington and his family are here. . . . You are progressing well in your work, I hope. . . ."

Thus talking, he was compelled to accompany Mr. Jaspard and give up the idea for the present of confronting Fan. He was certain, both from the rapidity of her movement and the fact that in the ordinary way the family never used the ante-room, that Fan did not wish to be seen.

On Sundays the Jaspards invariably sat in the magnificent Reception Room which, upon the first floor, ran the whole length of the rear of the house. The conclave now gathered there, though a goodly number, looked like forgotten guests at the end of a ball, with the shining floor under three vast chandeliers stretching emptily away.

Only one of the two fireplaces held a fire, and round this, in a wide semicircle, were seated Mrs. Jaspard, Delia, Kitty, Creswell, the Earl and Countess of Manvington, their six daughters, the Ladies Amelia, Maria, Lucinda, Georgiana, Louisa and Charlotte; also Lieutenant Carlton Stafford. The latter, in his red regimental coat, stood out vividly even against the far from sombre group. He was the flamboyant poppy in a flower-bed which makes lovelier the softer blues, pinks and yellows of the lupins and the snapdragons.

Carlton Stafford was a handsome man in an arrogant way. His complexion was very dark, so that although he wore a powdered tie-wig, the blackness of his hair could be deduced from his jowl and chin which showed blue-grey beside his ruddy cheeks.

Barney followed Mr. Jaspard in, made his bows, and was soon being asked by Kitty and Creswell how he had fared during his first few days at the Office of Trade and Plantations.

Mrs. Jaspard made no attempt to listen to his description of his new life—which, indeed, with the General standing by, he portrayed as a good deal more agreeable than in fact he found it. She continued her conversation with her sister-in-law whom, although she was a Countess, she tended to patronize. Poor Lady Manvington had managed to bear only daughters, six of them, while she, Mrs. Jaspard, had three sons living, and the Earldom was all but a certainty for Mr. Jaspard or his heir.

There was an extraordinary resemblance between Lady Manvington and the Ladies Amelia, Maria, Lucinda, Georgiana, Louisa and Charlotte, none of whom had been so fortunate as to inherit the Jaspard looks. All were rather taller than average, with long, narrow, sad faces, eyes set close together and tending to redness at the rims. None was very young, as female age was considered at that time, for Lady Charlotte, the last of them, had recently had her twenty-third birthday.

Only Maria had married, and a year after her wedding her husband had been killed fighting against the rebels in the 1715 rising. They were not a lucky family matrimonially. Lady Lucinda had been promised, in desperation, to a man nearly three times her age: he died of gout in the stomach shortly before the wedding. Lady Georgiana had been betrothed too, but, regrettably, her man jilted her and ran away with a pretty young miss to be wed by a Fleet parson; as much to the wrath of his people as to the Manvingtons. But the marriage was valid and there was no undoing it.

His lordship then accepted defeat. Though his wife sometimes complained to him, he refused to try and arrange any more matches for his daughters. If anyone, he said, cared to approach him with proposals, he would consider them. But as the Ladies, though they had rank, lacked to an unusual degree charm or any sprightliness of manner, no one had yet come forward. So they were to be seen trailing behind their Mamma from one assembly to another, as alike as sheep and as little gifted with social grace. What they themselves thought of their situation and their absolute failure to establish themselves in life, no one took the trouble to ask himself. By their cousins in Hanover Square they were always referred to collectively as their ladysheeps. Creswell had coined this name long ago, and at the time the occupants of the schoolroom had rolled about with unquenchable mirth. Though now they no longer saw the feeble pun as so excruciatingly funny, the name had never been allowed to relapse.

The Earl of Manvington was, in every respect, a lesser man than his brother. Less handsome, less splendid, less able, less lavish, less voluptuous, less overbearing. Far from jealous that his younger brother should so outstrip him, he admired him with all his heart; but he did confide to his countess that he was glad he did not have to live in the same house with him.

His lordship's family seat was in Buckinghamshire, but he lived the greater part of the year in London, for he was a conscientious member of the House of Lords, and indeed his chief interest in life was centred in that noble body. He was not a brilliant speaker, but experience had given him an aptitude and a fluency that passed, among his well-wishers at least, as oratory. He himself considered that public speaking was his outstanding accomplishment.

When Barney had done answering Kitty's questions and hearing Creswell giving him advice, he noticed that Mr. Stafford had unobtrusively disappeared. He knew, as certainly as if he could see through the walls and down the stairs, that he was in the ante-room with Fan. He looked again towards Kitty, and saw that she, too, was aware of Mr. Stafford's absence. Her young, unguarded face showed misery and uncertainty. Fearful lest she might go in search of Mr. Stafford, or rather Fan, he renewed his talk with her. He was not concerned to allow Fan success of her plan—indeed, he felt angry with her for flirting with Stafford, whose attentions to Kitty were considered by everyone to be serious—but he knew Kitty must hurt herself more if she found those two together than if she could still allow doubt of their being so to console her, however slightly.

In the ante-room it was exactly as he had supposed. Fan had been prowling about the narrow space of the floor, sometimes coming to the door to listen. When she heard footsteps on the tiles, she gave her bodice a smoothing and set her face in an expression of seductiveness and welcome. She heard the steps pause, and guessed Carlton was giving the porter vails that he might not mention the rather odd fact of a guest retiring to the ante-room. When he came in, she smiled, all meltingness and invitation in her eyes.

"Dear love, no one noticed me go, I am sure. Your brother has just come, and they were talking to him. Fan! Fan, how lovely you are!" He had her in his arms and was kissing her. . . .

"Do you love me?" asked Fan presently. She was not so tidy now. Her cap was ruffled, her ringlets out of place, and the neck of her dress awry where an inquisitive hand had been feeling.

"You can ask me that?" Carlton Stafford looked at her with tender, searching brown eyes. His voice, which was deep, had a tremor when he spoke to women, which he had discovered seldom failed to move them.

"Why do you not ask me to marry you, then?" demanded Fan practically. She moved away from him, and looking into a mirror on the wall began to put herself to rights.

"If I only could!" groaned Mr. Stafford.

"Unless you have a wife already, I do not see what is to prevent you."

"Your uncle would never consent." His sentence might be said to be unfinished. What he really meant was: Your uncle would never consent to give you the dowry I hope to have with Kitty."

"Because you began by wooing Kitty—in fact, are still considered to be wooing her, and she must be married first. Is that what you mean?"

"Yes, darling. . . ."

"No, I will not kiss you again. I wish to talk. Leave go of me, sir."

"You dear little kitten . . . Let me just hold your hand. There, we can talk as well like that."

"What you say is true. I do not think my uncle would consent. So a fig for his consent! We'll be married in spite of him. You have only to find a parson from the Fleet, and the thing is done."

Her lover did not answer.

"You either want to marry me or you don't. If you do, I am showing you the way. If not, let us go upstairs."

"It is not so simple as that, dear heart."

Carlton Stafford's mind was working with the thoroughness of a hen scratching through a midden. Fan ravished him, her beauty was perfection: but—as a wife she was not to be compared with Kitty, whose birth was above conjecture, who would bring £4,000 as her dowry and, as valuable at least, would almost certainly become one day, when her father inherited the earldom, the Lady Catherine. Mr. Stafford had lived long enough in the world to know that those are solid advantages beside mere loveliness of person. And yet . . . and yet . . . How could he resist Fan? Could he not be content all the rest of his days looking at the provoking line of her nose, her slanting deep-blue eyes, the flickerings of the thick black lashes, the quick changes about her mouth as her humour changed? He thought: It is not often one speaks truth in saying one cannot take one's eyes off a person. With Fan it is absolutely true.

While the seconds ticked away and he gazed at her, his hen-mind still seeking busily for possibilities and ways out, he reviewed and rejected the question of seducing her. It would not be difficult, he was sure of that. She was hot-blooded, and when he held her close her pulses beat in tune to his. But to seduce the ward of Robert Jaspard was to bring upon oneself disaster as certainly as to stand in wartime before the mouth of a cannon. It was said about London that Mr. Jaspard had no enemies: as soon as one appeared he had him removed.

Fan began to talk rapidly. "It is quite simple. I have thought it out. It is better, perhaps, that we do not run away together, for if I was immediately missed, the General might find us before we could be married. He is more thorough than you could believe. I have a better plan. I shall disappear this week—Wednesday would be a good day, I think. That will give you time to find me some respectable lodgings. You must keep on calling here—oh, for a few days more, so that no one will suspect that you have anything to do with my running away. Then we can be married. And after that it will be too late for anyone to interfere with us."

Carlton was not so sure of the flawlessness of this plan. But Fan, as though she knew that the closeness of her person was more persuasive than any words, leant herself against him, pressing her breasts against his chest, her thighs against his thighs. His heart pounded till it seemed to shake his body.

"Dearest, how happy we shall be!" whispered Fan.

He forgot prudence, caution, honour: he was flesh against flesh; man against woman.

"My love," he said, and the tremor in his voice now was unconsidered. "My little love! We shall, we shall!"

When he was again able to be coherent, they discussed more fully the scheme. She would go on Wednesday. On Tuesday he would come to Hanover Square, but they would not speak together privately lest they should be seen. He would leave a piece of paper with the address of the lodgings she was to go to at the bottom of the vase on the chest here in the ante-room. If it were to be found by anyone else, it would seem but a forgotten, crumpled note of no significance.

"Have you some money for me?" said Fan at length, and this she asked quite without embarrassment. "I shall need some for a coach, you know, and necessaries. A few guineas will make shift for that. But when you come to me I shall require immediately enough to buy myself an outfit. I can take nothing with me from here, except a few laces and small things. For I shall have to escape when it appears I have merely gone for a walk. I will take Jenny, the maid; we will go into some shop for a purchase I will tell her to make, and while she is about it I shall slip out." She put her head on one side, calculating. "Fifty guineas, I think, at the very least."

The lover looked taken aback.

"But we will collect your clothes after we are married. We must return here and ask Mr. Jaspard's pardon. Whatever his fury, he cannot deny you your property."

"He might. Kitty will send it after me, at all events."

He wondered whether she were so insensitive as she seemed. Could she really ask Kitty, whose accredited lover she had stolen away, to pack her clothes and send them after her?

"The fifty guineas, dear. You will not forget? You want me to look nice on my wedding-day." She kissed him. "And now something for my coach fare and a little over. I cannot be penniless till you come."

"I have not—a great deal on me." His hand went slowly to the inner pocket where he kept his purse. "Have you no money at all?" he asked, and was not able to keep a note of injured surprise entirely out of his voice.

She hesitated. "A little," she said shortly, "for emergencies."

He gave her two guineas.

"I had better have more than that," she said, seeing the purse was not empty. "I can always return it to you if I do not spend it. But of all things in the world it is uncomfortable to be short."

"I am sorry, love, I cannot. I have this evening to go through and can get no more before morning." He spoke firmly, and put his purse away.

Fan put her two guineas in the pocket which was hidden between her bodice and hoop. They fell down to knock against another one and a heavy weight of silver coins.

"We must return upstairs," she said. "We have been absent full long. But not together. You go first. Send Gray into the street on some pretext or another——"

"Gray?"

"The porter. He did not see me go in, his back was turned, and he must not see me go out. You can never trust servants."

"I don't suppose he imagines I have been in here alone all this time."

"Oh, you might have been meeting one of the maids."

"A maidservant! I?"

"Why not? Do as I say. And don't come to the Reception Room for several minutes. I will go at once."

Fan's late appearance on the family scene was not in the ordinary way remarkable, as she and Barney all their lives had been inclined to avoid for as long as possible gatherings which included their father and Mrs. Jaspard. But Barney wondered, looking at her bright, excited face that he saw she was endeavouring to keep demure, whether in conjunction with Stafford's prolonged absence, someone might not think it curious.

It was Delia who asked: "Where have you been all this time, Fan?"

Fan's eyes were wide and innocent. "In my bedroom preparing a flounce. I tore it, and Jenny has gone to see her mother who is ill." The last part of the sentence was perfectly true, and Delia let the matter drop.

Ten minutes later Stafford appeared in the doorway. He came, rather slowly, over to Mr. Jaspard, and Barney heard him say: "I must beg your pardon, sir, for my unmannerly disappearance. The truth was I felt unwell and had to retire. . . . Thank you, I am recovered now, but with your permission I will leave after dinner, and not stay the evening."

"As you wish," answered Mr. Jaspard indifferently. He supposed the young man had been drinking too much the day before, and thought it of no more account than if he had grazed his finger.

Stafford then went over to Kitty, and it was to her he talked exclusively until, at three o'clock, dinner was announced.

By that time Kitty was revived like a wilting flower given water. She looked, thought Barney, sitting opposite to her, pretty and fresh. For once she was neat, and her hair and her dress in place. Since church she had had no chance to lay her hands on a book, and sitting upright in the presence of her parents and her noble uncle and aunt was not conducive to disarrangement.

But her conversation remained, unlike her Sunday trimness, true to herself. She was repeating to Mr. Stafford some views of Miss Dale on the subject of education for girls. Poor Kitty! She held a pathetic belief, gained through wrongly interpreting her conversations with Gertrude (who understood men too well to harbour such an idea of them), that at heart men liked for a life-companion a thoughtful woman who could enliven their leisure hours with intelligent conversation. With the pretty, brainless things, believed simple Kitty, they only flirted lightheartedly.

Kitty, however, took care not to mention Miss Dale by name, for that clever lady was under a heavy cloud in this house since Mr. Jaspard had been informed that she did not choose to marry his son. Kitty did not despair of seeing her friend and paragon when the General had a little recovered from his mortification, and his disgust that she should be permitted to make her own decision and overthrow a plan made by wiser heads than hers. This last, his children suspected, nettled him more than the fact that she had jilted Stephen. Mr. Dale, Gertrude's uncle and guardian, was Mr. Jaspard's close friend and club companion. It was therefore not probable that all intercourse between the families was permanently over.

To her ridiculous, pompous remarks—as they appeared to him—on the desirability of a knowledge of Latin and Greek for girls, Carlton Stafford listened with the profound attention of a lover. He nodded his head, he supported her contentions, he took his eyes from her face only so often as it was necessary for him to fill his fork and put the food into his mouth. Barney, watching him, admired so masterly a performance of double-dealing; and felt sorry for Kitty who, touchingly ingenuous, accepted it as sincere.

Further down the table Creswell was acting a part no less than the young officer. Seated next to the Lady Amelia, he was talking to her with liveliness and apparent pleasure. Yet afterwards, as Barney well knew, he would make fun of his cousin, pull his face into long folds and take her off to the life. Well, those were the social graces. Aware that he himself had been neglecting them too long, he turned to address his neighbour, the Lady Charlotte.

Dinner lasted a long time. The table, of no mean length, was crowded with dishes. Before Mr. Jaspard was a pair of geese. At the other end an enormous joint of ribs of beef. Down the sides a plate of veal cutlets, sweetbreads, a ham, vegetables and hard-boiled eggs. Only the main dishes were handed round by the olive-coated and silver-laced footmen, and the diners helped themselves indiscriminately to the side ones. When this course was removed, there were brought in a plum-pudding, an apple tart and jellies. Sherry had been served and mountain wine. At the finish everyone's colour was higher, and the quietness of repletion settled upon them.

The gentlemen did not, however, waste time over their port. The company of his brother, his sons and Mr. Stafford was not enlivening to Mr. Jaspard, and as soon as he decently could, he suggested that they move.

Lord Manvington rose reluctantly, for he liked to get through his bottle; but the younger men were not sorry to be free of the restraint of sitting in such a small company with the intimidating General. At the same time they saw this early dispersal as no compliment to themselves. The General was not of abstemious habits, and could, had he wished, have drunk them all beneath the table. Whatever quantity of liquor he himself took, he never lost his dignity. The worst that befell him was that he dropped quietly asleep in his chair. More often, the only sign that he had had his share of the mounting empty bottles was a slowing down of his movements; no longer were they so neat, precise, graceful. In short, it was very hard to tell when the Hon. Robert Jaspard was drunk.

Mr. Stafford, remembering his illness—though he had eaten as Barney had observed, a hearty dinner—excused himself. Mr. Jaspard and his brother retired to the library. Creswell declared he had to go, and asked Barney to carry a message to his mother for him: he could not face Aunt and their ladysheeps again. He contorted his face and mimicked Lady Amelia's slow, sad voice: " 'I hope His Majesty's health keeps good.' Will you believe it? She actually did say that to me by way of beginning our conversation."

"I am not going in there again," said Barney, "till it is time for me to say good night. I am going to the Grey Room. *You* tell Fan I want to see her."

"Damme! you inconsiderate dog!" said Creswell good-humouredly. "But I dare say Mamma will be grieved if I don't give her my fare-wells." He went towards the door of the Reception Room while Barney continued upstairs.

He waited for Fan a long time. But she did not come. She is too crafty, he thought. She knows I guess she has been up to something, and she don't mean to be scolded for it. At length, tired of being alone, and Miss Finch coming into his mind, he went down the passage to the nursery. He would pretend he was visiting Jacky and Dorothy.

As he entered, the two children who had restlessly been looking at Bible pictures made a rush at him. He was not particularly popular with them, but through the long tedium of a playless Sunday afternoon

D

any visitor was a diversion to be uproariously welcomed. It was some moments before he could disengage himself to give a somewhat stiff greeting to Miss Finch.

He asked her then if the mystery of the money-box had ever been solved. The question brought forth even more volubility from Jacky who, with many repetitions, and assisted by echoing words from Dorothy, gave his version of the whole affair. All that Barney could gather from it was that the thief had not been found.

Then Barney, who disliked children's chatter as much as most young bachelors when a young woman is present, had an idea.

"I will wager you one penny," he said to Jacky, "that you cannot sit without opening your mouth for the space of ten minutes."

Wagers were, from hearsay, part of life to Jacky. "Make it two pennies," he said, after consideration.

"No. You cannot do it, I know you cannot."

"Can, sir! Can."

"Me, too," said Dorothy.

"Good. Both of you. Ten minutes."

The pair sat mute, fingers clutching lips, while their shoulders wriggled, their legs waved, with the enormity of their efforts.

And for ten minutes Barney was able to talk reasonably to Miss Finch, and was gratified that she showed an interest in how he lived and in the nature of his work.

That was the beginning of many such visits to the nursery on Sunday afternoons.

CHAPTER V

CRESWELL ABDUCTS A LADY

THE light was fading out of the midwinter sky, and it was growing very cold. Creswell, standing in Pall Mall with his friend Tom Brabazon, blew on his fingers as he felt the warmth of the punch he had recently drunk stealing from him. They were pretending to hold a conversation like two acquaintances who have just met by chance, when in fact both were watching a certain house, outside which two chairs were waiting.

"She must come out soon," said Brabazon. "It is ten minutes past time already."

"It would happen Pinelli should keep her late to-night. I shan't be able to kiss her for sneezing if I stay here much longer."

` "She's coming!" exclaimed Brabazon in an excited voice.

This evening or never Creswell hoped to win the wager of 500 guineas he had made with young Lord Penge. Brabazon, to whom he had promised a fifth of it for his help, had gladly lent his brains, and many schemes these two had turned over for the temporary abduction of the young woman under Lord Comberley's protection. They had learned by now that she was called Miss Tarquin, and passed as his lordship's niece. She had to be taken on her way either to or from her singing lessons, as those were the only occasions when they could come at her. Their first idea had been to cause a commotion in the street, in the course of which, under pretence of protecting her, they would remove Miss Tarquin to a private room in one of the coffee-houses. But in this case the problem of disposing of the old gentle-woman who always accompanied her had proved beyond their wit to solve. She was bound to raise the alarm at once; and they assumed, over-hopefully perhaps, that Miss Tarquin would enjoy her hour or two away, returning unobtrusively to Cleveland Court before Lord Comberley was back from the Palace. Even should she prove unaccom-modating, she would not know any of them by name, and could not therefore denounce them. For Creswell and Tom Brabazon were not alone in this prank. Several of their friends, including Penge who had made the wager, were even now awaiting them —and Miss Tarquin—in an upstairs private room of the *Green Periwig*, in St. James's Street.

Over many bottles of wine their plan had been perfected. When Miss Tarquin left Pinelli's, which she did every day at half past four, Creswell, waiting until she was in her chair, was to step forward, bow very politely, and give her a verbal message to the effect that Lord Comberley had been excused his waiting at the Palace and desired her to follow him to the *Green Periwig*. Before she had time to consider whether the message was not a strange one, he would direct the chair-men to move on. They, knowing him by sight (but not, as he hoped, by name) as one of the gentlemen about the Court, would have no suspicion that he did not bring a genuine communication from his lordship. The waiting gentlewoman, who would have heard the message too, would then be told that she was to return to Cleveland Court. Since the duped Lord Comberley really was in waiting at the Palace and would be detained there till midnight, she would naturally assume that he was at the *Green Periwig* as she had been told, and know no uneasiness.

Though every detail had been considered as carefully as if it were strategy for a battle, Creswell was almost surprised to find that the plan did go through without a hitch. Before Miss Tarquin could question him, she was jogging on her way, while he walked beside the chair, taking care to be, though attendant, too removed for conversation.

Brabazon followed. It was his part to see the gentlewoman carried across the foot of St. James's Street and deposited unsuspectingly at Cleveland Court.

At the entrance to the dubious but well-appointed *Green Periwig*, which was tavern, coffee-house and gaming-room in one, Creswell offered his arm to the girl, then led her inside and up the stairs. In the light of the chandelier on the landing he first looked closely at his prize.

"Is my lord having supper here?" she asked.

What a minx! thought Creswell. She looks so demure in her dark dress, and innocent as she is lovely. If I didn't know better, I'd swear she was so. I wonder how long she will hold this immaculate pose?

He did not answer her question, from diplomacy, not abstraction. This lack of manners evidently surprised her, for she glanced at him, and a fine line appeared between her eyebrows.

Here Brabazon caught them up. He threw open a door directly in front of them.

A roar of male voices in shouting, laughter and cheers went up. Seven or eight young bloods were standing round a table on which stood a bowl of hot punch, the steam from it swirling upwards and giving blue veils to the candles. It was a long room, rather narrow, with the fireplace opposite the door. The main furniture was the table, covered with a stained cloth, and a few ladles and glasses scattered round the punch-bowl; chairs; and on either side, fixed against the wall, a comfortable couch upholstered in red velvet, each of the length and width of a small bed. The velvet of these and of the cushions which adorned them was a little rubbed, and the gold ornamental fringing had here and there lost some strings.

The girl gasped as she found herself upon this scene of merriment; colour poured into her face and her eyes stretched wide. She tried to back out. But Brabazon pushed her forward, and the door swiftly slammed behind her and was locked. She opened her mouth, but if she said anything it was lost in the clamour of the men. Early as it was, they were all the worse for drink.

"No one's going to hurt you, my pretty," said one voice.

" 'Fore gad! I believe the wench is really frightened. Never seen a man before, dear heart?"

"There's safety in numbers, I dare say you have heard. Nothing much can happen to you with so many of us present." Coarse laughter followed.

"Have a glass of punch," said Creswell, "and you will feel better."

He was a little ashamed of himself; unnerved at the sight of so much beauty suffering stark terror, as the girl, whatever her experience of life, undoubtedly was. To steady himself, he drank deeply of the punch before ladling some into a tumbler for her. This idea of Brabazon's of holding a party, he was thinking, was perhaps a mistake. But at the time he had suggested it, his reasoning seemed sound. "If you bring the girl to an empty room," he had said, "she will at once think you intend to lie with her, and that may alarm her so that you do not even get your kiss. These high-class trulls pretend they expect to be wooed like an honest woman."

Creswell's draught, as might be expected, did not steady him. Instead, it wiped out the pity he had been feeling and made him as foolish and truculent as his companions.

"You must drink," he said to Miss Tarquin. "You must. I command you." He had driven her on to one of the couches, where she sat, her back braced against the wall. Her hands pushed against the tumbler of overflowing punch which he was holding as near to her face as he could get it. The lap of her dark dress was blotched with darker marks where the liquor had spilled. She seemed unable to speak, or even to cry out.

"You will feel better," he repeated wheedlingly, and he truly believed what he said.

"She shall have it, she shall!" cried a boisterous, red-faced fellow. "We'll have no sobersides here, not even if she be a lady. Hold her hands, Will."

His friend did as he was bid, and the bully, who had a full tumbler in his hand, put it to Miss Tarquin's mouth, tilted her head up, and forced her to drink.

Creswell thought that he ought to stop this, it was going too far. But while his fuddled brain revolved slowly on the matter, the tumbler had been emptied.

"More, more!" cried the man called Will. "I love holding her hands, dainty, white little hands!" His speech was slurred, it was not easy to hear what he said.

"Let her alone," said Creswell, "she's mine!" His aggression vanished almost as it appeared. "I—must have another drink. Then— I'm going—to talk to her. Tell her she mustn't be frightened. Not frightened. Pretty, so pretty! A shame. . . ." Muttering, he returned to the punch-bowl.

While he was refreshing himself, the unfortunate girl was made to swallow another tumblerful. And now it seemed that Creswell's words were fulfilled. She did feel better. As he returned to her, she put her hand across her eyes and began to giggle.

"I told you it would do you good," said Creswell very solemnly. He sat down beside her and stared into her face. He was not looking his best. His eyes were bloodshot, and he had spilled punch down the white ruffles of his shirt; this dirtiness gave him as much as anything else a dissipated appearance.

His friends, drunk as they were, retreated to the table. They understood she was Jaspard's girl, and they would not interfere if he was ready now to begin his philandering. Penge, as he went, patted his pockets and smiled ruefully. "The rhino's as good as yours, Jaspard," he said with a wink.

Creswell ignored him. Still staring at Miss Tarquin, he said gravely: "You are very, very beautiful."

She giggled a second time. "I don't suppose you can see very well. I cannot. It—it is hazy in here or—I don't know. I think I am giddy. I should like another glass of that nice sweet, hot drink."

"I shouldn't have any more," said Creswell, shaking his head. He hiccupped and looked surprised.

"Why not? Everyone else is. I—*will* have some more."

"Presently I will get it for you. What is your name, beautiful one?"

"Tarquin, *you* know that. Rosalind. I am called Rosa. . . . Where *is* my uncle?"

"Somewhere," answered Creswell vaguely. "May I kiss you, Rosa?"

She drew away from him, back towards the wall. "No, no! Please."

He did not try to force her, but sighed deeply with the maudlin sadness of the intoxicated. "Some more punch, then? Yes. It has been known to make people kinder." He stumbled away from her towards the table.

An hour went by. The punch-bowl and its successor were alike empty. The young men, in varying states of noisiness or sleepiness, began to go. It was too early yet for these gay blades to wish to leave their insensible bodies in the *Green Periwig* till morning. A half hour in the streets would fan them to vigour again, and so on to a stew, if a not more respectable entertainment. Creswell, in a haze that was now more and more impenetrable by considerations of either prudence or decency, bade them a good evening and locked the door again upon himself and Rosa. He deserved a little dalliance; besides, he had yet to win his five hundred guineas. Well, Penge could hardly doubt, in the circumstances, that he would win it.

When he turned to Rosa, he saw that she had fallen fast asleep. Like an abandoned doll thrown on the couch, she lay limp and ungraceful. Her mouth, flanked by scarlet cheeks, was slightly open, and noisy breathing came from between her lips. Her cap had fallen off, and her golden hair lay in disarray on the red velvet. He bent over her; and twisted about his fingers the golden strands, stroking them, pulling them gently. She did not stir. He remembered how he had lain awake and thought about her. Not seeing her as she was now, it was true. But once in his arms she would be as desirable as in his dreams. He shook his head as though his eyes hurt him. What a fool I was, he said to himself, to drink so much . . . but 'tis early yet. I'll sleep too, awhile, and then I'll be another man. She can't escape, for I've the key.

To make certain she would not steal a march on him, he transferred it from his outer pocket to one inside his waistcoat. Then, having removed his sword, he laid himself down on the opposite couch, and almost as his head fell on the cushion, he was asleep.

.   .   .   .   .

He awoke stiff, and feeling cold. The room was nearly dark. The candles had burned down to their sockets, and only two were still flickering. In the fireplace were grey ashes and a little redness. His head was aching. Memory came back haltingly, and then at a gallop whose hoof-beats seemed physically to pound, so that he put his hands to his throbbing temples. He was sober, and he wished with all his heart that he could be drunk again.

He became aware now that the girl was awake too, and probably as sober as himself. At all events, she was crying. She was sitting on the edge of the couch, her face huddled over her knees, sobbing with a low, insistent wail. Heard in this dim, chilly room, with the two lonely candle-flames twisting, there was something so heartbreaking in the sound that he was moved as he had been moved by nothing in his life. In a second of crazy remorse he wished he could have died before he had so grieved this unhappy young girl. . . . But it was absurd, indefensible, he told himself, to feel so for a whore.

Getting up, he went over to her.

"Don't cry so, my dear."

She neither ceased her crying nor looked up. Indeed, he might never have spoken.

"I'll take you home now, and——" He stopped. She was probably terrified of meeting Lord Comberley, as well she might be. What explanation was there to give him? On his own account as well as the girl's, there was solid reason for the gravest apprehension. It must be very late. He pulled his watch from his pocket and carried it to the feeble light of the candles. As he did so, one went out. It was twenty minutes to three.

"Damnation! We'll be in the dark in a minute. You must compose yourself, Rosa. I am going to call the drawer for some candles—and a pot of coffee."

It was as if she were remote. Her odd, wailing sobs continued undiminished.

Saying oaths under his breath, Creswell fumbled for the key, unlocked the door, and going out on to the landing, bellowed for the drawer. Not till he had called two or three times did the man appear.

"Your honour calls?"

"Bring me candles quickly, and coffee for two. Make haste."

Creswell came back into the room which now, except for the red of the fire, no more than a great glow-worm, was pitch-dark.

Rosa was at last making an effort to control herself. Her sobs were intermittent, and she blew her nose several times. He did not speak to her, partly for fear of bringing on again her wild crying, but mostly because he was cudgelling his brains as to how the deuce he was going to get her back into Comberley's house without himself being discovered as responsible for her absence. Oh, the crazy, accursed fool he had been to let the punch get the better of him the way he had! Like a green, inexperienced boy. And now he was probably ruined, his Court career finished; and the General's anger to face, too. He recalled Stephen's scornful question: Was it worth it for a kiss from a trull? It was not, nor worth five hundred guineas neither. And, drunk looby that he had been, he had not so much as won his wager. She had given him no willing kiss, though he remembered that he had taken one, forcing her back against the wall. She had wriggled her head this way and that trying to avoid him, but she had drunk her punch by then and had little strength of muscle or purpose of mind left her. Gad! he and the rest had been like brutes, even to a girl of that sort.

His uncongenial reflections were interrupted by the appearance of the drawer with a three-branch candlestick which he placed upon the table.

"Will that be sufficient light, your honour?"

"Yes, yes. Where's the coffee, man?"

"Here, sir, just outside." In a moment he returned with a tray.

Creswell flung him a coin. "Keep the change."

"Thank you, your honour, thank you." He went out, bowing.

"Now, ma'am, a cup of coffee." He poured one out and brought it over to her.

She was dishevelled, and her eyes closed up with weeping. Tears had blotted out her beauty, yet there was in the motionless, desolate figure an air of grace and innocence (how ridiculous! he thought) that was appealing.

"I apologize to you," he said. "We made a vastly nasty mess of this night's work. It was to be only a harmless prank, and you should have been home before Lord Comberley missed you. What we must now consider is: what are you going to say to him?"

She did not answer at once, but drank her coffee reflectively. Then she asked a question which astonished him, so unexpected was it.

"Are you married, sir?"

"I? No. No, I have not got an angry wife to make *my* explanations to, if that is what you mean."

"Thank God!" she said, and he had just time to puzzle over her fervency on his behalf (as it appeared) when she added: "You will have to marry me."

"Marry you!" He decided to take it as a joke, and laughed.

She put down her cup carefully and stood up. "I mean it, sir. I hate you and despise you. You are a dishonourable, depraved and wicked man; but we must be married after what you have done."

"After what I've done!" he repeated, little pleased by the strongness of her abuse, although he had been willing to admit to himself that he had behaved unchivalrously. "I have done nothing," he went on with vigour. "And if I had, you have not been over-particular before to-night. Marry you indeed! There's no use your trying to dupe me, madam."

"Not—been—over-particular." She repeated the syllables slowly as though she were speaking a foreign language. Then, and with a suddenness that made him start, her voice rang out angrily. "How dare you say that to me, sir? How dare you? You took advantage of me. You told me lies to get me here. You—and your vile friends—made me—take too much to drink, and now—now you are so dastardly a villain you try to make out I am not—not—over-particular. O-oh!"

"I will beg your pardon," he said reasonably, "for using a word which seems to have upset you. Perhaps it was not quite the right one. But that you, who are under the care of Lord Comberley, should set up——"

She interrupted him. "And why should I not be under the care of his lordship? As his ward and niece——"

"Let us be done mincing matters, madam; and that I speak bluntly is your own fault. Though why you should affect such squeamishness I do not for the life of me know. The *mistress*, then, of Lord Comberley."

"The mistress? *Mistress!* Are you mad? Are you trying to drive me mad? Do you know who I am sir? Do you?"

"I do. You are Rosalind, or Rosa Tarquin, the friend of his lordship who, for convention's sake, passes in the world as his niece." Though he spoke calmly, Creswell felt his stomach queasing in fear of what he was going to hear next, a fear which outdid in magnitude and horror any of the other fears that thoughts of his meeting with Lord Comberley had harboured.

"I *am* his niece, sir. The daughter of his sister, and whoever says differently is a liar. A liar, sir!"

He saw she was too angry even to cry—or perhaps all her tears were spent. She stood very erect, her head thrown back; and her voice was as convincing as a queen's.

"Great God!" said Creswell, and because he was so overwhelmed by the enormity of his mistake, repeated blankly: "Great God!" Then he went down on one knee before her and bowed his head.

"Madam, I swear, I swear on all I hold sacred, I believed you to be —not Lord Comberley's niece—but his—but—living under his protection. I—I surely do not have to say I would never have presumed, had I known the true circumstances, to—to have behaved as I have. It was a mere prank, for a wager—oh, foolish, but young men will be foolish."

"*Why* should you have thought I was—was what you are saying?"

"We all believed it so. It was the mystery with which Lord Comberley surrounded you. You never appeared anywhere, never in the Drawing Rooms, or at the assemblies in private houses. When we asked him questions about you—for we were much struck with your beauty, madam, as we saw you coming and going in Pall Mall—he told us you were none of our concern, and his manner was so abrupt, even furtive, that—that we put that construction upon it. 'Pon my soul! it was Lord Comberley's own fault."

"Do you call it his fault he should take good care of me? Yes, he was afraid of you all for me. And the reason I never went to Court or appeared in public places was because I am in mourning. My father died recently"—he saw her hands twist and knew this was a grief had hurt her sorely—"I lost my mother some years ago. She had appointed my lord my guardian in case of my father's death. My lord was afraid the gentlemen of the Court would come around me because—because I am young and—and rich now, and he said you were all worthless, unthinking puppies, not fit for me to meet. I do not believe, though, that he could have known how very true he spoke." Her voice shook.

Creswell got to his feet. "I must take you back directly, madam. I cannot ask you to pardon me, for I see my fault is beyond pardon. . . . What are we going to say to him?" he ended on an almost childish note of desperation.

"There is only one thing that we can say to him," she answered coldly. "That you have used me as ill as a man can use a woman, but that you will make what amends you can by marrying me."

He put his hands to his aching head. "Madam," he said, speaking slowly as with difficulty he chose his words. "In—suggesting marriage you—you do me too much honour. . . . Wait, please listen."

"He will not let you avoid it," she broke out; and the digust and scorn of her tone was such that Creswell quailed as only before his father had he ever quailed.

"It is no question of avoiding it, madam. I cannot see that you can possibly wish to spend your life with me, despising me—very rightly—as you do. There is"—he floundered—"I—madam—I believe you are under a misapprehension, owing to—to the punch you had. But on my honour, there is no *need* for you to marry me."

She looked at him, and though her tear-red cheeks became redder still, her eyes did not falter. "It is true I do not remember everything that happened to-night, and I may be very young, but I am not such a baby as not to know that a man and a gentlewoman cannot spend the greater part of a night locked alone in a room without its being imperative on the man to marry her. And if he will not, her male relations shall flog him into his duty."

"Yes, madam, yes. If I had seduced you. I admit this night will take much explaining to your uncle." He groaned, and his agitated hands pushed his periwig crooked. "But this I do swear to you, madam, and would on the Holy Bible, that you are the same now as when you were brought here several hours ago. You do understand me? While you slept, I slept. That was all."

"I do not believe you," answered Rosa flatly.

Creswell, perhaps seeing himself convicted for rape by the unappeasable Lord Comberley, and so coming to the gallows, became wildly exasperated.

"But you *must* believe me. You—oh my God, madam! What am I to say to you? Do you not know that you would—would—would *feel* different. You would *know*."

"I *do* know. You kissed me. And it wasn't the way my uncle kisses me, or my father ever kissed me."

Her innocence, he saw, was more formidable than any guile or cunning.

"For the love of Heaven, madam, why should it be?" He began to pace up and down. "You don't know anything. You are an infant, a miss in the nursery."

"I know men and women do not spend the night together unless they are married. So you will have to marry me."

"But if you hate me?" He tried a new line. "Think what it will mean. Seeing me every day, ay, and every night. How will you bear it?"

"I do not expect to find any pleasure in being married to you, I can assure you, sir. It is simply a question of what is right."

"Then, I have to get my father's consent to marry. He is a man of some standing. I believe you do not know who I am——"

"I do. You are Mr. Creswell Jaspard."

He was surprised. So, even had she been the whore he supposed her, she would have had it in her power to denounce him to Lord Comberley.

"How did you know?"

"While I sit in the window in Cleveland Court my uncle points out to me all the ladies and gentlemen of the Household as they go to and from the Palace. Do you suppose, if I had not known your face, I would have gone so readily with you when you gave me that lying message? Please take me home now. We shall have to knock my poor uncle up."

Slowly, as though more time could help him, Creswell picked up his sword-belt and buckled it on, straightened his wig in front of the mirror.

"Come then." With his hand on the door-knob, he paused and gazed at her. He said gravely: "You will never believe me. I consented to this wicked joke because I was half in love with you. I wanted so much to know you. Now I am wholly in love with you——"

"It is quite unnecessary to make pretty speeches. Indeed, I find them offensive. Ours will be solely a marriage of convenience."

"Please let me finish. I am—deeply in love with you. In other circumstances it would have given me all the joy in the world to woo you and to win you. But to marry you like this, because I must, it—it breaks my heart."

"Never dare to speak to me of love. *Love*! and to have treated me so!" She walked swiftly past him and down the stairs.

The hall was now in darkness, except for a small oil-lamp. From behind a closed door came a hoarse, tired voice saying: "Seven's the main!" and the rattle of dice. Otherwise it was very silent. Only the sleepy drawer was about. He unlocked the door into the street for them, and let them out.

St. James's Street was still, too. A dark figure slipped into the alley running into Crown Court, and Creswell, his hand on his sword-hilt, guided his charge to the opposite side of the road. In Pall Mall a boy began to whistle, and the glow of his link as he lighted some reveller homeward bobbed away amid a welter of black shadows. In the Palace windows the last light went out.

It was but two minutes' walk from the *Green Periwig* to Cleveland Court. Creswell wished it had been miles. Frost was in the air, but he did not notice it. He was sweating with nervousness, and weak as a sick man from the turbulent agony of his emotions. As they reached the corner of the Court, the watch, a few minutes late, went by.

"Three o'clock of a cold, fine night, and all's well!" His steps beat loud in the silence as he went on his way.

Now they were at Lord Comberley's door, and the evil hour had come. The banging of the knocker sounded, in the quiet night, of dreadful portent.

CHAPTER VI

BARNEY MAKES EASY MONEY

AT the moment when Creswell was lifting Lord Comberley's knocker, Barney lay wakeful in bed in his lodgings in Beckford Court, between Tower Street and Thames Street.

He had come in but twenty minutes since and, late though the hour was, his mind was too exalted for him to think of sleeping.

He was in love. For the first time in his life madly, deeply in love. Till now he had never much considered women; nor had he often had the opportunity while living in Hanover Square to visit such haunts as a young fellow of his age might be expected to choose for an evening's entertainment. The deprivation had not bothered him, for on the very few occasions when he and Stephen, prompted both of them less by desire than adolescent notions of what it was proper for them to do, had made a night of it, he had been less entertained than abashed. His passion, thus developing late, came upon him with the more violence.

Lucy Brook was the sister of a man he had met one night in a coffee-house in the Haymarket. Barney had been flattered when the gentleman with whom he had got into casual conversation had invited him to his home. This new acquaintance would have been handsome in a rough, virile manner if at some time or other his nose had not been broken. It had mended badly, and lay with a twist which gave his face a slanting, devilish look. His dress was sumptuous, and the gold lace on the coat, the Brussels lace at his throat and hanging over his hands, were even more lavish than Barney was accustomed to see adorning the person of the General. In fact, he suspected that the General would consider him garish. He was not, for all his affectation of splendour and the lordly way he threw his guineas about, quite the sort of gentleman who would be received in Mr. Jaspard's house. But Barney was here in full agreement with Fan: wealth in friendship was as much to be desired as breeding.

He promised to call at his home the following evening, and then it was that he met Lucy. Lucy was dark and thin—too thin, Barney thought at first—and not remarkably pretty, except for her very large brown eyes which were more expressive than any eyes he had ever seen, even Fan's. Her manner was at once vivacious and friendly, so that everyone who came into her presence was set at ease in a moment.

That had been five days ago, and he had seen her twice since. But it was only this evening that the sorcery of her attractiveness had fully worked upon him. Perhaps it had been strengthened by the realization, which had not come to him earlier, that Miss Brook might not be entirely unobtainable. Certainly, her manner with men was very free. Every glance from her eyes that were like brown pansies, every gesture of her olive, graceful hand, contained a half-promise. However it was, he was lost, captivated, her slave (as he foolishly believed) for ever.

The Brook household had done nothing to allay his suspicions that the family was not a gentle one. Harry, Lucy's brother, was the master of the house; for Mrs. Brook, their mother, if she were not a widow had mislaid her husband. It cannot be said that she appeared to feel this as any loss. She was a surprisingly young-looking woman with a sprightliness that was only just behind her daughter's; and a certain Mr. Raikes stood in the position of constant companion and admirer. Even excluding this somewhat raffish middle-aged cavalier, the little family was never seen by Barney to be alone. On each occasion that he had visited the house there had been present three or four young men besides himself. On this evening two jolly girls had also made up the company, but he had an idea that Mrs. Brook and Lucy were not much in the habit of entertaining female visitors.

The young men were less showy than Harry, though their dress, Barney imagined, was as expensive as they could make it. He himself felt insignificant in his untrimmed velvet and meagre lace. All these men had a certain similarity of expression which puzzled him. They were lean-faced, with quick-moving eyes, and had a trick of becoming for a second immovable when a door slammed outside.

Only one did he succeed in dissociating from the others. He was more often at Lucy's elbow, a wild, rakish fellow intimately called Dick by everybody, and indeed Barney never caught his surname. Early on he saw, with a good deal of gratification, that Dick was jealous of any notice Lucy bestowed upon himself; and with her suggestive eyes and gestures she was not inclined to pay solitary attention to any one of her visitors. He would glower when Barney came into the room, and when he was called upon by Harry (who seemed to exercise a mysterious authority over all these young men) to be about his business, he made his farewells with a reluctance and sidelong glances that caused Barney to enjoy a sense of triumph—and one which he very foolishly, as it was later to be proved, delighted in showing rather than concealing.

The Brooks' house was situated in a street running from the Strand down to the river. It was commodious and suited to a gentleman, but it struck Barney that very few servants were employed for a house of its style. There appeared to be, besides a dumb black boy who waited upon the family as to food and drink, a burly footman—one whose thick, short figure would not be tolerated in the livery of a gentleman living in St. James's—and a very old woman-servant whom he had once passed in the hall as she made her way upstairs.

An hour passed before he fell asleep, so occupied was he over the perfections of Lucy and assessing his chances of winning them. It was, therefore, not surprising that when morning came he was more than usually unwilling to rise in time for the day's work. He was dressing in the haste his sloth had made necessary, and had just cut himself for the second time while shaving, when his landlady knocked on his door.

Thinking she had taken it into her head to summon him personally to breakfast—though ordinarily she merely rang a bell—he called out with a note of irritation:

"Yes, Mrs. Stokes, I'll be there directly."

"There's a—young woman waiting to see you, sir." And in Mrs. Stokes' plummy tones were both curiosity and disapproval.

"A young woman! What sort of a young woman?"

"She could be a young gentlewoman, sir," answered Mrs. Stokes very guardedly.

"At this hour!" For a wild, gay moment he thought it must be Lucy, so full was his mind of her. But she would not be visiting him, and even should she ever condescend to do so, it would not be at this extraordinary time.

"It is a strange hour of day to be calling," Mrs. Stokes confirmed dourly from behind the door.

"What is her name?"

"She would not say, sir. Said you knew her well enough." Mrs. Stokes sniffed. "I've no doubt you do," he heard her mutter.

"Tell her I shall be down as quickly as I can."

It must be Fan, he thought. Nobody else. Fan who had disappeared from Hanover Square nearly a week ago, and on whose account he had endured one of the more withering of the General's storms. He had been questioned and bullied, and questioned again, for at first Mr. Jaspard refused to believe he did not know where she was. Driven, he had indeed admitted that she had spoken to him of running away from home, but—he had quickly added—he had not supposed her to be serious.

He splashed at his face, put on his coat and went downstairs to the sitting-room. Sure enough, standing by the breakfast table, in her outdoor clothes and as neat as if it were noon, was Fan.

'What a pox are you doing here?"

"Don't be cross with me, Barney," she said in her wheedling way. "I had to see you early, before you went out. It is very, very important."

"Where have you been? What have you been up to? I can tell you there's been a fine to-do at home since you went away, and I've had my share of the General's displeasure, I assure you. You are not staying here, miss, that I promise."

Here Mrs. Stokes bustled in with Barney's breakfast. "I've brought two cups," she said, and stared at Fan in a manner that was only a little less than insolent. "The young woman would like a drink of coffee, I dare say, after being out so early on a cold morning." She banged the door behind her.

"You see," said Barney, "what she takes you for, and it's no wonder. If you had to come here, why the deuce didn't you say who you were, and bring a maid with you as a lady should?"

"A maid!" Fan began to laugh. "I did not wish her to know who I am. Now, if the General comes here asking questions, she cannot tell him that I have visited you. I was thinking of you, Barney."

"I am quite sure you were not," he said, sitting down and beginning to eat his rolls and butter. "Pour out the coffee."

She did so. "Barney," her tone became grave. "I am in trouble. Something has happened to Mr. Stafford; he must have had an accident. I want you to find out. You will go to his lodgings as soon as your work is over?"

"I have better things to do than call on Mr. Stafford. I do not care if he has met with an accident. What is it to me?" The oddness of her request seemed only then to strike him. "And pray what is it to you either?" he demanded.

"Everything. Barney, don't be angry. Listen patiently. I left home because—Mr. Stafford and I are to be married. We did not run away together for fear the General should suspect and go after us. I mean, if anything had gone wrong with our plans he might have caught us before we could find a parson. Now he has no idea that Stafford has any connection with my disappearance. Not the least in the world, for he has been going to Hanover Square since I left. . . . *Listen*, Barney, don't interrupt. I have not seen him myself since I went. He was coming for me yesterday with everything arranged for us to be married immediately, but—but he did not come, and I have had no word from him. He *must* be ill. *Something* has happened."

"Maybe, like other gallants before him, he has changed his mind."

"No. No, he would never do that. Perhaps—perhaps the regiment was ordered away suddenly or—or he has been hurt in a duel. You *will* go and find out for me, Barney? I cannot go myself; he lives with four or five other officers. I can give you the direction."

She was evidently agitated, and Barney was forced to the conclusion that she truly believed harm had come to Stafford. Her vanity, he reflected, would never allow her to accept the alternative he had suggested.

"Please, please do this for me," she said, and began to cry. Delicately and prettily, with little dabs at her long wet lashes.

He was not much moved. All her life Fan had cried for what she wanted, and usually, out of good-nature, her brothers had given in to her. And that coming evening he was particularly unwilling to go on an errand—for Fan or anyone else. He had planned that as soon as he was freed from his work he would call upon Lucy Brook.

"You will get a letter from him to-morrow, I dare say."

"How can you be so cruel?" she sniffed. "Don't you see—what a position I am in? Suppose he has had to leave London, go to the Continent, perhaps. What is to become of me? Suppose—suppose he has been killed."

"He won't have been killed. It serves you right for poaching from poor Kitty. No, I have no sympathy with you, you should be downright ashamed of yourself." He gave her a further and terse account of his opinion of her behaviour, both in running away from home and treating Kitty, who had done her no harm, in so scurvy a fashion.

Fan, while looking penitent, did not waste time in making excuses for herself. She had seen Barney glance at his watch and attack his breakfast the faster.

"Yes, yes. But you cannot see your sister, your own, own sister, Barney, left f-friendless in the city."

He supposed, very reluctantly, that he could not.

"There's more, too, Barney," she went on, managing to make even her sniffs attractive. "I am in trouble about money. Stafford was going to bring me some yesterday. I bought several things, my wedding clothes, you know, and of course I had to leave home without bringing any more than a few laces. The shopmen gave me credit, but—I think my landlady must have said something to them after Stafford failed to come early yesterday. In the afternoon they were calling and—and they were very unpleasant, Barney."

"Wedding clothes? You must have spent a lot."

"I did. Stafford was bringing me fifty guineas, I knew; and besides, there were a few other things I wanted. I owe—over seventy pounds. So you understand how—how very important it is that I should know what has happened to him."

"Your creditors are probably on the doorstep at Hanover Square by now," he remarked drily.

"Oh no! They do not know who I am. I am in my lodgings under

E

the name of Miss Debonair. It was my landlady who persuaded them to give me credit. She *was* very agreeable to me, and is highly respected, it seems. But now—since Stafford has not come—she has changed her manner to me quite."

"I have to go," said Barney. "I shall be late."

"Here is the direction, I wrote it down for you." She dabbled in her silk bag for a piece of paper. "You will find out, Barney, and then come straight to me? I have written underneath where I am lodging. Don't forget to ask for Miss Debonair. You will do this for me, Barney dear?" She was clutching his sleeve with one hand, while the other waved the piece of paper before him.

He took it and put it in his pocket. "Oh very well. Debonair! What a name!"

"Don't you like it? I thought of it. Dorinda Debonair." She gave her usual happy titter.

He was at the door, and he said to her sternly: "You had much better go straight back to Hanover Square and confess everything."

"No, I cannot go back. Never—whatever has happened. Neither the General nor Madam would ever believe I had not been away with a man. You could not blame them, for that matter. Girls as pretty as I am do not usually run away from home except it is to go with a man."

He made a sound of exasperation, for he could not refute what she said. "If you come out with me now, I'll see you into a hackney coach."

As he slammed the door on her she called through the window:

"I'll be waiting for you. Come as soon as you can."

He walked on, frowning. Fan was certainly in a worse pickle than any he had supposed even she was capable of getting into. If, for whatever reason, it should happen that Stafford did not marry her, what—as she herself had asked—was to become of her? Even if the General could be persuaded by her landlady that her conduct while in her lodgings had been unimpeachable, it was unlikely Madam would choose to credit it. She might well be glad of the opportunity to get rid of Fan altogether. Then, who was to pay all the money she owed? Well, she could hand the things back, he supposed. But what a devil of a nuisance she was!

He had come by now to Thames Street, with its familiar malodorous smell of cheese; and the hurly-burly of this centre of trade distracted his thoughts. Here the river was as thick with masts as though some calamitous thunderbolt had struck a long narrow wood, stripping branches and leaves alike, leaving only stark, straight trunks, decorated with trails of denuded creepers. As if, too, a constant frolicsome wind played among these poor vertebrae of trees and set them rocking and bobbing, rocking and bobbing, ceaselessly.

Shouts and oaths sounded from among the masts and seemed to be echoed back in the streets, so that between the two was an incessant, similar clamour. Horses and carts clattered by, coaches, hand-carts, porters, throngs of people; mostly men in labouring or seafaring dress; a few neat, now scurrying clerks akin to Barney; sometimes a portly, prosperous merchant with red face and beaver hat; small boys making weird calls and winding in and out among the traffic. It was a population preponderantly male. Very few women had occasion to come to this part of Thames Street, at least in broad daylight. What stealthy, hooded figures might slip aboard the ships when night had fallen was another matter.

As backcloth to this busy, noisy scene stood the magnificent Customs House which had been put up after the Great Fire: a long, two-storey building, with two wings jutting forward, the whole in pillared, classical design. In the broad space before it were piled barrels of liquor, bales of merchandise, sacks of goods, boxes, packages. Over these the Customs officers stood guard, or directed the lading of them into wagons that they might be taken into the customs hall. And round and about busily passed the coaches and the carts, the clerks and the merchants, the porters and the boys, each intent upon his own affairs, most noisily vocal according to his needs.

It was in a back room upstairs of this great building that the particular department of the Office of Trade and Plantations in which Barney held his clerkship was situated.

Twice that day he was scolded by his superior for carelessness and inattention. But it was not Fan's problems which were coming between him and his work: of Lucy Brook he dreamed.

The clerks in the Office could never be certain at what hour they might have their freedom. If many ships had come in, they could be kept at their letters or their figures till eight o'clock at night, even later. In the ordinary way, however, they might hope to be released by six. That evening Barney was fortunate. There had not been a great deal to do all day, and at half past five he was in the street.

Having first—heedless of Fan's impatience—gone to a nearby tavern for some refreshment, he picked up a coach and had himself driven to Stafford's lodging, which was in the district of St. James's.

He did not know what he had expected to learn here, but he was certainly surprised when the soldier who opened the door gave him no indication that anything unusual had happened to Lieutenant Stafford.

"I think he has gone out, sir. But if you will step inside I will make certain. This way, please, sir. What name shall I say, sir?"

Without thinking, Barney gave it. Only when the man had gone did it occur to him that possibly he had been foolish. If Stafford wanted to avoid him, he had made it easy for him to do so.

He had been shown into a small room, the furniture of which, such was the precision of its placing, appeared as well drilled as the soldiers who presumably looked after it. A rank of chairs lined each wall, except at the further end under the window where a round table, a little pulled out, stood exactly central. From the opposite wall, above the fireplace, the fleshy, unhandsome face of George I watched him. In these un-homely surroundings he walked up and down for a minute or two.

When the door opened, it was not to re-admit the soldier or to let in Carlton Stafford. A young officer greeted him formally, then said in a friendly manner:

"I am sorry, Mr. Jaspard, you have had the trouble of calling here for nothing. But if you go to Hanover Square I am sure you will find Stafford there. He mentioned to me that he was calling at your home this evening."

"At Hanover Square?" Barney repeated, astonished. "Are you sure?" he added.

"Unless he has changed his mind since. But I think that is not likely. We know—if you will pardon my saying so, sir—that there is a magnet in Hanover Square draws him thither." He laughed pleasantly.

"Er—yes," said Barney. "Yes. Oh, thank you." He made as if to go.

"You will drink some wine with us, Mr. Jaspard?"

"No, thank you. It is very kind of you. But—but I want to see Stafford rather urgently. If I linger, I may miss him."

He got himself away from the proffered hospitality of the officer, who seemed genuinely disappointed that he would not stay, and walked rapidly towards Hanover Square. Now he could make nothing of the situation. Obviously, Stafford was uninjured and in London. Why, then, had he failed Fan? And—an even less answerable question—what could he be doing this very evening under the General's roof? He knew Fan pretty well, and was sure that, whatever trimmings her story may have had, she had not been lying to him in essentials—an explanation which, in view of the cunning that went to make up her character, he had not overlooked.

He did not need to go home, for as he entered the Square he saw Carlton Stafford coming towards him. Mr. Stafford did not bear the look of a guilty man. To Barney's further surprise, he quickened his steps and was so eager to speak he scarcely bothered to make a salutation.

"You are the very man I want to see."

"I want to see you, too," said Barney truculently.

"Let us go into a tavern where we can talk. I have a great deal to say to you. I—er—would have called on you this evening, had I not been so fortunate as to have this chance meeting. . . . No, no, my dear fellow, wait till we are in the *Flying Unicorn*; it is here just round the corner. I cannot say what I have to in the street."

Morosely, though full of curiosity, Barney went with him to the tavern. They came into a long room, so partitioned that as one walked down the centre it was not dissimilar to passing between a double row of horse's stalls. But each was furnished with a laid table surrounded by chairs, a four-branched candlestick fixed to the central wall, and on the remaining two walls large wooden pegs waited the accommodation of hats or swords.

Only a few of the tables were occupied when Barney and Stafford arrived, and they chose one at the further end, removed from any neighbours.

"What will you take?" asked Stafford, seating himself. His tone was as affable as that of a man who has nothing on his conscience, yet Barney suspected a hint of nervousness in it.

He replied stiffly: "I do not care to drink with you."

Now Stafford looked disconcerted. "Oh, come," he said, "we can be so much more comfortable over a bottle."

"I have come here to talk, not drink."

"As you wish. You will excuse me if I do not follow your example. Besides, we cannot come in here and call for nothing . . . Oh, there is the drawer. A pint of October, and be quick."

"And the other gentleman? Your honour?"

"One pint of October, that is all for the moment."

The man gave Barney a very disparaging look, and departed to carry out the meagre order.

"You have guessed it is about your sister I want to speak," said Stafford, showing signs of embarrassment. "I have been nearly worried out of my mind over her. Er—you have seen Fan?"

"Yes," said Barney, and would help him no further.

"Well, you must know then that I intended, that it was the desire of my heart, to marry her. We had arranged that she should go from home——"

"Yes, yes," interrupted Barney, "I know all the plans you made. What I do not know is, why you did not go to her yesterday and marry her."

"I am coming to that. I was at your home in Hanover Square yesterday morning. I thought it wise to call there at the very last opportunity so as to allay all suspicion. The most unexpected, the most calamitous thing occurred. Mr. Jaspard called me into the library and——"

Here the drawer returned, and put down a tankard. Stafford raised it and took a long drink.

"Go on," urged Barney impatiently.

"Yes. Where was I? Mr. Jaspard called me into the library and—to be brief—he *commanded* me to marry his daughter Kitty. I—I have not behaved too well in that quarter, I'll admit. As you know, I was paying my serious addresses to Miss Kitty until I was captivated by your enchanting sister. So—er—Mr. Jaspard had reason on his side. What could I do? What could I say? You know how ungovernable he is. He is not a man one can dispute with——" Stafford's words tailed off.

"You are telling me," said Barney slowly, "that you have abandoned my sister and propose to marry Kitty?"

"In substance—er—yes. I do apologize. I am desperately ashamed. I know just how you feel just now that you wish to flog me, to kill me. But, my dear sir, do try and put yourself in my position. What could I do? I was Miss Kitty's accredited suitor. Mr. Jaspard said to me: 'You are going to marry my daughter. I have written to your uncle concerning settlements.' If I had defied him"—Stafford faltered, and then went on with energy—"if I had defied him, told him the whole truth, he would still never have allowed me to marry your sister. I do not need to tell *you*— one of his own family—how he sets his face against insubordination, whatever the cost or the consequences may be. The *only* chance for Fan and me was for us to have been married before he discovered we had any inclination that way. There lay the reason for all our careful plans, why she went away alone, why I continued calling on Miss Kitty. No, he would have come between us. I would have been—removed in some way. . . . Sir, I do not wish to impute anything to your—your uncle. But you must have heard stories of him, too. If people cross him or anger him, they—disappear. Oh, I do not mean he has them killed—there are other means. My aunt remembers some such strange story concerning Miss Delia——"

"Concerning Delia!" Barney's interest was momentarily deflected from Fan.

"Yes. Some man who loved her was never heard of again . . . What was I saying? Yes, you see we *could* not have married, once he had learned that we wished to be so, and Fan would have been disgraced, her reputation ruined. *Now*, she may come home, and bear perhaps a great scolding, but Mrs. Craft, at whose house I have lodged her, will vouch that she has behaved herself decorously in these few days, and in every way as becomes a modest young woman. It will seem she went for a mere prank, and there was not a man in the case at all." He leaned back with a sigh as one who has given his evidence and hopes for a lenient judgment.

"It will not be as easy as that for her," said Barney, scowling. "A young woman, whatever you may say, and particularly one as pretty and lively as she, cannot vanish from home for a week and no one blow upon her name."

It did not occur to him to doubt that Stafford had told him the facts as they had happened, and he saw, in spite of himself, the young officer's position as a very difficult one. What he had said of the General was probably true: out of malicious caprice, if for no better reason, he was perfectly capable of preventing an unwanted marriage in his family by any means. (His imagination darted for a moment after Delia before it returned to the problem in hand.) Further, should he discover Stafford's duplicity, he would for sure, his worldly prospects notwithstanding, forbid him alliance with his family, whether through daughter or putative niece. Yet, even allowing the complexity of the situation, Barney felt that Stafford's behaviour was hardly excusable. He said, while still considering what his best course of action would be:

"At least you could have written to her, or found some means of informing her that you could not come. Naturally, she expected you all day."

"To have written would have been proof that we had been in league together—should the letter have miscarried," answered Stafford lamely. "And obviously I could not send a verbal message."

"You would not damn yourself with any written evidence, is what you mean," said Barney coldly. "Might you not, then, have gone in person and explained the reason of your defaulting? That, it seems to me, would have been a more gentlemanly thing to have done than leaving her wondering and anxious. 'Pon my soul! it was monstrous."

"How could I have gone to see her? Her—her beauty would o'erset any resolution I had coolly made. Besides, to save her reputation I have never visited her there, and it would be but to undo all my caution—for you never know who have eyes to see, or tongues to tell."

Plausible as this excuse sounded, Barney could not feel himself satisfied.

He was wearing a sword, for although this gentlemanly addition to dress by no means formed the usual equipment of a clerk, he refused to forgo it. It was his sign for himself, if not for the world, that in spite of his comparatively humble way of life he was a man of breeding. Now his hand was fiddling with the hilt.

Stafford, noticing his restless fingers, said: "Do not let us quarrel over this, Jaspard. Were we to fight—and I can see it is in your mind to call me out—you can only harm your sister the more. Now, as I have said, she must go home, and if there is a little talk it will blow over. But should we fight, there is material for a first-class scandal. You show the world she has been wronged when her brother stands up to defend her."

Stafford had a glib tongue, and he enlarged upon this theme until he had won Barney to his view. This was the easier done since Barney was not of a quarrelsome disposition, and moreover reflected that Stafford was almost certainly both a better shot and a better swordsman than himself. For his pains he would but get wounded, and nothing, so far as he could see, could rescue Fan from the consequences of her folly.

But Stafford, he determined, must make amends in one direction. He told him forthrightly of the debts Fan had incurred through buying wedding clothes; and mentioned £80 as the sum she required to discharge them. This was a round figure, and he could do with the change himself and deserved it for his trouble.

"I cannot pay out all that," said Stafford with determination, yet with a craven air. "I am not a wealthy man, and—and only consider what expenses I shall have with my new condition. A home to set up, and so on. She—your sister—must take the things back to the shops where she bought them. She cannot have worn them."

"No. And I dare say she could take them back. But, before the Lord! sir, you have treated her scurvily enough, and you'll not be so mean as to back out of *that* commitment."

"My good fellow, you do not consider what you are saying. How can Fan come home with new dresses, new laces? The first question will be: where did she get them? And no one can be expected to believe that she—er—did not make another kind of payment for them."

This was so true that Barney was dashed. Yet he was loth not to obtain this £80, part of which he had seen in his own pocket. He believed that Fan had meant it when she had said that, whatever had happened, she would never go home. In that case she would need her clothes. . . . Perhaps he could send her to Mrs. Fletcher who had been Barbara Jaspard, married, conveniently, so very far away in Northumberland. Barbara, though he had not seen her for some years, he remembered as kind and smiling. . . . But Fan's future would have to be settled later, and on no account must Stafford be allowed to suspect that she might not return to Hanover Square.

"I understand you," he said. "But you give me the money, and I shall find a way how she may have her dresses and no one be surprised."

"Indeed, then, you will be very clever."

"I may give my sister presents, I suppose."

"Presents! I do not pretend to know your circumstances, sir, but I cannot think it very probable you could give her dresses to that value without your family wondering nigh as much how *you* had come by them."

Barney could never brook allusions to his poverty, which stung him almost as much as would expressed doubts about his birth have done, had anyone been bold enough to make them to his face.

"May I remind you, sir," he replied grandly and without a shred of justification, "that so near a relation to Mr. Jaspard will not remain indefinitely in a subordinate position? I repeat: you have done my sister enough wrong, grievous wrong. Such meanness as to withhold money that was spent solely upon your account is little becoming a gentleman. It savours to me of a tradesman and his wench."

Stafford passed his tongue round his lips. He was wondering if he dared ask for Barney's silence as a condition of the payment.

For the story he had told had been lies from beginning to end.

During the few days following his last meeting with Fan, he had, freed from the enchantment of her presence, had time to reflect upon the many and grave disadvantages of making a runaway match, and with a young woman in her equivocal position. Not only would he have Mr. Jaspard's wrath to contend with—and, as he had hinted to Barney, he had been hearing tales of his implacable temper—but he had to consider, too, his great-uncle who, though he could not prevent him inheriting his title and estates, yet could make the intervening years a good deal less pleasurable for him than they might be.

Only when Fan was near could he lose his caution and hard-headedness. Her presence was an intoxicant that robbed him of reason.

Yesterday (that was to have been his wedding-day) Mr. Jaspard had not called him into the library. He had gone there of his own free will. Of his own free will asked for the hand of Catherine Jaspard.

That Fan would have a shocking and highly discreditable story to tell against him had, naturally, occurred to him. He had determined to meet it with lies. Fan could produce no evidence against him: he had never written her a word except for the scrap of paper left in the ante-room vase, and that he had taken care to print in block capitals. He could count on Mrs. Craft, who had been his nurse, to deny that he had ever engaged rooms in her house for her. He would admit, since everyone knew it, that he had flirted with Fan, and let it be seen that now, regrettably, she was jealous of Kitty, and had chosen this violent way of bringing him into disrepute. He expected his story to be accepted because it would suit Mr. Jaspard, who wanted him for a son-in-law, to accept it; and Kitty was too much in love with him to stumble over obstacles in the way. Nor was such an irresponsible action on Fan's part beyond credence. She was known to be headstrong, and very restive at being kept subordinate to the younger Kitty. Lastly, a fact to be reckoned much on his side, Mrs. Jaspard would never champion her.

There had remained Barney. He had guessed that Fan would go to him, and it would therefore be necessary to give him a version that would throw as little unfavourable a light as possible upon himself. That Barney might repeat it in Hanover Square was a risk that he had assumed he must take. If he did, he had planned to meet it with more lies: in short, flatly to deny that he had ever made any such revelation to him. His word would be as likely to be taken as Barney's if only because the Jaspards would prefer to take it. And if Barney, enraged, should challenge him to a duel, well, there was time enough to bother over that when he was face to face with it. But he did not want a duel, or the risk of Barney's tongue.

He put both his hands round his tankard and stared at him. "If I do give you this money, may I ask you for one condition?"

"What is that?" His tone was not encouraging.

"Only that you do not discredit me with Miss Kitty." His eyes shifted, he went on: "May I have your word that you will repeat nothing to anyone of what I have said to you here this evening?"

"I certainly intend to tell my sister."

"Oh yes. Yes, she must know, to be sure. But it will go no further? And you will do what you can to persuade her not to speak either. It—would make Miss Kitty so unhappy."

Barney was not deceived by this last plea. He saw Stafford was ill-at-ease, and though he did not suspect the extent of his double-dealing, neither did he suppose he was suffering any concern for Kitty's feelings. It was enough that he had good reasons for wanting this evening to be forgotten. Barney's lashes lowered over his eyes and he leaned a little forward.

"Perhaps you would be wise," he said quietly, "to make it £100."

"A hundred! Are you mad, sir? I am not made of money."

"I said—perhaps you would be wise," repeated Barney, still gently but with an obstinate undertone.

Stafford writhed. He raised his tankard and, seeing it was empty, put it down again.

"Oh—very well," he said awkwardly. "I have your word as a gentleman?"

"I give you my word."

"I—have not the money on me."

"I did not suppose you would have. You shall write me a draft . . . Drawer! Pen and ink! And bring me a pint of mountain." He threw a glance at Stafford. "Are you drinking?"

"Thank you. The same."

The wine was soon brought, but the pen and ink, unusual objects to be called for, did not follow very closely. Stafford now appeared anxious to resume the friendly footing upon which he had first met Barney. He proffered his snuff-box, and said with a self-conscious laugh:

"I believe I am not the only one in trouble to-day. I suppose you have not seen Creswell?"

"I saw him on Sunday. Why?"

"Oh, he's in some scrape or other. Miss Kitty told me that when they were at breakfast this morning a message was brought to Mr. Jaspard. It concerned Creswell, she knows, because he said to her mother it was on his account he was called away, and he must go at once. Mrs. Jaspard was alarmed, and asked had any harm come to him. 'Not what you infer by harm,' he said in his abrupt way. 'My Lord Comberley has asked me to go to his house immediately.' Later in the morning he came back for Mrs. Jaspard. Miss Kitty watched them go, and she said her mother had been crying and the General was at his fiercest. And they have not been home since, that is, they had not when I left half an hour ago. Indeed, it was for that reason I came away as early as I did, for Miss Kitty is so anxious as to what has befallen her brother that she would give scarcely any heed to me."

" 'Tis probably a trivial matter," said Barney, without showing much interest. "Mr. Jaspard's sense of proportion is not always to be trusted. . . . Where is that man? I want to get back to Fan."

At mention of her name, Stafford lost the look of ease he had been wearing as he discoursed of Creswell. He fell silent, and busied himself with taking a piece of paper from his pocket-book.

"Coming, sir, coming!" The breathless drawer laid the pen and ink and a small container of sand upon the table.

With ill-concealed reluctance Stafford wrote out the draft for £100.

Barney read it through, and only nodded as he took it. He got to his feet, picked his hat off the peg, and with a cold "Good night" walked out.

In the street satisfaction brought a happy glint to his brown-green eyes. He would give Fan £75 to pay her debts—or rather, lest her extravagance again get the better of her discretion, he would pay them for her. That would leave him £25 for himself. He could give Miss Brook (and of course her mother and Harry) a right royal entertainment, and still not have emptied his pockets.

This was the first time he obtained money by what might be called unconventional means; and though often in the future he was to resort to extortion, perhaps never again was he so joyous of his gains as of the £25 he had squeezed from Carlton Stafford.

CHAPTER VII

CRESWELL'S MARRIAGE

CRESWELL'S first knock was not answered, and three times more he had to bang before he and Rosa, standing in the cold wind, heard shambling footsteps from within, followed by the rattling of bolts. The door, still on a chain, opened only a crack.

"Who's there? Who calls?"

Creswell was relieved of making any reply by Rosa's instant:

"It is I, Miss Tarquin. Hodge, open the door!"

"Miss Tarquin?" came an astonished murmur, as the chain was loosed. "I am sorry, ma'am, indeed. No one told me you was out. I thought you'd a' come in with his lordship. Davies didn't say ought to me as you wasn't in. I'll be after 'im in the morning."

By the light of the one candle, evidently just put down on the hall-chest, Creswell saw that it was an old man who had opened the door, probably Lord Comberley's steward. It was plain to be seen he had got hastily out of bed, for he had an overcoat about him, and under it could be seen his thin, bare legs, the feet in shabby felt slippers. A green woollen night-cap covered his bald head.

"It was not Davies' fault," said Miss Tarquin decisively. "Pray say nothing to him about it."

"No, madam. As you please, madam. The gentleman?" He looked questioningly at Creswell whom, very obviously, he expected would take his departure.

"Close the door, Hodge, and bolt it. Yes, I said bolt it. His lordship is in bed, I presume?"

"Yes, madam, these three hours gone."

"Please wake him. Tell him I have something very urgent to communicate to him. It will not wait."

"Y-yes, madam." The old man looked very doubtful. "He will not care about being disturbed," he added, with the familiarity of an old servant to a very young member of the family.

Creswell, who during this time had been standing awkwardly by, his hat under his arm, found the courage to say, with a good deal of firmness:

"The man is right, madam. I think you will be advised to let his lordship sleep. I will return in the morning at an hour more convenient both to him and to yourself." Miss Tarquin, he was calculating, could hardly, in front of the servant, argue with him along the lines she had used in the *Green Periwig*. As it was, he wondered what the devil the steward thought of his young mistress returning home at three o'clock in the morning in the sole company of a gentleman.

Miss Tarquin, however, paid not the slightest attention to his suggestion. She did not even look his way. To Hodge she said: "Do as I say. Wake his lordship immediately. Immediately."

Such was the imperiousness of her command that the old man turned towards the stairs, shaking his head in worry and bewilderment.

But there was no need to wake Lord Comberley. The voices had disturbed him, and now he appeared on the landing, holding a candle-stick over the banisters. In truth, he was a comical figure, had anyone been in the mood to see him as such, clad only in his nightshirt, with a red wool night-cap on his head.

"What's that? What's that?" he called in the irascible tones of one roused suddenly from sleep. "Who's there? Who is it?"

"Uncle! Uncle!" Rosa ran towards him. As she overtook Hodge, who had not got beyond the first steps, she said to him: "Go down again. See the gentleman does not leave. Oh, Uncle, my lord!"

"God bless my soul! You, Rosa dear, and fully dressed! What is it? What has happened? One moment, my child, till I get some clothes on."

Lord Comberley vanished into his room, and a moment or two later reappeared in a dark-blue brocade dressing-gown. He was a very thin man, with a long beak-like nose, and strange wrinkled eyelids that looked as if they were originally too big and had been puckered up to make them fit over his eyes. It was these more than the nose which helped to give him the aquiline appearance upon which Creswell had commented to Stephen.

Rosa now leant over the banisters and said, in a manner no less commanding than that she had used to Hodge:

"Please come upstairs, Mr. Jaspard."

"*Mr. Jaspard!* What the devil is *he* doing here at this time of night?" He peered down into the feebly lit hall. "*Which* Mr. Jaspard?"

"Mr. Creswell Jaspard. Are you coming, sir, or must we come down to you? . . . You may go to bed now, Hodge, there is nothing else. Yes, take your candle."

"Eh, but wait a minute," said Lord Comberley, not however directing his remark to Hodge, who, thinking only of his bed, picked up his candle and shambled off. The hall was now left in darkness except for a long pale streak of moonlight coming through a window. "I don't want to speak to Creswell Jaspard to-night. And what in damnation's name is he doing here anyway? Explain yourself, sir, explain yourself!"

Creswell still stood there, looking, had there been light enough to see him, quite as foolish and hang-dog as he felt. This was even worse than anything he had anticipated. That Miss Tarquin should speak of her wrongs in his presence he had not supposed possible. He had concluded she would tell her uncle in private, and that he would be alone with that nobleman when he let loose his condemnation.

"What the devil! Has the man gone deaf? Creswell Jaspard, is that you? Speak up, sir!"

"Yes, my lord, it is."

"Come here, then, come here. Am I to go shouting at you all the night?"

"I beg your pardon, my lord." He ascended the stairs slowly, and every step was a muscular effort of which he was conscious.

"Well, well! We need not talk on the landing. Pish! I'll have caught a cold, see if I haven't." Lord Comberley shivered ostentatiously.

It was certainly warmer in his bedroom. Dull red still showed in the fireplace. He threw some sticks on, and at once a crackle started. He then lit a pair of double-branched candlesticks standing on the chest of drawers. The room now—in strong contrast to the feeling of everyone in it—looked cosy, cheerful and friendly. The large bed, completely surrounded by red curtains except where his lordship had thrust them aside to arise, stood solid and comfortable near the door, leaving a wide free space between itself and the heavily curtained windows.

"Now what the devil is all this? Rosa, where have you been? Why are you not in bed?"

To which questions Rosa, who undoubtedly had a sense of the dramatic, pointed at Creswell and said, simply: "Ask him!"

Creswell, however, was tongue-tied. Not one sentence could his mind frame which it was in the least possible for him to utter. He crushed his hat, which he was still carrying, even closer against his side, and stood with an abject air before Miss Tarquin and her uncle.

At his silence, and as well perhaps at his obvious air of guilt, Lord Comberley became not only more angry, but alarmed. He was beginning to see, as he could hardly fail to do, that some sort of harm had threatened his Rosa.

"You have been crying, my darling. . . . 'Fore gad! sir, will you speak?"

Racking his bemused brain for some appropriate answer to this urgent command, Creswell managed to say: "I had the misfortune, my lord, to mistake your niece for—somebody else."

"And whom did you mistake her for?" asked Lord Comberley in a voice more dreadful than a prosecuting counsel's.

"It—is a very difficult story, sir." He glanced at Rosa. "If I might speak to you alone? It is not very fitting for a lady's ears."

For a moment Lord Comberley looked undecided. Creswell hoped

he was about to tell Rosa to leave them; but whatever his intention may
have been, before he had put it into words, she said in a low, bitingly
contemptuous tone:

"He will only lie to you, sir. I will tell you."

Creswell moved now to take his handkerchief from his pocket. He
feared that, to add to his mountain of humiliation, he might be going to
be sick. Nervous apprehension and too much punch were, between
them, turning his stomach. But to ask to be excused at this juncture,
even in the unlikely supposition of his request being granted, was
purchasing privacy and a degree of physical ease at the price of appearing a coward. Flight was out of the question: he must either control
himself or be sick as discreetly as was possible.

Rosa, in the candlelight and with her tear-daubed face, looking
more like a little girl than a woman, was saying in a shamed
voice:

"He gave me a message as I was coming from Mr. Pinelli's that you
were awaiting me at—I don't remember the name of the place, some
tavern or coffee-house, and that I was to join you there. I knew him by
sight as one of the Gentlemen-in-Waiting, so I believed him. Mrs. True,
of course, believed him, too; she was told to go home. He—he took me
to this place. There were several gentlemen there. They were all drunk.
They—held me and made me drink. Then, later, all the others went
away, and—and Mr. Jaspard stayed with me there—alone—with the
door locked—till—till a few minutes ago." Now she sounded like a
spent runner, her breath came so fast and the words jerked.

The effect of this revelation on Lord Comberley was—though for
different reasons—to make him feel as ill as Creswell. He went as white
as a dried bone, and as the pale colour slowly came back to his face it
was in small rings and patches so that he looked as if he had a rash. His
hands trembled. For several moments he could find no words. When his
voice returned to him, it was changed, half-sobbing, and let out oaths
and abuse.

"You foul scoundrel! You black-hearted villain! You filthy spawn
of Hell! My niece! My little Rosa! By Heaven! I'll see you hanged for
this. I will. And your father shan't save you. No, by God! I have more
power than Robert Jaspard. You'll hang, like the dog you are!"

Creswell swallowed down his nausea and, prompted by self-
preservation, said with nearly as much heat and vigour as Lord
Comberley:

"I have done nothing for which I can be hanged. I have not—not
touched your niece. I give you my oath."

"Not touched her, and you have been alone with her half the night!
Do you expect me to believe *that*?"

"I was asleep, and so was she. I took too much to drink, and fell asleep."

Unlikely as this statement sounded, Creswell was relieved to see that Lord Comberley at least looked as if he wished to believe it.

"Is that true?" he asked Rosa.

"We did sleep," admitted Rosa, it seemed to Creswell with unnecessary reluctance. "But—but all those gentlemen know—we were locked up in that room. And—he behaved in a—beastly way to me."

"I did not," contradicted the goaded Creswell, seeing that her remark was bound to be misinterpreted by Lord Comberley. "I kissed you against your will, I will admit, but nothing more."

"Nothing more!" shouted his lordship. "You enticed my niece with a false message, you compelled her to drink punch with half the town looking on, you remained with her in a public tavern until three o'clock in the morning, on your own admittance you forced your loathsome kisses on her. But you did nothing more. *Nothing more!* Egad! where's my horsewhip? You are going to be thrashed, sir, as you've never been thrashed in your life." He began looking about him.

"I told him," said Rosa very calmly, "that he would have to marry me."

Lord Comberley stopped his search abruptly. "*Marry* him! Be tied for life to a libertine, a selfish profligate! Oh, Rosa! Rosa! I would sooner see you dead."

"I know, Uncle dearest. But—I *have* to marry him. The gentlemen there—at that dreadful place—would know me again. I can never hold up my head before the world, nor marry any other man."

"That is true," agreed Lord Comberley, after a long, sad silence. "My poor unfortunate child! But you are right. There is nothing else, it must be so." His voice rose, and he shook his fist in Creswell's face. "You *shall* marry her!"

"My lord, I am willing to make all amends in my power. May I—say something in my own vindication?"

"Nothing can vindicate you."

Though this could hardly be construed as permission, Creswell plunged on. "I told you, sir, I had the misfortune to mistake Miss Tarquin. You will surely believe me, my lord, when I say I should never have dreamed of offering insults to a lady whom I knew to be your niece."

"If you did not think she was my niece, how is it that you told her that I—I, Lord Comberley—was awaiting her at this tavern? Answer me that, eh? You are a liar as well as a knave. Heaven help my sweet girl!"

"He says he thought I was your—your—I cannot say it, Uncle—your—woman." Rosa's tones trembled.

Creswell would have done better not to have offered his vindication. Lord Comberley's fury was now so great that his words came, not in complete sentences, but scattered like leaves falling in an autumn gale.

"My woman! Rake! Profligate! Because *you* keep women. *I!* Your evil, wicked mind! The Jaspard blood! Satan himself! Oh, all lies, lies! A-ah! You'll wish you'd never been born!"

During this tirade his eye had fallen on a heavy horsewhip laid on top of the tallboy. In his quivering hands it shook like the tail of a pleased dog.

At sight of it, degraded and ashamed as he was, Creswell felt his temper rise.

"Have a care, sir, what you do! I do not wish to forget that you are much older than myself and for many reasons entitled to my respect. If you touch me, my lord, I'll not be answerable for what I do."

"Do you think I am afraid of you, you puppy! you coxcomb!"

But as he raised the whip, Creswell took a quick step forward and, using both hands, wrenched it from him. He threw it, clattering, on the floor behind him. They glared at each other, stiff and angry as snarling dogs.

Creswell had reckoned without Rosa. She ran and picked up the whip. He had no notion but that her intention was to give it back to her uncle. Instead, holding the butt in both her hands, she lashed at him herself with the energy and incompetence of an angry child. At the first stroke, the tail of the lash, curling round, caught him in the corner of the eye. The pain was so intense he was able to think of nothing but holding his handkerchief to it, while it watered freely. Perhaps three times more the whip fell across his shoulders or his legs, but he scarcely noticed it. He thought he heard Lord Comberley protest, and then, as suddenly as she had picked it up, Rosa threw the whip down, burst into a torrent of tears and ran out of the room.

Creswell continued to mop at his eye. He was bereft now of all emotion except only the desire to be allowed to go to bed. Though the nausea had passed, he felt far from well; his head ached, and his eye was extremely painful.

"Will you excuse me, my lord? Your lordship too must be in need of sleep."

"She is right," said Lord Comberley, as if he had not heard him. "You will have to marry her. Though I would to God—but it is done now. You may live a hundred years, Creswell Jaspard, but you'll never live down the dishonour of this night."

Creswell made no reply, since it seemed useless to do so.

F

"I'll send for a clergyman first thing in the morning. . . . Who were your friends who saw you with my niece to-night?"

"It was nothing to do with them, sir. I take full responsibility."

"You do indeed. But I must know who were witnesses of her shame."

"I am sorry, my lord. I cannot tell you. It *must* prejudice you against them."

Lord Comberley railed at him for a few minutes, but Creswell was not to be moved. Penge and Brabazon, both of whom were employed at Court, would be dismissed their places for sure, and Lord Comberley might find means to injure the others. Luckily, his lordship was by now nearly as tired as Creswell and he gave up his inquisition.

"Have I your permission to go, sir?" repeated Creswell. "I am in waiting at nine and I must get some rest."

"In waiting at nine, are you? You will not be. My Lord Penge must do it for you. I will get a message to the Palace early. Your father must be sent for first thing in the morning too. *And* you needn't look to him to get you out of doing your duty by my niece. *This* time Robert Jaspard will not do as he pleases. Though, damme! quite the contrary, he will congratulate you. No, Robert Jaspard won't help you."

"I can take a message to Lord Penge now, sir. It will save your sending anyone else."

"You, sir? You are not leaving this house—no, nor this room neither. I don't trust you, you rascal! If I let you go, for all I know you'll be off to the Continent instead of marrying my niece. No, here you stay until you two are man and wife. . . . Now let me see. A note for Penge. My man comes in at half past six. Time enough for him to take it then." He was talking to himself.

"My lord, I give you my word I will come back in the morning at whatever hour you say."

"I do not choose to take your word."

"Very well, my lord. Yet I think you have forgotten something. A Gentleman-in-Waiting cannot marry without His Majesty's permission."

Lord Comberley looked momentarily nonplussed. He was not a man who cared to sin against Court etiquette. But now he had only a very short struggle with his conscience before he put Rosa before the Monarch.

"His Majesty will understand the urgency of the case when I explain it to him. Indeed, Jaspard"—his wrinkled lids came down threateningly—"it will depend entirely on how I put the matter before His Majesty whether you will be allowed to retain your position. And that decision I shall make to suit my own plans, not yours. I will have to give it some thought. Employment of a sort you must have——"

Here Creswell, foreseeing that if once they embarked on the topic of his future his hopes of bed would recede yet further, yawned politely behind his hand and interrupted with: "I must beg your lordship to excuse me. I am too tired to hear or to think. If you will show me where I may retire to——?"

"Did I not say you shall not leave this room? Wait. I must see my wretched, unfortunate niece."

Since Rosa's door was opposite and Lord Comberley left it open, Creswell could hardly have escaped even had he felt inclined to do so. For a few minutes he heard whisperings, and then his lordship returned.

"Where am I to sleep, sir?" persisted Creswell.

"Sleep? You can make do with a couple of chairs for anything I care." He locked the door as he spoke, then removed his dressing-gown, and climbed the three steps up into his bed.

"Thank you, my lord . . . I am sorry to trouble you, my lord, but I require toilet necessaries. I am not accustomed to——"

"Damn you! I don't care what you are accustomed to. You will find everything you require in that closet there. And make what haste you can, I wish to sleep."

Creswell wiped his face over with cold water which, though it struck chill, soothed his inflamed eye. He was very angry now. Whatever he had done, he had the right to a bed: even a condemned murderer was not denied boarding to stretch himself upon. It would serve Comberley right, he thought blackly, if I did murder him.

As he emerged from the closet, Lord Comberley, who had evidently been having somewhat similar thoughts, said:

"Take off your coat and breeches, and be quick. You may lie in bed with me. I hope you don't snore."

"I—hope not, my lord."

So Creswell lay down beside his prospective uncle-in-law, and thought he had never had so ill-matched and fearsome a bed companion in his life. Still, the bed was comfortable, and the dark and the silence were healing. Though he did not expect to do so, he fell asleep almost immediately.

But it seemed to him that his eyes had only just closed when he became aware of stirring and movement in the room.

Lord Comberley, with his dressing-gown thrown over his shoulders, was sitting up in bed writing against a tray laid upside-down against his knees. A manservant stood by; on the table next the bed was a cup and a silver jug. His lordship folded his notes and gave them to the man.

"See that these are taken to the Palace at once. My Lord Penge must be woken, do you understand? If Mr. Pratt should be engaged, he must arrange for one of the other chaplains to come. That is all for the moment. There will be a note to take to Hanover Square later."

"Very good, my lord. Will the gentleman take chocolate?"

Creswell, who had been listening with his eyes shut, continued to feign sleep. He felt Lord Comberley look at him.

"Er—no. He wants no chocolate. He will be breakfasting, of course."

Creswell dozed again, and this time he was brought back to the unpleasant realities of the morning by Lord Comberley shaking him urgently by the shoulder.

"Wake up, sir, wake up! 'Tis time you were stirring. The clergyman will be here at half past ten, and I have sent for your father, too."

In spite of the fact that he had missed supper the night before, Creswell brought but a poor appetite to his breakfast, a meal he ate in the sole and dour company of Lord Comberley. Fortunately, his lordship busied himself over some papers, and Creswell was thus spared the ordeal of conversation. But his own thoughts were very little more agreeable. He kept saying to himself: This is my wedding-day. In an hour or two I shall be married. Married, and to a woman who both loathes and despises me. It was as fantastical as a nightmare, but alas! unlike a nightmare, it was real, it was happening. Was it only twenty-four hours ago he had been breakfasting with a heart as carefree as his dog's, talking to Brabazon and laughing over the coming evening? Well, he had nothing to laugh about now, and as far as he could see, he never would have again.

My wedding-day. These three words recurred through his thoughts like drops of water falling, falling. My wedding-day. He had always planned he would be married in silver brocade, and be as magnificent as royalty. Here he was instead, admittedly in the best of his evening coats (not counting his two especially grand ones for Drawing Rooms at Court), but with a borrowed lace cravat about his neck of far inferior workmanship to his own soiled one now lying upstairs in his lordship's washing-basket. And, to boot, his appearance marred by a red and weeping eye. An injury, he recollected grimly, inflicted upon him by his future wife. There was a good start for a happy marriage, heigh-ho! She was a turbulent child, no more. Could last night never have happened, he might have wooed her, patiently, so that she came to her flowering slowly as Nature intended, instead of his having roughly forced open the bud. . . .

Lord Comberley rustled his papers together, scowled furiously at Creswell, so that he looked more than ever like an eagle, and said: "I am truly sorry to have to tell you, sir, that my niece is mistress of a considerable fortune, a very considerable fortune. But I do not intend that it shall be dissipated by you, sir. No, indeed. The settlements will see to that. And what is more, I shall expect your father to treat you handsomely."

"I am sure he will do what is right," murmured Creswell; though indeed he was by no means sure that the General's standards of rightness would agree with Lord Comberley's. What the General would have to say of last night's work was not a subject he cared to contemplate.

"You shall live here with me, at any rate for the present. And by the Lord, sir, if you do not treat my niece well, you shall rue it! I have power and influence, as perhaps I do not need to tell you, and I can so discredit your name that no man of honour or decency will speak to you."

"I hope I shall not fail in my duty to her, my lord," Creswell answered stiffly and automatically.

" 'Fore Gad! Jaspard, if you break the heart of that good, lovely, girl, I believe I shall kill you with my own hands."

Upon this somewhat extravagant pronouncement, Lord Comberley rose to his feet. He rang the bell and asked the footman if Mr. Pratt, the chaplain, had arrived yet.

"He is in the ante-room, my lord."

"Take away these things," he waved at the table, "and show him in here."

"Yes, my lord."

When Mr. Pratt, a portly, short man arrived, Lord Comberley introduced him to Creswell, and said:

"This is the bridegroom. Pray inculcate in him a state of grace, if you can."

In spirit Creswell groaned. This was really too much. But he could not escape. He and the clergyman, after exchanging civilities, sat down, one on either side of the fire.

"Holy Matrimony, as you know, Mr. Jaspard, is a Sacrament. It is, therefore . . ."

On and on went his monotonous voice, with its slight yet irritating nasal accent—due, Creswell deduced, to his over-indulgence in snuff. Stains of it made an irregular and unpretty brown pattern down the front of his black coat. He kept interrupting himself to take a pinch of this stimulant, and more than once begged Creswell to accommodate himself from his box. Creswell, suspecting the strength of the mixture, declined. He was not paying much attention to Mr. Pratt beyond giving him the politeness of appearing to listen.

After twenty minutes or so he was distracted from even this slender duty by the sound of voices beyond the door. One was raised, demanding, unmistakable. His father had arrived.

During the next half-hour Mr. Pratt gave up. One could not address with any degree of fervour a man who constantly turned to stare at the door. He remarked finally, with a heavy playfulness that made Creswell wince, that, to be sure, he had lighter aspects of matrimony upon his mind. Ah, well! one was a bridegroom only once, and it was but natural. If he would but remember. . . ."

Creswell was saved from further advice by the summons he had, in no happy anticipation, been waiting for. Lord Comberley at once left him alone with his father.

The General did not rant or rage. Yet Creswell was not deceived by his calmness. Indeed, it indicated to him the depth of his displeasure. When the General began to be abusive, the interview was usually nearing its end.

"Give me *your* version of last night's doings, if you please."

Haltingly, Creswell told his discreditable tale: his belief that Miss Tarquin was Lord Comberley's mistress, how for a wager he had undertaken to have a kiss from her, and that the whole unlucky evening was the result of this. It sounded, under the General's disdainful face, as foolish and puerile as it well could. When he had finished, the General said, in tones of absolute scorn:

"I should have supposed that a son of mine was capable of discerning between a young, sheltered woman and a whore."

"Yes, sir. If I had not been a little drunk at the start—that is to say, not exactly drunk, but I had been drinking and—I found, I suppose, what I expected to find." He could hardly remind his father, it crossed his mind with wry humour, that it was in his own home he had learned to doubt the genuineness of avuncular relationships.

"The trouble with your generation is that you cannot carry your liquor. None of you. I have got through my share of bottles in my time, and more, but, egad! never in all my days—or nights—have I insulted a lady because I was the worse for drink. Never, I give you my word."

Creswell, looking at his magnificent father, was sure that he had not.

"Things have certainly turned out better, a great deal, for you than you deserve," continued Mr. Jaspard in a different tone. "Miss Tarquin has an excellent fortune——" he went into some details. "The estate in Somerset is a good one. The house is let at present, however. Ah—he intends to be rather stiff over the settlements—we have yet to go into those when he returns from the Palace. Our respective lawyers will be here by then, too. I will do my best for you, but after your boorish and vulgar behaviour you have not left me free to insist too vigorously."

"No, sir. Thank you, sir."

"Hm! Lord Comberley is seeing the King now, I understand—we had time for a short talk only. He is informing His Majesty of your marriage and, I presume, making such excuses as seem proper to him for its precipitancy. Has he told you his intentions towards you? He can direct the King on all matters of his Household as he pleases."

"No, sir. He told me he—would need to think about it. But that it was necessary I should have some employment."

"You are a fool, Creswell, a bigger fool than I ever supposed a Jaspard could be. There I placed you at Court with every chance, if you behaved yourself, of making a name in the world, and you choose to offend the one man in London, other than His Majesty himself, that it is fatal for you to offend. 'Pon my soul! you deserve to go into the gutter."

"As I shall be—so closely connected with him, he must make some interest for me," suggested Creswell reasonably.

"It is to be hoped so. For though fortune—and you will have *that*— may advance a man, a reputation of being well at Court will do more for him still. I do not want to see you a rich nobody. You must get into Parliament, become a power in the country."

Though Creswell felt quite unable to imagine himself—he, who could not manage sensibly his private life—fulfilling these rosy hopes, yet he was grateful to the General for harbouring them. He murmured as much.

"Eh? What have you done to your eye? You don't look as handsome as *I* should like to on *my* wedding-day."

At this abrupt change of topic, Creswell was a good deal further disconcerted. Foolishness, even lechery if necessary, he was prepared to confess to, but not that humiliating scene in Lord Comberley's bedroom. "I hurt it," he mumbled, " 'Tis nothing."

Fortunately, Mr. Jaspard, whom no one could accuse of having a condolatory nature, was not much interested in his injury. "Yes," he said, following a train of thought, "your lucky star was in the ascendant last night. As well as a fortune, you get a demned pretty girl. Demned pretty!"

"You have met her, sir?"

"I saw her a few minutes ago. No, Creswell, I have no objections at all to the match, only that you have managed it so clumsily. How do you imagine I like owning to a son who doesn't know how to behave himself like a gentleman?"

"I am very sorry, sir."

Mr. Jaspard put his head on one side and gave Creswell a shrewd look from his slanting blue eyes. "You did have the girl, I suppose?"

"No, sir, I did not. No one will believe me. But I did not."

"How do you expect anyone to believe you? Not ill, are you, eh? You understand me? Answer me, boy, are you?" There was a touch of genuine anxiety in the General's voice, bullying though it was, which confused Creswell more than ever.

"No, sir. I am—perfectly well," he said miserably.

"I am glad to hear it. But, 'fore Gad! If *I* had been locked up with a pretty wench from—from what time?—about eight o'clock till three in the morning I would have had her. 'Pon honour, I would!"

Once again Creswell was quite sure his exuberant father was speaking no less than the truth.

"Now listen to me, my boy." He took Creswell by the arm. This was, for him, a strong gesture of affection, and Creswell was so surprised he turned his head to look into his father's face. "Remember that you are a Jaspard and my heir, and that one day, please God, you'll be the Earl of Manvington. Don't let my Lord Comberley down you. Your blood is as good as his, and better. He should be proud his niece is marrying into our family. That's all. My lawyer has arrived, I dare say, and we can discuss the papers Lord Comberley has left with me till he returns with his own man of business. When the lawyers have finished their confounded blood-sucking, I'll fetch your mother, and the ceremony can go forward. . . . No, you had better keep away. You may be sure I shall look after your interests."

It was characteristic, thought Creswell, of the General's attitude to his offspring that they were allowed no voice in affairs that concerned them, it mattered not how deeply. Even he, the heir, twenty-two years old, was excluded from discussions on his own marriage settlements. But he bore with this—which must be the last paternal tyranny—with the more patience because the General's previous words had given him much comfort. To his father, so little given to commendation, he was not simply a despicable coxcomb, but a Jaspard, a future Earl, even perhaps, a future Minister of England. His self-respect began to return.

Presumably Lord Comberley supposed he would be unlikely now to try to escape from his fate, for there seemed to be no arrangements made to have him watched. During the next two hours he was left to his own devices. Even Mr. Pratt had disappeared. The breakfast-room, whither he had been bound to return not knowing where else he might sit, proved mercifully to be empty. Distasteful as his own company and thoughts must be in his present circumstances, yet every time there was a step in the hall he started, fearful lest his solitude was about to be interrupted. The heavy time passed quicker than he wished. . . .

When the door at length opened, it was to admit his mother and father, with Lord Comberley behind them. Mrs. Jaspard kissed him, and had time only to murmur reproachfully: "How could you, Creswell, how could you?" when his lordship said abruptly:

"Are you ready, Jaspard? I think we have kept Mr. Pratt waiting long enough."

Mrs. Jaspard's maternal attention was now caught.

"Your eye, dear child! What have you done to it?"

"I—had something in it," said Creswell foolishly, and heard his lordship gave a noise that might have been a snort or a malicious chuckle.

"Oh dear! It looks very sore."

But there was no further opportunity for her to enlarge upon remedies, as her son feared she was about to do, for Lord Comberley's gestures could no longer be ignored, and the little party trooped upstairs to the drawing-room.

Near the window someone had arranged flowers; and a table covered with a white cloth stood as an altar behind the surpliced figure of Mr. Pratt, who was kneeling in prayer. As they came in, he rose to his feet.

"Will you stand here, please, Mr. Jaspard?" He indicated to Creswell a hassock, beside which waited another for the use of the bride. He disposed in the most deferential manner imaginable the other members of the party at a little distance, excepting for Lord Comberley, who was to give his niece away.

Lord Comberley now handed Creswell a gold ring, which made him start, for he had forgotten this necessary adjunct to a wedding.

After that there was a long silence. Then the door opened. Creswell turned his head and saw his bride, accompanied by Mrs. True, coming towards him.

She no longer wore black, but was robed all in white and silver. Her dress was of white brocade with a self-pattern of roses, and the bodice and the skirt of the petticoat showing between the looped-up sides of the dress were of palest silver tissue. On her hair, gleaming golden, was a lace cap threaded with white and silver ribbons. She appeared to him so beautiful that he drew in his breath audibly. His heart began to pound. Though she hated him, though she held him in contempt, he was in love with her and all his life would be kneeling at her feet. So he fervently believed.

She did not look at him; with a slow, proud grace which made him think, incongruously, that just so some brave and lovely woman, perhaps Lady Jane Grey, had walked to the scaffold. For there was on her young, undefended face an expression of fear being overcome, of a terrible resolve being carried out for honour's sake. It was not the face a bride should be bringing to her wedding, and it cut him to the heart.

He wanted to cry out: "Don't do it! Don't do it, if you don't want to! It isn't too late yet." But he could not. They already were as inevitably married as if the words had been said over them.

As she reached the hassock by his side, she turned her head towards her uncle and gave him a weak, uncertain smile.

The clergyman's voice began: "Dearly beloved, we are gathered together here in the sight of God . . ."

Her hand, when he took it in his, lay cold and unresponsive to his pressure. As she made her vows to him, he watched her face.

"I, Rosalind Elizabeth, take thee, Creswell Robert George . . . to love, cherish, and to obey . . ."

So in her cool, remote voice she promised to love him, but he knew that her heart was making an exception to her private God of this, and she would not.

The service seemed to be over very soon. Mr. Pratt was shaking him by the hand and wishing him joy. Lord Comberley was kissing Rosa; the General and his mother both kissed her; his mother kissed him as well. There was much kissing, but the bridegroom did not kiss the bride, and no one made any comment on this extraordinary omission. Creswell, indeed, had advanced upon Rosa with the intention of doing so, at least for form's sake, but she had turned her head sharply and begun to talk to her uncle. . . .

Creswell began to reckon how many more hours there were of this day, which already seemed to have lasted a week. Now they would have the wedding dinner, tea afterwards, and conversation. Tedious and all but unbearable as each one of these things would be, he could not wish the day to end.

He wondered whether any man had ever dreaded as he dreaded the hour when he should be left alone with his bride.

CHAPTER VIII

AT THE MASQUERADE

BARNEY, with his new wealth in his pocket, did not scruple to hail the second hackney-coach of the day to take him to Fan's lodgings.

"What has happened?" she greeted him, before he was well into the room. "Answer me, Barney! What's the matter?"

"It is not very good hearing, Fan." He was in a hurry to be gone, but he had not understood, while talking to Stafford, how difficult it would be to break the news to her. He could not in decency blurt it out, and then say: "Excuse me, I have an engagement I wish to keep." No, he must make up his mind not to see Miss Brook to-night. Fan would need comfort, and her future had to be decided upon, one way or the other. Stafford was right. She *must* go home. But would she?

"Tell me!" said Fan impatiently, and with the slight ugly shrillness that came to her voice in moments of stress or excitement. She had come over to him and was shaking him by the arm.

"I am sorry to bring you bad news, but—he will not marry you, Fan."

"Will not——? Why not?" She sounded, not desolated, but angry.

"The General——"

"Did he find out?" interrupted Fan sharply.

"No. Let me finish. Er—you know Stafford has been paying his addresses to Kitty—the General called him aside yesterday morning and told him—commanded him were the words Stafford used—to marry her."

"He is going to marry Kitty?" A blend of incredulity and indignation was in her tones.

"Yes." He repeated to her all Stafford's extenuations as he himself had put them forward, not with any wish to exonerate Stafford from dishonourable conduct, but to lessen the blow to her pride by the suggestion that his desertion of her was unavoidable. He ended: "I have got the seventy guineas odd from him, however, with which to pay your debts."

Her face changed at once. "You have!" She drew in her breath with delight. "Oh, give them to me, Barney!"

"No. You give me the bills, and I will settle them."

Fan was furious, and they argued wildly for some time. But the angrier she got the more doubtful he became that she would not use the money to incur further debts instead of ridding herself of those she had; and he remained immovable alike to her pleas, her wheedling and her tantrums.

He said at length: "You are more concerned, to be sure, to have your guineas than you are over the loss of your lover."

"Indeed I am. Why should I not be?"

He looked at her in real amazement. "You do not mind that you are not to marry Stafford?"

"I do not break my heart over it, if that is what you mean. Heigh-ho! that is one thing finished, and now I must consider what the next adventure is to be."

"You did not care for him at all?" Barney's brow was still wrinkled in puzzlement.

"Not two straws!" She flicked her fingers. "He is a conceited, sly creature."

"But if you do not love him, why in Heaven's name were you going to marry him? Why did you run away, and make the General irreparably angry with you—all for a man for whom, from what you say, you have neither respect nor affection?"

"Oh, simple, simple, Barney! I told you I wanted to run away from home. Stafford was in love with me—I could do what I liked with him. He offered me a way of escape—the only, or at least the best—way that I could see then, and I decided to take it. But now he has failed me I do not intend to repine, I assure you. There are plenty of other men in the world besides Lieutenant Carlton Stafford."

"You are a worse little fool than I thought. If you hold so poor an opinion of Stafford, how do you think you could have borne your life with him? He *is* a conceited, sly creature I dare say, and if you knew it you must have known also that you could not be happy with him."

"Still so simple, Barney? If I had married him, I would have been *Mrs.* Stafford, and so free of all the stupid restraints that surround a *Miss*, and particularly a Miss Jaspard. If he had become insupportable, I should have had my consolations." She waved her lashes at him. For Fan could not help flirting, even with her brother.

"I see you'll very soon get into trouble, miss, if you are left to your own devices," said Barney sternly. "You must go back to Hanover Square now, to-night, and we must make up what excuses for you that we can."

"I shall not go back to Hanover Square. I am never going back to Hanover Square."

"And what do you intend to do then, pray?"

"The first thing I intend, Barney dear, is that you and I shall go to the masquerade to-night."

"I wish you would be serious. If you will not go home——"

"I am serious. See, I have the tickets here. You will take me, Barney? It wouldn't be quite proper for me to go alone, now would it? And if you refuse to accompany me, perhaps I shall. With a mask on no one will know who I am. Oh, it will be vastly amusing!"

"Where did you get these tickets?"

He had taken them from her and was studying them. They were for a masquerade to be held that night in the King's Theatre in the Haymarket, under the direction of Mr. Heidegger. He had seen similar tickets before; they were issued to subscribers only at White's Coffee-House in St. James's Street.

"Mr. Folkes gave them to me." Fan, in anticipation, was already doing the steps of a dance.

"Mr. Folkes?" Then he remembered the wealthy tradesman who had so irritated the General by calling upon him for a subscription to a charity for bastards, and at whom Fan had blinked with such good effect.

"Yes, and he gave me a purple rosette to wear on my shoulder so that he may know me in spite of my mask. He is to wear a similar one."

"When did you see Mr. Folkes?"

"Do not look so fierce, Barney. It does not become you, indeed it does not. You look at your best when you are being simple and kind. Your eyes are rather sweet . . ."

"Never mind my appearance. Where did you see Mr. Folkes?"

"Don't grasp my wrist in that silly fashion, it hurts. I met him, and *quite by chance*, in a linen draper's in Cheapside on Saturday."

"He must have been very surprised to have seen you unaccompanied."

"He was. But I told him I was married."

"You told him you were married!"

"It seemed the simplest thing to say. Of course I swore him to secrecy. So he gave me these tickets for myself and my husband. As I haven't got a husband, you must come instead, Barney."

"Do you mean to say you would have taken Stafford to-night?"

"Why not?" Her apparently innocent eyes gazed at him.

"Why not? Married a day, and you would have gone to a ball on purpose that you might flirt with Mr. Folkes. You are quite unprincipled, Fan." But he found himself laughing.

"You will come, Barney? He gave me the masks, too."

"Don't be ridiculous, child! We have to decide seriously what you are to do. I have been thinking that, if you will not go home, you might go to Barbara. That is sufficiently far away, and——"

"Mrs. Fletcher! I don't know her, I have not seen her for years. What an extraordinary notion!"

"I do not see that it is so extraordinary. She is a close relation, and I remember her as a kind and pleasant creature."

"She may be the kindest and pleasantest creature in the world. But if you think that I am going to bury myself in Northumberland, where I might as well be in the wilds of North America for any civilized diversion I would get——"

"They must have some diversions in Northumberland."

"Oh, I dare say. Rounding up the sheep on the fells, perhaps. I am sure her husband is a red-faced squire who thinks of nothing but horses."

"His face is rather red," admitted Barney, who had met him when the couple had stayed at Gartonby a few years before at a time when

Fan was indisposed with an attack of measles. Since then, poor Barbara had yearly planned to revisit her parents, but as each summer came she found herself pregnant or suffering a miscarriage; and in winter the roads from Northumberland were too bad for her husband who, in spite of his red face, was a delicate and cautious man, to care to venture the journey.

"I never heard a more fantastical suggestion in my life," interrupted Fan with great definiteness.

Barney tried to argue with her, but she would not heed him. She kept repeating: "Let us go to the masquerade to-night, and to-morrow we shall talk." On one point only did she express her opinion with vigour: she would not go back to Hanover Square.

He stood out against going to the masquerade for some time, but when it became clear that Fan really meant she would slip away and go alone if he would not oblige her, he gave in. Miss Brook was not, after all, expecting him, and perhaps it would be more politic not to appear too impetuously eager to see her again. Besides, as Fan had said, the masquerade would be vastly amusing, and this extra money in his pocket called loudly for celebration.

"Very well. Give me your bills, and I shall take you."

Pouting, Fan went to a drawer in the table and brought out several sheets of paper. "They are all in Cheapside," she said. "Except one in the Strand. You are mistrustful and horrid, Barney."

"You may think yourself lucky you did not have to return the things." He glanced through the bills, then put them away in his pocket. Suddenly he looked at her sharply. "You like to feel money in your hand, don't you, Fan?"

"I should be a fool if I did not."

"It was you, I suppose, who broke open Jacky's money-box and stole his guineas? I don't know why it never occurred to me before."

She giggled. "I needed them more than he did, and the silly little boy would go on boasting about the guinea Mr. Osborn had given him. And then, besides, the General intended taking the money to punish Jacky for breaking a vase. And *he* has plenty of his own, where I have not."

"It was downright wicked of you. You did not stop to consider that unfortunate Miss Finch might be blamed?"

"Oh, she!" Fan's tone was dismissive. "To tell you the truth I never gave it a thought. I wanted some money. I was not *absolutely* certain then that Stafford would ask me to marry him, and if he did not I meant to run away—not immediately. But I had decided to save till I had enough."

"That is a new name for stealing."

"Oh, don't sound so virtuous, Barney! It ill suits you . . . Very well, I was wrong. I am very sorry. Will that do? Kiss me to show you forgive me." She stood on tiptoe in front of him, her face turned up.

He could not help smiling at her. "I don't waste my kisses on my sister. If we are going to this masquerade, I must go and change. You will not be wearing a fancy costume, I hope; for there I don't mean to keep you in countenance."

"No, it is not necessary. Some do, but there are more, they tell me, who are content with only a mask for disguise. Not but what I should not like to go as—as"—her lashes went up and down—"as Venus rising up out of the waves."

"You rate yourself highly. *I* would not accompany you in those circumstances. How long will it take you to dress—demurely?"

"Come back in an hour, or an hour and a half, if you will. It begins at nine, but no one of the highest fashion arrives much before eleven. One of my new dresses is just the thing. : . ."

"I shall wear my best apricot brocade coat, and I have those new clocked oyster silk stockings Lady Mavington gave me for Christmas, which I have not worn yet." Barney showed nearly as much enthusiasm over his attire as Fan. The male sex had not yet learned to be ashamed of finery.

.   .   .   .   .

As the coach in which he had fetched Fan took its slow place in the line of vehicles drawing up outside the portal of the King's Theatre, Barney forgot that he had ever hoped to spend the evening in the company of Lucy Brook. He was as excited as Fan herself. They donned their masks and commented upon each other's appearance, which from time to time they could see, not by the light of the street lamps which flickered at the top of rare posts, pale and useless, but in the lurid glare cast by the link-boys who, their links held well aloft, pushed a way for their pedestrian patrons. Fan had cut the eye-holes in her mask bigger than ordinary, so that she might the more effectually make use of the most devastating weapon at her disposal. These big rounds, through which her eyes, blue nearly to violet, glistened darkly, gave her a surprised and, somehow, an ingenuous air; as if everything happening about her was matter for astonishment.

There could scarcely have been more confusion and tumult had the theatre been on fire. In the roadway the coachmen shouted unavailingly at those in front to move on, instructed them in impolite terms to guide their horses a little more to the left or to the right; cursed the boys who dodged between the wheels to cross the road; flicked their whip lashes gently but with good aim at any pretty young woman of the lower orders, whether escorted or not, who happened to pass within reach. On the footpath, divided from the road by posts and chains, sedan-chair-men, who in fact had no business to be there, jostled the walkers against the walls of the buildings or left them clinging to a post in peril of being crushed by a passing coach wheel.

And as the masked gentlemen and ladies in their gorgeous, rustling coats, their sumptuous crackling petticoats, here and there an Eliza-bethan courtier, a harlequin, shepherds and shepherdesses—as these descended in the little space kept clear for them by the burly footmen of the theatre, the rabble who had come to stare let their comments, usually of a coarse nature, fall freely on their ears. This in spite of the fact that the masquerades were advertised as being sufficiently guarded within and without against the committal of any disorders or indecencies.

The stage of the King's Theatre was brilliantly lit by a huge chan-delier suspended from the rafters. More candles outlined the stage-boxes, and the hundreds of still flames drawing bright colour from the coats and the dresses of the massed dancers, assembled where at other times the actors walked, made so vivid and fairylandish a scene as to cause the stranger to masquerades to draw in his breath with wonder and delight.

In the plush benches of the pit were scattered such of the assembly who did not choose either to dance or to seek the refreshment-rooms opening off the foyer. They formed as fine an audience, if a sparser, as could be seen in the seats at any theatrical representation, and their attention was as little given to the stage. Only now, instead of seeking acquaintance in the boxes, or posing and preening for the edification of anyone so sensible as to be looking upon their splendour, heads were bent to heads, fans fluttered playfully, provokingly; eyes behind masks rolled and languished, tender words were whispered, pledges exchanged, and all the world for a few minutes forgotten.

When Barney and Fan entered, the company was taking places for a country dance, and they hastily joined in at the bottom of the line. Fan attracted attention immediately. All the gentlemen in her neighbour-hood turned to stare at the big-eyed mask which left uncovered a naughty mouth, smiling promises. The partners of the gentlemen, on the contrary, tossed their heads and renewed their conversations with added sweetness and dash.

The dance was barely over when a tall, burly man dressed in green velvet and silver lace, with a purple knot upon his shoulder, came up to Fan and bowed. Barney heard him say in a low voice: "I was watching by the door for you to come." He gave a quick look in Barney's direction; it was not, he felt, exactly unfriendly, but it was certainly appraising.

"This is my brother," she said.

"Your servant, sir," murmured Barney.

"Your brother! I am glad to meet you, sir." Mr. Folkes bowed.

"You are surprised, to be sure. Oh! it is a tedious story. I want only to dance, to dance!"

"If I may have the honour——"

They seemed to be swept away from Barney rather than have left him of their own free will. The man's head was bent close towards hers. Fan's masked face was raised, and he could imagine how her eyes were darting their charms into Mr. Folkes'; darting them so deep that they must go down—if not into his heart at least into his passions. For a moment or two Barney felt ill at ease. The shadow of Fan's future seemed to fall across the lovely candlelight, the brilliance of the scene that was brighter in colour than any summer flower-bed. But he had brought her here now, and he could not take her away again. In any event she was not to be controlled. Already he recognized that Fan was mistress of her destiny, and neither he nor even the General could prevent her from clutching with both hands at what, in the minute and without thought for the future, she wanted.

He felt a tap on his shoulder, and started. At once he shook off his passing inquietude. Was he not young, too, and should he not enjoy himself?

The woman beside him was distinctive and exciting. She was clad in black velvet and black lace, a wide hoop of velvet looped over a petticoat of lace on satin; and the skin of her bare neck down to the distinctly visible twin risings of her bosom was smooth as cream and white as a snowdrop. Close about her throat, on a black velvet band, a diamond ornament reflected the flames of a hundred candles and flashed changing brilliance with every slight turn of her head. Her mask, unlike most others, was hung with lace at the bottom, so that all her features were covered, and her mouth appeared only mistily behind its veil.

"This is no place to stand in a dream, sir." Her voice was low and husky; it reminded him of the black velvet that she wore.

"Then may I have the honour and delight of dancing with you?" he asked, with a low bow.

To the thin, plaintive wail of the violins and french horns they paced two minuets, jigged three gay country dances. Then, warm and laughing, gazing at each other's eyes behind the masks much as Fan and her gallant had done, they went from the crowded stage to a room off the foyer, where supper was being served.

G

Because he gave a footman a guinea, they were bowed to a secluded table, and quickly served with cold chickens, wine and fruit. The lackey's obsequiousness was more intoxicating to Barney than any liquor. I throw him a guinea, he thought, and he gives me deference and service such as I can never command when I am without money in my pocket. Money! that is the lord of life! But it was no time to consider this now. . . .

"You have not told me your name," he said, turning his eyes and his attention to his partner.

"My name? O-oh! Call me Phillis, that is enough, and I shall call you Corydon."

"We are very far from Arcady among this throng," he said practically. "But I wish we might wander in the meadows with our sheep. A crook in your hand would become you, sweet Phillis."

"And a leopard-skin vest you, dear Corydon."

They amused themselves for a few minutes with such harmless and foolish fancies.

But behind his banter Barney was pondering seriously her identity. Her diamonds proclaimed her a woman of means and—the bent of his mind being always towards romanticism—he played with the idea that she might be a lady of the very first quality: a Countess, even a Duchess.

"Are you married, Phillis?" he asked presently.

"Widowed," she answered, with a tremor in her velvety voice that conveyed not so much sorrow as pathos: it implied she was in need of protection.

"And you, Corydon?"

"No, I am not married."

"Heart-free?"

Barney finished a large mouthful of chicken before he answered. With that elasticity of heart which is perhaps a trait commoner in male lovers than in female, he had temporarily forgotten that he was pining for the favours of Lucy Brook.

"To-night—quite heart-free," he said, with a smile.

She must have noticed his qualification, for she fell silent and continued her meal. This was accomplished with some difficulty, as with one hand she had constantly to raise the lace that fell over her mouth. But for all his peering Barney could gauge little more of her appearance than he had before. That her mouth was small and her eyes a hazel that accorded with her light brown hair was the sum of his knowledge of it.

When supper was over and they had emptied the better part of two bottles of wine, he shuffled his chair closer to hers, as close indeed as he could get it. He bent his head and laid his lips on the creamy skin just above the line of her dress.

"Fie, sir! and with all the world looking on!"

"They are not looking at us, they have themselves to look at," he replied, though very indistinctly, as his lips remained close against her skin. She had a pleasant perfume, like roses on a hot summer day; this was a little mingled with the smell of her sweat, a mixture of odour that in no way repelled Barney who, on the contrary, found that it excited his senses the more. His lips moved lower and pushed, as far as her dress would permit them to do so, down the crevice between her breasts.

She tapped him gently on the cheek with her closed fan.

"That will do, sir. Pray, sir, remember where we are. You make me blush, indeed you do. . . . We had better dance, Corydon." She tapped him more smartly.

Barney, not unlike a dog who has been sniffling after rabbits, reluctantly raised his head.

During the next set that they danced he looked up and down the lines in search of Fan, but he could not see her. His restless gazing did not go unobserved.

"Whom are you seeking?" asked Phillis, as they walked across the floor to find seats. "There is a lady upon your conscience, I believe. Have I made you desert your true partner all this time, Corydon?"

"The only lady on my conscience is my sister. Do you mind if we walk round once to see if I can find her?"

"Not the least in the world. But is she truly your sister, Corydon? Phillis grows a little jealous."

"On my oath she is my sister. For my part, why should I not be jealous too? Have you not a gallant who is gnashing his teeth in search of you?"

Phillis only laughed.

They circled the room twice, and returned to the supper-room; but of Fan there was no sign.

"I dare say she does not want to be found," said Phillis sensibly.

Barney feared that this was only too true.

"Is she with somebody you know?" pursued Phillis.

"Er—yes. Yes, she is."

"Then I should not worry over her. One must presume he is respectable, or you would not have committed her to his care in the first place."

"No," he agreed, but with a noticeable lack of conviction.

The music was beginning again, and Phillis urged him back to the dance.

Much later, they were sitting again at their secluded table, drinking more wine. They had recovered their previous seats without resort to bribery as the room was emptying, many of the guests having already left.

Barney had been kissing her bosom again, and with greater hardiness now thrust his fingers down that tempting valley until Phillis rapped his knuckles painfully with the hard edge of her fan.

"Ow!" he cried, and while pretending to be distracted by a tingling hand made a sudden movement and kissed her on the lips. True, the lace came between them and marred the sensation, but it was a hearty buss for all that.

"Corydon! Corydon!" she chided him. "Must I remind you again that we are not alone?"

"I wish we were. . . . Unmask for me now. Please, Phillis. I want to see you, I want to know you properly. There!" He pulled off his own mask. "Now you must do the same for me."

She appeared to be studying his revealed features: the blunt nose, the thick-lashed eyes that, for all their boldness, had a gentle, self-depreciatory expression.

"Say you like me," he begged. "Say you are not disappointed, that you did not expect a paragon of male beauty?"

"No," and her voice was sweet and thrilling. "I am not disappointed. Oh, no! Put a leopard-skin in place of your apricot brocade, and you are just as Corydon should be."

Barney was not quite sure that he was entirely pleased to be considered so like a shepherd, even an Arcadian one. But he did not dwell on this. He raised his hand as though he would remove her mask himself.

"No," she said. "Please humour me, Corydon. If you will agree to meet me again, you shall see me unmasked then. But not here."

"You tease me and tantalize me. What have I done to deserve it?"

"Do you—wish to see me again, or shall to-night be forgotten—remembered only as a little pleasant episode?"

"Phillis! How foolish a question! When am I to see you? Where?"

"I will write the direction for you on a piece of paper—oh, the back of the card will do." She took from the velvet bag that dangled at her waist her card of admission to the masquerade. "Have you a pencil?"

He found one in his pocket. "At least you will have to tell me your real name," he said as she was writing.

"Ask for Mrs. Randal."

He read the address on the card. It was in Bond Street. He was not disappointed in her neighbourhood. A pity she was not a duchess after all; on the other hand it might have its inconveniences to be received on intimate terms by one quite so high among the nobility.

"You will come—one week from today?"

"Not till then! Oh, take pity on my impatience!"

"It is now Wednesday, is it not? A week today. Perhaps I shall explain when we meet why I wished to wait a week."

"A week! Seven days! You are very cruel!"

"Do not say that, Corydon." Her husky voice lost its playfulness. "I await our meeting as eagerly as you can. Do not expect too much. You—may be disappointed in me when I am unmasked."

"Never, madam!"

"In the meantime I may trust to your discretion? You will not inquire after me from curiosity, and so let it be known that I made an assignation with a stranger at the masquerade? A woman, alone as I am, cannot be too careful to protect her reputation."

Her throaty wistfulness roused all that was chivalrous in Barney's heart. He swore not to let her name pass his lips.

"Dear boy! I shall expect you then to dinner next Wednesday, at three o'clock."

Barney would not admit he was not the wealthy gentleman of leisure she evidently and naturally supposed him to be, and that as a clerk it was not possible for him to dine with her at that hour.

"May it not be supper, madam? Three o'clock is a practical, unromantical time of day. Let it be seven, Phillis."

"You silly fellow! If you wish. And now, Corydon, you must tell me what name you go by when you are out of Arcady."

"Jaspard. Barnabas Jaspard."

"You are related to my Lord Manvington?"

He had been afraid that his name would connect him with that nobleman, if not with his brilliant and notable father.

"I am." But he did not specify his relationship. "Do you know him?"

"Only as all the world knows him. . . . Now, Corydon—I shall continue to call you Corydon—I must leave. Will you perform one more kindness for me, and see me to my coach?"

The ballroom was half empty as they crossed it, and Barney looked round again for the blue dress and purple rosette of Fan.

Phillis's equipage pleased him. It was drawn by a pair of fine horses, and a footman in livery attended her. As he watched her drive away he was looking forward keenly to the meeting a week hence.

He returned inside and again sought Fan. So thinned were the numbers now that he knew he could not miss her. Yet nowhere was she to be found. He crossed and recrossed the stage, he searched the seats, going even into the gallery, lest she and her partner should have had a whim to be alone in that common and deserted place; through the foyer again, and the other rooms. She was nowhere. His own pleasures over, he was irritated and sleepy. He looked at his watch. He would be fortunate if he got two hours in bed before he had to prepare himself to go to the Customs House.

For another half-hour he waited, by which time the musicians had packed away their violins and french horns, and all but a dozen or so of the dancers had left the theatre. Forlorn were the empty rooms with chairs untidily awry; scraps of paper, a mask or two, and torn pieces from the hem of some lady's dress stained the shining stretch of the stage boards; the candles in the chandeliers were guttering, while here and there thin lines of smoke ascended from soot-blobbed wicks in need of the snuffer's hand. Round the walls flunkeys, openly yawning, waited for the last of the guests to depart.

Mr. Folkes must have seen Fan to her lodgings, he said to himself; but as he went out into the lessening bustle of the Haymarket and raised his hand in acceptance of the clamouring offer of two hackney-chair men to take him home, he knew that he did not really believe this.

To-night Fan had chosen her own way of life. Finally and for ever she had shaken the dust of Hanover Square from the soles of her slippers, and henceforward would walk apart from the family of Jaspard.

CHAPTER IX

CRESWELL'S WEDDING NIGHT

THAT part of Creswell's wedding evening which was spent under the eyes of the family passed exactly as he had foreseen. Even at dinner there was no assumption of gaiety, beyond the formal drinking of the health of the couple; and he thought it hard that he should pass from a bachelor to a married man without the support of a single friend. He wondered whether Tom Brabazon and Penge yet knew what had befallen him; and never did debtor imprisoned in the Fleet long more passionately for his freedom than did Creswell to be sitting with a crowd of his cronies; laughing, drinking, planning wild escapades, with no thought that Nemesis might some day descend to diminish their exuberant spirits.

The contrast of the reality here in Cleveland Court was a sad one.

The ladies left the table, and the port went round between the ill-assorted quartet of Lord Comberley, Mr. Jaspard, Creswell and Mr. Pratt. Mr. Pratt alone showed any pretensions to joviality. He related, between his copious snuff-takings, tales of his country parish, before he came to Court; these, to judge from his laughter, highly amused himself, though to Creswell they were as tedious as the discourses of a godly, elderly spinster. Lord Comberley and Mr. Jaspard were talking politics, and the words "Whig" and "the Prince" were scattered through their conversation like pepper sprinkled into a soup.

Since things could not well be worse, or his personal esteem fall much lower, Creswell decided that he might as well get drunk. But he soon saw that even this consolation was to be denied him. The port stayed obstinately in front of Lord Comberley, and though Mr. Jaspard's glass was filled many times, the decanter passed but intermittently to Creswell and Mr. Pratt. This was due, he was certain, to no oversight or lack of manners on Lord Comberley's part. His lordship was determined to send the bridegroom to bed sober. If Mr. Pratt suffered as a consequence it was no matter, and in any case he should think himself honoured to be at Lord Comberley's table.

At long last the gentlemen retired to the drawing-room, where Mrs. Jaspard and Mrs. True were chatting in a comparatively animated manner, while Rosa listened with an air of demure attention. Creswell tried to smile at her, but she still refused, as she had done all day, to look at him.

Tea was brought in presently, and insipid and constrained conversation followed. Then, with the stately pageantry with which, in a great house, every service, however slight, was rendered, the two wigged footmen, seeming an extension of the furniture in their red plush and gilt, their wooden stiffness, carried out the china. A minute later they returned, stood one on either side of the double door like sentinels, bowed, turned with drilled precision and marched out again, closing the doors behind them.

Mr. Jaspard, who was not given to hiding his feelings unless it suited him to do so, had been showing signs of impatience for some time. He was, Creswell suspected, as heartily sick of this day as he himself. But at least the General would end it in the comfortable dullness of the company of a woman who had been his wife for nearly thirty years.

It was not nine o'clock when Mr. Jaspard got to his feet, shook out his lace cuffs with the gesture habitual to him, and said, addressing himself to Lord Comberley:

"I dare say the young pair are impatient. Will you not excuse your niece, Comberley, and I will play groomsman to my son? My wife and

I should like to see them bedded, and we must be on our way within the hour."

It must not be supposed that there was anything shocking about this speech: it was one perfectly conformable to the polite usages of the age. Yet Creswell, though he had known that they must be publicly bedded, found himself blushing like a schoolboy. He did not dare to raise his eyes towards Rosa. Her uncle spoke to her, and he heard the rustling of her dress as she made her curtsies and, with Mrs. True and Mrs. Jaspard, withdrew.

Creswell was at least spared the coarse humour that a bridegroom marrying under more auspicious conditions must inevitably have had thrust at him. His father, to be sure, did make one waggish and mildly obscene remark, but upon noting Lord Comberley's expression of disapproval, he recollected that the disgraceful circumstances surrounding Creswell's marriage did not make it a suitable subject for jest.

Ten minutes after Rosa's departure, a footman was summoned to accompany the groom and Mr. Jaspard to the chamber where the former was to disrobe. Creswell, who had not given any thought till now to such a trivial matter as that he had no night-clothes with him, found a new night-shirt laid over the back of a chair, together with slippers, a dressing-gown and a night-cap.

"Your mother packed a portmanteau for you," said Mr. Jaspard when the servant had left them alone. "I told her no man wanted a night-shirt on his wedding night, but she seemed to think it would not be the thing to go naked to bed. Well, it may be the young ladies are more squeamish than in my day . . ."

Creswell was just ready when, with a perfunctory rap at the door, Lord Comberley walked in. He carried a candlestick, and led the way, a few steps down the passage, to another door. This he opened, and ushered the bridgeroom in.

Rosa, as pale as the pillow supporting her, was sitting up on one side of a very large bed. Beside her stood Mrs. True and Mrs. Jaspard. Creswell, still wearing his dressing-gown, climbed into bed beside her. There they sat, he thought, like two puppets on show, while formal expressions of good will, including the embarrassing hope that they would soon be blessed with progeny, were once again offered to them.

Mrs. True curtsied deeply, and left the room. Mrs. Jaspard kissed the bride upon the cheek, then walked round the bed, and more warmly embraced Creswell. Lord Comberley kissed his niece, but bestowed on his new nephew no more than a minatory glare. Mr. Jaspard in his most gallant manner, and that included movements both of beauty and grace, picked up Rosa's hand and placed upon it a warm kiss. Creswell he shook by the hand and gave him—to his son's unutterable astonishment—a significant wink, as who would say: "You are a lucky fellow! make the most of it." Then he and Lord Comberley drew the bed curtains, blew out the candles, and at the door all three wished the pair a final good night.

The bride and bridegroom were left alone.

Creswell for some seconds lay lost in contemplation of his father's wink. Never before, not in all his life, could he remember the General unbending so. But of course, he reflected, to be the success he has been —he is—with both men and women, there must be a side to him he does not choose to show at home. And that wink, he suddenly knew, had held more than a lewd suggestiveness: it had signified that his childhood—and childhood for the General had little to do with years— was at an end. He was accepted as a man of the world.

But this was no time to be considering the ramifications of the General's mind. He and Rosa were still sitting up, straight and immovable, still like two puppets. That they might slide the more easily into intimate conversation, he said pleasantly:

"You wore a lovely dress to-day. I wish I could have been as grand for you. How did you happen to have one to hand so suited to a wedding?"

"I was to have worn it at my first Drawing Room. My lord thought I might soon go out of mourning." Her tone was polite, but as of one answering the query of a total stranger.

"So I had the pleasure of seeing it first, instead of His Majesty? . . . Oh, Rosa!" he turned towards her. "Don't hate me, please don't hate me!"

She did not answer. Her stillness could be felt through the darkness.

"We are married now," he urged in a low, gentle voice. "You have vowed to love me. You can at least try." .

"I told you last night I never wish to hear you speak of love. I hope you understand now that I mean it. I will endeavour to do my duty as your—wife before the world, but when we are alone I think we may forget that we have—these obligations towards each other."

Creswell pondered upon this quite impossible view of matrimony which she apparently expected him to adopt. Then he said: "I should like to say, madam, that if your behaviour towards me all to-day is an example of how you intend to show the world you are a dutiful wife, it is a very strange one. You would not so much as look at me, let alone give me a smile."

"I did not feel like smiling."

"Neither did I," agreed Creswell, "but I know my manners, I hope."

It was not a happy remark.

"If you had known your manners," came her cold little voice, "we would not be married now."

"I am sorry," said Creswell, sounding however more sulky than penitent. "I have begged your pardon, I have apologized. You cannot spend the rest of your life reminding me of how we came to be married." For fear that she might tell him that indeed she could, he went on hastily: "We were talking about your manner towards me before the world. I hope you will manage to assume a more convincing air of— I shall not say affection, but companionableness—than you did to-day."

"I hope as time passes I shall not find it so difficult to wear an expression I am not feeling."

"I hope so indeed." He kept his tone light. "I am told that the graces of society are based on the ladies smiling at each other, when, in fact, they might like to scratch each other's eyes out. . . . Do you think, if I were to light a candle, you could start practising to smile at me now?"

"No," she said decisively. "I am going to sleep."

He heard her rustle down in bed.

He removed his dressing-gown and lay on his back, considering what it would be wisest for him to do next. She was such a baby she probably had no idea what marriage meant. It had certainly sounded so from her confused accusations of the previous night. But had Mrs. True enlightened her since? From the calm way she was settling herself to sleep it did not appear very likely. Or was she behaving in this cold, detached way on purpose to perplex him and to add difficulties to a love-making that was already beset with them? It was impossible to say.

At first he decided he would try to sleep himself, and forget, if it were possible, that a young and lovely female lay beside him in the bed. When he abandoned this plan—which he did in a very few minutes—it was not solely because the pounding of his pulses would not let him rest. If he postponed making her his wife in fact, it would be but to spend another wretched day on the morrow, and be faced with the same problems the next night.

He knew, without undue vanity, that he had charm for most women, and it seemed to him, lying there between the small four walls of the big bed, that the only chance of his happiness with Rosa was to triumph over her now, to love her and to win her.

This resolve made, he put his hand out and touched her. He knew she was wide awake, for he felt her body shake.

"My darling," he said, "don't be frightened. Be kind to me, Rosa!"

He moved to her and took her in his arms. She lay still as a dead thing, stiff as a dead thing.

"Little love! little bird! I'll not hurt you. I'll try not to hurt you."

.   .   .   .   .

She had cried out once, but now she was sobbing without restraint.

Creswell, exhausted, defeated, degraded, not, as he had seen himself, the triumphant lover—and he had brought to his love-making all the sweeter side of his experience—joined his tears to hers. He turned away to his side of the bed and cried as he had not cried for more than fifteen years.

She was sufficiently surprised that her own sobs were halted. "If you find me," she said snifflingly, "so great a disappointment, it—it serves you right."

But Creswell's only answer was a choking groan as he endeavoured to control his weeping.

So ended their wedding night: each asleep upon a far side of the bed, with tear-stains on their faces.

CHAPTER X

A SUNDAY AT HOME

KITTY let her book drop onto her knee and, without being guilty of the bad manners of opening her mouth, allowed herself the pleasure of a yawn. She was thinking how very odd it was that since she had not had Gertrude to talk to the savour had gone out of reading. There was no one to discuss her books with, no one to whom she could point out those passages which moved her, no one to sympathize with her indignation should she disagree profoundly with her author. It was a shame of the General to be angry with Gertrude because she had courage enough to refuse to marry Stephen when she did not love him. But Mamma had told her after breakfast this morning that on Saturday she and Papa had met Mr. Dale in the street, and Papa had added a curt good morning to the stiff bow which had lately been his sole acknowledgement of Mr. Dale's presence on the occasions when they happened to meet. Here were the beginnings, both mother and daughter hoped, of a reconciliation. Mamma, as Kitty knew, whatever may have been her feelings towards Gertrude for jilting her son, approved highly of Mr. Dale as a friend for Papa. He was a gentleman whose morals and politics were alike irreproachable.

Mrs. Dale, too, would assuredly do as much as lay in her power to being her brother-in-law to friendliness. Though she would not coerce Gertrude she still hoped—so she had confided to Mrs. Jaspard—that when Stephen returned from his travels the quarrel or disinclination, whichever it was, might be ended. Kitty, however, gave little considertion to Mrs. Dale's point of view. By comparison with the intimacy with which Gertrude, until this breach, had come and gone in the Jaspard family, her mother was a stranger to the younger members. She was a woman given much to card-playing, though not in an extravagant or vicious manner, and a great part of her day was passed in this occupation. In appearance formidable, with her long plain face; in manner, when one knew her, she proved to have the charm and humour her daughter had inherited.

So very short a time ago, continued Kitty's train of thought, she had believed that if only she would be left alone to read, she would have no other demands to make from life. But now that Stephen had gone on his tour, Barney no longer lived at home, Fan had vanished (and though she had good reasons not to be sorry for this, yet she found she missed her companionship), and Gertrude was in disfavour with the General, there were many hours of the day when no one questioned her doings, no one spoilt the silence with chatter, and she might read till her eyes were tired. But it was unconscionably dull. . . .

Perhaps her books had become tedious, not because Gertrude was absent, but because she herself was in love. However one looked at it, real life was more exciting than anything in a book. Yes, that must be it. How handsome he was! What romantic compliments he could turn! She suppressed a passing unworthy thought that it was a pity that Carlton—for so she now called him in her meditations though not to his face—a pity Carlton did not read the books she enjoyed—if indeed he read any books at all. When she was married she would have a salon, and all the intellects of the age, upon a special evening in the week, would be seen jostling upon her doorstep. It was a delightful vision, but perhaps in her heart she could not really see the wife of Lieutenant Carlton Stafford of the Foot Guards the centre of such a scene, for there was no room in it at all for Stafford himself.

She sometimes wondered how much Carlton's thoughts dwelt on the subject of Fan's mysterious disappearance. The General would not allow it to be discussed, but there had been a recent evening which Kitty could not easily forget. Four or five days had passed since Fan had run away, and Carlton, who had seemed distrait from the moment he arrived, upon the first opportunity asked Kitty in a casual manner that could not hide the earnestness behind the question, whether there had been any news of Fan. Kitty's jealousy, happily dormant since Fan went, awoke refreshed.

"You had better ask Papa," she said coolly, "*I* know nothing."

"But you must be gravely disturbed. Your cousin and playmate, and so pretty a creature! I conclude Mr. Jaspard has sought her far and near?"

"He has not told me what steps he has taken," answered Kitty, quite unmoved by the reference to her lost and pretty playmate.

"'Od's fish!" Carlton fiddled with the gold tassels of his sword-hilt. "Were I her relative, I should have no peace of mind till she were found."

"Mr. Stafford," said Kitty, looking directly at him with eyes so much less lovely than those he had foresworn, "I am not allowed to talk of Fan. She was headstrong, and chose to leave home and bring disgrace upon us. I must ask you not to force me to go against Papa's wishes by continuing this conversation."

Carlton had obeyed her, and talked of other things; but during the remainder of his visit he paid her no compliments, and his demeanour was not such that a stranger would have guessed he was Miss Jaspard's lover.

Yet Kitty, though she had been so cool on the subject to Carlton Stafford, was nonetheless wildly curious to know what indeed had become of Fan. She must have had very little money, and she could not go to any friends known to Mamma and the General, for they would very soon send her back to Hanover Square. Barney had denied any knowledge of her . . . but she was not absolutely certain he was speaking the truth.

Now Kitty glanced at Delia, seated near her, whose needle was going in and out of her material with the speed and efficiency of a paid sewing-woman. It was not strictly Delia's hour for sewing, but it was raining too hard for her to think of taking her morning's walk; therefore, at the minute when she would normally have gone to put on her outdoor clothes, she had changed her tapestry work for charity-sewing.

Kitty, enclosed as she had been for some hours with her formidable elder sister, longed for conversation. So much had happened, and there was no one to talk things over with. It had become insupportable.

"Do you never get tired of needlework, Delia?" she asked by way of an opening.

"Yes," answered Delia surprisingly, but added no more.

"Then why do you not stop?"

"If I stopped, what should I do?"

"You might read," suggested Kitty, "or talk to me."

"Sewing is useful, and neither of your alternatives is."

"One cannot for ever be doing something useful," objected Kitty.

To this observation Delia made no reply.

"I wish Stephen had not gone away, then I should have somebody to talk to," said Kitty, speaking her thoughts aloud.

"If he had not gone away, he would not be here to amuse you, but at the Court."

Delia, upon those occasions when she condescended to make a reply longer than a few monosyllables, always answered with withering practicality.

But Kitty could contain herself no longer. "Do you like Creswell's wife?" she asked.

Yesterday had been the Sunday following their marriage, and the couple had dined at Hanover Square, the first occasion upon which Rosa had been introduced to her new family.

"I can hardly like someone I have seen for a few hours only, but she appeared agreeable."

Kitty was encouraged. Delia was being, for her, quite chatty. "But Creswell——" and Kitty's eyes opened wide. "What was the matter with him? He was so quiet, so unlike himself—he seemed a different person altogether. When he smiled it—it reminded me of the way sick people smile, a sort of patient bravery, with no pleasure behind it."

"You are ridiculously fanciful."

"Oh, you *must* have noticed, Delia." Kitty spoke with some exasperation.

"I consider it was an improvement on his usual ebullience."

"I don't. He is so amusing and gay. . . . Perhaps he had a pain."

It will be observed that Kitty, for all her wading through many tomes, yet retained a simple outlook on life.

"Delia, *why* do you think they were married so suddenly, so secretly?"

"I have no idea."

"Perhaps he eloped with her, and the General and Lord Comberley did not want it made public. Do you think so?"

Kitty was startled at the change that came over her sister's face. Delia had stopped sewing. She was staring straight in front of her. Her eyes had a wild look and her fingers were trembling.

"I do not know," she said without expression, and her mouth closed in a prim line.

Deciding that Creswell's marriage was not a topic to pursue, Kitty tried to return to *Some Thoughts Concerning Education*, by Mr. John Locke. But she could not attend to it. Other incidents from yesterday clamoured for expression.

"I think Barney is falling in love with Miss Finch," she announced.

Again Delia's needle—for she had resumed her sewing—faltered and paused; but she made no comment.

"Are you never interested in other people?" asked the baffled Kitty despairingly.

"No," said Delia flatly.

"I don't understand you. I don't understand you at all. For instance, do you never wonder where Fan is, what has become of her? You must!"

"I can guess without much wondering what has probably become of her."

"Oh, what? Tell me."

"I do not choose to tell you."

"Oh dear! Well, tell me this: have you noticed anything between Barney and Miss Finch?"

"Certainly not."

"I have. Do you know where he was after dinner yesterday—and after dinner the Sunday before?" Though she paused dramatically, there was no response from Delia, and she was forced to answer her own question. "In the nursery with Miss Finch."

"He plays with Jacky and Dorothy."

"Plays with Jacky and Dorothy!" echoed Kitty scornfully. "Have you ever known Barney play with the children before? And that's not all. I mentioned him to Miss Finch this morning, and she went quite pink, she did indeed."

There was no reply to this from Delia, and Kitty belatedly feared that her zeal to talk had outrun discretion.

"Delia, you will not tell Papa or Mamma?" she said anxiously. "I am sure there is no harm in it, and poor Miss Finch would but be sent out of the house in an instant. And she is a nice creature if dull. Barney could not care for her seriously, she is not pretty and her hair is red. You will forget I told you, Delia?"

"I do not usually forget things I am told," said Delia, "but if you mean will I not speak of it—no, I will not. Miss Finch is a fool, and Barney is a greater."

On this pronouncement Delia's needle went in and out faster than before; and despite Kitty's efforts she could not be persuaded into further conversation. She snapped at her sister, and appeared to be withdrawn into some far contemplation of her own.

With a sigh Kitty picked up the discarded Mr. Locke.

.   .   .   .   .

But Barney was not in love with Miss Finch. The greater part of that time yesterday when Kitty imagined he was in the schoolroom, he had been sitting in the gun-room with Creswell.

As short a while as it was since he had left home, it was with increasing reluctance that he spent his Sundays at Hanover Square. The habit of obedience to the General was still strong upon him, and tempting as it was to spend his one free day in the week following his own inclinations, he had not yet found the courage for such an act of defiance.

This Sunday he found more than usually tedious. Stephen and Fan, his two closest companions in the family, were, for their varying reasons, absent. Creswell, usually to be depended upon to keep the company lively, was subdued; as for his bride, she was as pretty as a man could want, but she appeared a haughty little thing. Kitty was a good creature, but he had nothing to say to her. The General and Madam, Delia, Lord and Lady Manvington and the two youngest of their ladysheeps were company which Barney found neither amusing nor stimulating. There remained, besides, Carlton Stafford, who was now treating him with unctuous politeness. He heartily disliked Kitty's betrothed, and had been at some pains to avoid finding himself alone with him, a situation it was obvious Stafford desired. No doubt but he wished to question him about Fan, and he had no intention of satisfying, or even snubbing, his curiosity.

Barney compared the stately meal, with its uninteresting discourse of family topics being bandied dutifully from diner to diner, with the exhilarating supper-party of two nights ago to which—thanks to Lieutenant Carlton Stafford—he had entertained Miss Brook, her mother, Mr. Raikes, Harry and a young woman of Harry's acquaintance. None of his easily-gotten money was left now, but it had been, he considered, well spent. He had gone home with the Brooks afterwards, he and Harry and Mr. Raikes singing at the tops of their voices, while the women giggled and made jokes. Then, in the Brooks' drawing-room, the others one by one made excuses to retire, and he was left alone with Lucy. It had been as simple as that. He had kissed her and tumbled her—for admittedly he had been rather drunk—but she, though acquiescent to a point beyond what he had dared to hope so early in their friendship, had nevertheless set very definite limits to his freedom. He had had to go home unappeased, if with high expectations for the future. . . . There was, too, the adventure of the masquerade, which had yet to reach its climax when he should see the adorable Phillis unmasked. Yes, Barney felt he was a dashing young fellow and—if only he was in possession of more money—worthy to follow in the Lotharian steps of Robert Jaspard.

It was this self-satisfaction, this cock-o'-the-walk jauntiness, that gave him the boldness to question Creswell on the mystifying subject of his precipitate and totally unexpected marriage.

When dinner was finally over and the men straggled from the dining-room, he accompanied Creswell to the house of office in the cellar. Creswell was a little drunk. It was scarcely detectable, yet he stumbled on the steps and Barney had to catch him by the arm. As they were coming back, Barney said to him:

"You were a sly one over your wedding, Creswell. Why did none of us know of it?"

Creswell looked at him with a slightly stupid stare. "Why should I have told you?" he asked aggressively.

"I think it is a case rather of why you should *not*," answered Barney undeterred.

"It was no more of a surprise to you than it was to me, I assure you," said Creswell drily. In milder tones he added: "You'll hear of it, you are bound to hear of it. So—I may as well tell you the true version." They were still in the servants' part of the house behind the green baize door, and had paused by the gun-room entrance. "Come in here."

There had been a fire lit earlier in the day, and the room, though comfortless, was still warm. They sat down on a hard bench, opposite a rack full of firearms of every sort. A faint and not unpleasant smell of oil filled the atmosphere.

As soon as he began his story, which he did only after some encouragement and urging—for once in the gun-room a silence had settled upon him—Barney soon saw that in spite of this reluctance it was a great relief to Creswell to unburden himself. He reflected that had he been perfectly sober he would not have done so; certainly not to him, Barney, for whom his natural brotherly affection had always been mixed with an unbrotherly condescension. Obviously, he had been longing to talk. But he could not, for the sake of his wife, discuss this extraordinary adventure with even his closest friends outside the family, not Brabazon or Penge themselves, who had been both instigators and witnesses of the greater part of it.

Creswell's tale, which was not perhaps strictly accurate in every detail and glossed over that part of the night when he and Rosa had been alone in the *Green Periwig*, ended, it should not need to be said, with the marriage ceremony.

"She is very beautiful," said Barney politely and consolingly.

"And very rich," added Creswell, but gloomily.

"You won a wager of five hundred guineas besides," Barney reminded him, with a practicality that was already assessing what advantage this might be to himself.

H

"No. We agreed to speak of that no more. Penge said I did not win it in the circumstances which the wager embraced." For the first time he smiled slightly.

But he did not tell Barney that even yet that wager had not been won, nor did it seem at present in the least likely that it ever would be.

"You are still in waiting?" asked Barney, who did not wish to rush his fences.

"Yes. His Majesty, on the supplication of my beloved uncle-in-law, condescended to overlook my breach of etiquette in marrying without his permission."

"Shall your wife go to the Court—I mean, become one of the Ladies?"

"I do not think so, not at present."

They spoke desultorily of Court matters for a minute or two until the time seemed ripe to Barney to take his leap.

"These South Sea stocks are worth buying, aren't they?"

"Why, so I believe." Creswell looked surprised. "Since when were you interested in investment, Barney?"

Barney ignored the implication. "A friend of mine," he said, and he was speaking of Mr. Raikes, "a good business man, told me one can make no mistake in buying them. I have heard other people—men in the Office—say so, too. They stand at 150 per cent now, and are rising every day." He went into figures with the enthusiasm noticeable in those who aspire to make their fortunes by easy means.

Creswell did not appear much interested.

"I was wondering," said Barney, coming at last to the point, "whether you could lend me, let us say £100, to buy some South Sea."

"A hundred pounds! My dear fellow! I have no spare money." Since incredulity, not to say irritation, was clearly to be read in Barney's face, he went on: "I know that must sound absurd to you when I have just married an heiress. But, 'pon my honour, what I say is the truth. In the first place, such are the settlements, that in her lifetime I shall never have the whole of her fortune in my power, and until I am twenty-five years old I am restricted to but a small portion. In the second place, that portion I do not in fact handle at all, since my Lord Comberley is pleased to take it for our housekeeping and to pay off my debts. Taking into consideration the style I have to live in, I am as poor as you are, Barney." He spoke with decision. ". . . And now, I suppose, we had better return to the ladies."

"Yes," agreed Barney, who was deeply disappointed. If only he had been more drunk, he thought, and passed me his word. . . .

Creswell, no doubt meaning to make some amends by being agreeable, asked in the same perfunctory manner that he did every time that he saw Barney whether his work in the Office of Trade and Plantations was becoming easy and pleasant to him. Barney, not deceived as to his interest, answered him briefly and unenthusiastically. They were standing up, ready to go.

"You know nothing of Fan, I conclude?" asked Creswell suddenly.

"Fan? No—I have no idea where she is." He wondered whether he should tell Creswell he had seen her since she ran away from home. It was possible he could give him the direction of Mr. Folkes's house—a piece of information he had not yet succeeded in discovering.

But Creswell had reached the door and opened it. The time for confidences seemed past. And perhaps it was better not. Creswell might well feel it was his duty to tell the General anything that he had learned concerning Fan. Then he, Barney, would get into serious trouble for concealing that he had any knowledge of her. Indeed, none of his behaviour in that direction would bear close investigation. And Fan was lost; beyond saving . . .

He had gone to her lodgings the following day at the earliest hour he could leave the Customs House, only to learn that, having been out all night, she had returned to pack her belongings, had paid Mrs. Craft what she owed her, and driven away in a coach with a gentleman who had waited outside for her. And Mrs. Craft's lips had closed in a manner which implied she could hardly hold a lower opinion of Miss Debonair.

Barney parted from Creswell at the door of the Reception Room, having told his half-brother frankly that he did not feel sociable and should prefer a half hour freed from the constraint inescapable among the gathered family. He thought that Creswell, as he put his hand on the door-knob, looked as if he wished he too might stay outside; but if this was so he did not follow his inclination. A gentle hum of talk drifted through as he opened the door, and silence came back to the landing again when he closed it upon himself.

Then it was that Barney made his way to the nursery. His desertion of the party was not, in spite of Kitty's surmises, prompted by any strong desire to see Miss Finch. Nor was it that he felt he could not again support the company of the Ladies Louisa and Charlotte, between whom he had sat at dinner, and whose entertainment since their arrival had appeared to fall exclusively on his shoulders. The truth was he could no longer bear to watch red-coated Stafford with his dark, arrogant face bending over Kitty and whispering—one must conclude—words of love in her ear. His conscience was not easy on Fan's behalf. Perhaps it would have been more becoming a man of honour not to have listened to Stafford's sauve arguments, but to have called him out.

Yet Barney was clear-sighted enough to see that Stafford had been only the accidental first cause of Fan's fall from virtue. She was pre-destined to be a whore. Still, if she had been Mrs. Stafford first, it would not have been so bad. . . .

Miss Finch greeted him with a surprised and an attractive embarrass-ment. She at once called to order Jacky and Dorothy who, in spite of having been set to pore over the Scriptures, were squabbling loudly; and bade them bow and curtsey respectively to their elder cousin. Once again Barney bribed them into silence, but found, having effected this, that he had little to say to Miss Finch. He might not have stayed above a minute or two had he not observed, with amused gratification, that same tendency to pinkness which Kitty was to comment upon the following morning. As well, she had a tender, appealing way of asking him questions about himself and his work. Did he not get very tired? Was he well looked after in his lodgings? Had he fire enough? Barney, who was not accustomed to anyone being in the least interested in his physical ease, found her concern for his comfort very soothing.

He did not make the mistake of again trying to take her hand, or in any way behaving in a manner not consistent with the proper deport-ment of a member of the family towards the governess.

This was no virtue in him. He enjoyed talking to her—and in his turn drawing her out on the subject of *her* daily life—but the truth was he no longer wished to hold her hand. He had, he said to himself, with a coxcombry pardonable only in one so young and inexperienced, incomparably more beautiful and attractive women at his disposal.

CHAPTER XI

PHILLIS UNMASKS

WHEN Barney stood upon the doorstep of the house in Bond Street, he was by no means so filled with excitement as, walking home in the dawn after the masquerade, he had believed he would be. The tumul-tuous impatience of that hour had dwindled to an unpassionate curiosity: his pursuit of Lucy Brook was absorbing all his energies and his emotions.

Nevertheless, it was with no dragging step that he followed the liveried footman up the stairs, glancing as he passed at his reflection in a tall mirror on the half-landing. He was a good-looking figure enough, he thought complacently, in his second-best coat of light-green

embossed velvet, trimmed with gold galloon, and the lace cravat that
was the most ample his wardrobe could produce.

The man, walking as quietly as a cat on the thick carpet, opened a
door, announced: "Mr. Jaspard," and waited with bowed head till the
visitor had passed in.

Barney found himself in a small room. It was obviously not the
drawing-room of the house, and must be Phillis's private cabinet. The
general impression was of warmth and redness, both from the red
hangings and the firelight which laid a ruddy glare upon all the furniture. This it did with the greater effect because the lighting was dim. A
pair of candles burned in each of the wall brackets, one on either side
of the fireplace, but in the central chandelier hanging from the ceiling
only every alternate candle sent up its flame. Before the fire, at a little
distance from it, stood a table covered with a white cloth; two places
were laid, the silver appointments gleaming redly. It was a scene set for
intimacy and romance. But where was Phillis?

He heard a noise, and turned. A door at the farther side of the room
opened, and a woman, with a rustling swish of lavender-coloured
taffeta, came through. She was carrying a three-branched silver candlestick in her hand, and the small, clear flames lit up her face. It was an
oval face, with well-defined cheek-bones, a straight nose, a neat and
pretty mouth. It was, too, a face carefully prepared and painted; but
art had not been able entirely to wipe out all trace of the fine thread-
lines at the corners of the eyes, the faint creases across the forehead, or
the slight droop of the flesh from nose to mouth. The skin of the
exposed bosom, below a ruched lavender-coloured ribbon tied about
her throat, was white; white as a snowdrop. And it was this that made
Barney, with a slowing of his heart-beats, suspect before she spoke and
removed all doubts that it was Phillis herself who stood before him.

"So, Corydon, you have kept your appointment?" she said in her
deep, attractive voice.

She put the candlestick down on the centre of the table, and
dropped him a graceful though slight curtsey.

"Your servant, madam." He took her hand and kissed it.

Years of training in polite behaviour prevented Barney from
showing anything of what he was feeling. To say that he was bitterly
disappointed would not be quite true. There was a part of him which
wished to laugh at himself for having been duped into supposing that a
mask who accosted him at a public ball must of necessity be a young
and lovely thing; he was a little angry, too, that he had been so fooled,
and for this reason was inclined to feel resentful towards his hostess.

As his eyes came up from his bow, he studied her more carefully,
which he was able to do under the pretence that he was bestowing on

her a bold and admiring gaze. Now that the first shock of the disparity of years between them was over, he admitted to himself that she was still a good-looking woman, and any girl might be proud to own that skin. He tried to guess her age: probably thirty-seven or thirty-eight; say eighteen years older than himself . . .

"Come and get warm," she said, "it is cold out, I am sure." She indicated to him a chair, and herself sat down on the other side of the hearth.

"Thank you. Yes. Yes, it is! I dare say it will rain before morning."

As he delivered this sentence, which could hardly be triter coming from a young man keeping a romantic rendezvous, Barney was ashamed of his inability to handle the situation. Though he could control his facial expression and betray no surprise that the fair Phillis was not a maiden shepherdess in Arcady, he could not for the life of him think of anything to say. It was impossible to begin with this stranger, this woman who looked as if she deserved not a lover's homage but filial respect, where he had left off with the glamorous masked Phillis on the steps of the King's Theatre at three o'clock in the morning.

She endeavoured to help him out.

"You found your sister that night, I hope, and learned that your uneasiness on her account was groundless?"

"Thank you. Er—er—my sister had gone home. She left me a message—which I received just after you and I parted." These necessary lies did not make Barney feel any more at ease. He wondered desperately how he was ever going to get through the evening. Could he pretend to be taken ill? Or——? But no. The barest gallantry demanded of him that he must endure a couple of hours at least of Phillis's company.

Then Phillis laughed, and the sound was so rich and gay, and the candlelight so subdued, that for a moment he was jerked back to the atmosphere of the masquerade.

"Oh, Corydon! Corydon, dear! You are trying so hard. You thought I would be a sweet thing of twenty, did you not? Yet I warned you not to expect too much. I warned you you might be disappointed in me."

"Madam——" Barney began in high confusion, thoroughly disconcerted by this direct attack.

"Must it be 'madam', Corydon?" she interrupted him. Now do not distress yourself, my dear boy. We will not talk of this any more. You shall see presently that though I am not all that you dreamed, I *am* still the same Phillis you danced with last Tuesday night, and whose company—if I may make so bold as to say so, sir—you appeared to enjoy. It was—precisely because I feared you might be—how shall I put it?—might be surprised, that I asked you to wait for a week before seeing me again. Had you come hotfoot the next morning your disillusionment would, I flatter myself, have been the keener. Time had a little dulled the first exhilaration, had it not? Indeed, I much wondered whether you would come to-night. And if you had not, Corydon, *I* should have been grievously disappointed." She smiled at him in a manner that could not but flatter a very young man, for if her beauty was slightly faded, she was a woman of the world, an experienced and delightful charmer.

"It would not of course occur to you," she went on, looking at him now rather archly, "that I, in my turn, might have been slightly—no, not disappointed, never that—but disconcerted, to see, when you unmasked, my gallant so very *young* a man."

This aspect certainly had never come into Barney's mind, and he looked rather foolish. He was not so vain that he could not see—now that it was pointed out to him—that a woman of her maturity might well not find all that she was seeking in one who would appear to her as a green and inexperienced boy.

Phillis laughed again. "We will talk no more of our expectations," she said. "Tell me now about yourself. Let us begin, for instance, with what you have been doing to-day."

"Oh—!" Then Barney suddenly laughed, too. "I have another disappointment for you besides my youth. Though I am a gentleman, I am not a leisured one. That is the real reason I begged to be excused from dining with you. I cannot be free then. In short, I have to earn my living."

"And you pretended it was because the evening was a more romantic time! I remember you called the dinner hour a practical, unromantical time of day—those were your very words. Oh, fie on you, Corydon! . . . Come, do not look so hangdog, I am only teasing you. Tell me, what do you do, what is your work?" She asked as one really interested, and with none of that lack of esteem which he so dreaded, and constantly experienced from visitors to Hanover Square when they were first informed that he was earning his living.

Thereafter the conversation ran smoothly, until she happened to ask him if he had many brothers and sisters. Barney was naturally accustomed to dealing with this common inquiry, but he never learned to answer it easily.

"I live in a large family," he said, "but they are my cousins. I have only one sister."

"Oh," she said, seeming to recollect something, "do you perhaps live with the Honourable Robert Jaspard? I do not know him, but a lady of my acquaintance was talking of him the other day, and she mentioned that he had a nephew and niece in his family."

"Yes," said Barney uncomfortably, "I am his nephew."

"Lord Manvington has a third brother, then?"

She asked this with so much candour that he was certain she had heard no gossip about him. He was relieved. And yet . . . and yet he had often wished that he might meet some woman, a woman who would be just about the age of Phillis, or a little older, who would say to him: "But Robert Jaspard is not your uncle, he is your father. I knew your mother well. She was so lovely and so witty." But he met no such woman. . . .

"Er—yes, my father died long ago."

"And your mother, too?".

He nodded, since he could not well deny it. In any case, for anything he knew, one answer was as likely to be true as the other.

"Poor Corydon!"

She led him—and he gladly followed—to talk of other things, and particularly of himself and his aspirations. She was a gifted listener, and knew the right moment to put a question, to add her own observations, or to remain silent.

By the time the footman brought in supper, he was perfectly at home, and no longer thought of the clock and how soon he could, with decency, leave.

All his life anyone was to be able to get round Barney, for a time at least, if they gave him their interest and their unpitying sympathy. Pity he would never stand; but there is a sympathy clean of this by which the hearer puts himself in the speaker's place, understands his motives, his wishes, his ambitions; and it was to sympathy of this sort that Barney, deprived all his childhood of love, invariably succumbed.

She had served a delicious supper: not dainty, for she knew the extent of a young man's appetite, and that no lady's boudoir finicalness could really please him. He had a choice of three sorts of cold fowl, veal or mutton; besides oysters, an open apple tart thick with whipped sour cream; and as the accompaniment to this good fare, champagne.

If Barney had been disappointed in his hostess, he certainly was not in this part of the evening. He ate with a gusto and an appetite which, though they would hardly be considered polite to later generations, were a source of gratification to Phillis, who had been at much pains to consider what her young gentleman would be likely to relish.

She herself ate only of three dishes, and as Barney was too engrossed to carry the conversation, she let it be her turn to talk. He learned that she had been a widow for five years. Her husband had been a Jacobite. ("I told him," she said, "that it was a lost cause, that the Stuarts' day was over, but he would not heed me.") He had been involved in some plot at the time of the '15 Rebellion. What happened was never discovered, but one night he left home, and he did not come back. Later, his body was found stabbed in a dark alley. . . . Their only child, a son, had died of a malignant fever when he was seven years old.

Phillis told this sad tale of her life without emotion, as though the events she related had happened to another person. Only, when she had been speaking of her boy, Barney noticed that she drank some wine quickly and blew her nose as though the bubbles had prickled it.

When the meal was over he did not, as he had on the last occasion when they had supped together, shuffle his chair close and proceed to kiss that snow-like bosom. But he did pick up her hand and put his lips to it. The champagne had had its mellowing effect.

"Thank you, Phillis, that was a wonderful feast you laid for me in Arcady."

But, rather strangely he thought, Phillis did not seem disposed to be sentimental. "Come back to your chair by the fire," she said. "I will have the supper things removed. The champagne we may keep at hand, but I do not like looking at used plates and soiled silver." She pulled at the bell-cord.

When the man had removed everything, made up the fire and snuffed the candles, she said to him: "That is all, Joseph. You may retire now. I will let Mr. Jaspard out myself."

"Very good, madam."

Barney caught himself wondering whether the man was accustomed to his mistress entertaining gentlemen of an evening and letting them out herself. But he stifled the thought as unworthy and in any case no concern of his. And now his eyes did go to the clock. It was nearly twenty minutes to eleven. Soon he could, without impoliteness, leave; especially as he had, to uphold him, the excuse of his having to rise early. He had not latterly been getting to bed before some time after midnight, and twice in the past week had suffered reprimand for being late in his place in the Customs House.

Phillis now rose, and crossed to a spinet. She began to play; a sweet, sad air which he did not recognize. From that she broke into one of Lawes' songs from *Comus*. Her voice was soft and a little husky like her speaking voice, yet pure and moving.

Barney, with his glass of champagne in his hand, leant back in his chair and let the voice and the high tinkling accompaniment become a soothing, vivifying background to his thoughts. His thoughts of love, and Lucy . . .

She sang two of Purcell's songs, and another air unknown to him.

He was warm, comfortable, well-filled, and had had enough champagne to feel that the world was a pleasant place, that in spite of the inconveniences and drawbacks which must from time to time beset one,

one was master of one's own fate, and circumstances could be twisted to one's desires. Lucy . . . he would make her his own soon; and by some means he would raise himself from a clerkship to one of those sinecure posts of the sort held by both Creswell and Stephen, whereby one drew a yearly salary and appeared in person once in many months, if at all. There was, for instance, a Clerk of the Market, who received £9 a week and had nothing whatever to do as the work was farmed out. But he could not bother to think now how the gaining of this or a similar emolument was to be accomplished. The warmth of the fire, the inner heat of the champagne and the big supper that he had eaten made him drowsy: contentedly, uncaringly drowsy, with the sweet singing running like a summer stream.

Her voice died away. The tinkling did not begin again. She had closed the instrument and come back to the fireplace.

"That was delightful. . . ." He paid her appropriate compliments on her voice, and filled her glass with what was left in the bottle—the second that had been opened.

They spoke of their tastes in music for a few minutes; then Barney, seeing that it was past eleven, got to his feet.

"Oh, 'tis early! You do not need to go yet." Her voice was cooing, persuasive. "See, Joseph has left another bottle for you."

"You are very kind. But"—he smiled—"I have to rise early in the morning, and that is a thing I still find hard."

She had turned to a small table beside her, and from a drawer in it she took a small box. This she opened, and turned out upon the palm of her hand a ring.

It was a man's ring, of gold and mounted with a ruby. The stone glowed there, on the white skin of her hand, with the red flashes changing as the flickering firelight caught them. Warm. Lovely. Rich. The General himself did not wear a finer ring.

"Do you have to go?" she repeated. "I should like you to have worn this ring—for me."

Barney looked at the stone, fascinated. The scent that she used, that was like roses on a hot day, came into his nostrils. He stammered in his confusion. "I—I could not accept such a present. It—you do me too much honour, madam—Phillis."

She moved her hand back and forth, and the rays scintillated more vividly.

"I should be honoured—were you to wear it for my sake. I am a lonely woman, Corydon. There is—much I might do for you."

He raised his eyes and they met hers: everything that could not be put into words was said then.

Barney was touched to a point of high emotion. With an unusually gentle smile that lit his rather ordinary face to distinction, he said: "You are too good to me, Phillis, far too good. I——" He could not go on. "I have to go," he ended abruptly. "Good night, madam."

As he walked to the door, he heard the small click of the drawer behind him.

"Before you go, Corydon, will you promise me one thing?"

"What is that?" Though he turned, he did not look at her, but stood with his head bent, near the door.

"If at any time—even if it should be a year hence—you feel you would like to see me—or if you are in any trouble or distress—you will come. You think nothing can hurt you now. You are young and proud, and the world is all yours. But—ah, Corydon! you too will have to learn that there are times when disappointments, chagrins, change our views. Perhaps you will—want to see me then. Will you remember?"

"I will—Phillis. Thank you. Good night." His words, he knew, were inadequate, lacking even a pretence of chivalry; but he could not bear to prolong this difficult scene.

"Please forgive me if I do not come down with you. You will let yourself out? The door is bolted, but not locked."

He murmured acquiescence. As he passed through the door he heard a whisper, so soft it might have been in his imagination, yet ringing with intensity: "I love you!" He felt his muscles stiffen before he decided to pretend that he had not heard. Very quietly he closed the door, and went slowly downstairs.

His emotions were so mixed he hardly knew himself what he was feeling. No one in all his life had ever said to him before those three sweet words: I love you. Though she was old, she was still attractive, and so kind . . . so generous . . . so understanding. If he had not been in love with Lucy, he would surely have stayed. . . . He looked down at his bare hands, and thought how well the ruby ring would sit upon his finger. . . .

CHAPTER XII

STEPHEN FALLS IN LOVE

STEPHEN fell in love in Hanover, and this he did so suddenly that the chance turning of his head in a ballroom was the opening of a gate into a different life.

He had stayed a month in The Hague with Mr. Osborn before they set out for Germany, and it had been for both of them a time of labour rather than of pleasure. Mr. Osborn had many private affairs of his own to attend to, particularly the ordering of his house in which he expected to spend the next four or five years. His official business, too, he was looking into, that he might be the readier to take it over from his predecessor as soon as he had seen Stephen on to the boat for England at the conclusion of his tour. As for Stephen, he spent his days most creditably in study of the various small Courts of Europe: their customs, their manners and, not least, the complicated interweaving of their lineage—a tapestry that had now, in the person of the Elector of Hanover, absorbed into its pattern the reigning house of England.

In the evenings he accompanied Mr. Osborn to assemblies at the various houses of the small English colony, or to sedate, formal Dutch parties, where he conversed in French with the blond, plump natives of the country and endeavoured not to yawn. For, though The Hague had engagements enough to offer of an evening, Stephen, perhaps because he read too much by day and was taking the educational advantages at his disposal very seriously, found little entertainment. He often wished Barney was with him. Having lived always in a big family, he missed very much having a companion with whom to discuss his observations. Mr. Osborn, to be sure, was at hand were it a question of architecture or even one of manners; but there were comments he would like to make on, for instance, the Dutch ladies; which were not such as could with decorum be confided to the middle-aged Mr. Osborn. He and Barney might often have laughed together, but laughing alone is a poor pastime. With the few other young Englishmen of his own age whom he met at the assemblies, he felt it behoved him to be discreet. From kindliness, if nothing else, he did not wish it to come to the ears of his Dutch hosts that he found their parties tedious and their persons dull.

It was on his last evening in The Hague, upon his return from an assembly, that Stephen found waiting for him a letter from his mother. Storms had delayed the packets, and this was only the second he had received. The first, written a week after his departure, had informed him very briefly of Fan's disappearance. It was therefore, in expectation of learning the sequel, that he picked up with more than ordinary eagerness the crackling, sealed piece of paper.

"Do not go to bed a moment, sir," he said to Mr. Osborn, who had thrown his own post aside as being business missives which did not require his immediate attention. "Stay, and see what news there is from home." He read his letters freely to Mr. Osborn, as an old friend of the family, and had not even hidden from him Fan's disturbing behaviour.

Stephen sat down on the settee, and drew the candelabra on the table nearer to him. Mr. Osborn also seated himself, but in the attitude of one who does not intend to linger. He had brought Stephen home before the end of the party, but it was already past midnight and they were making an early start in the morning.

" 'My dear Stephen'," [read Stephen in a skimming fashion, waiting till he should come to something worthy of Mr. Osborn's attention.] " 'I trust you are well and are enjoying the pleasures of The Hague.' Um .... um . . . um . . ." His voice suddenly took a high, surprised tone. " 'Your brother Creswell was married yesterday to Miss Rosalind Tarquin, a niece of Lord Comberley . . .'

"Creswell *married*! A niece of—what's that?—a niece of Lord Comberley. A niece! Good gad! but it can't be! A niece of Comberley . . . Oh, I beg your pardon, sir, I—I was thinking of something my brother said to me. But married—I can't get over it."

"It certainly appears to be very sudden," said Mr. Osborn. "Perhaps the letter will elucidate the matter further."

Stephen began to read again.

" 'They were married in Lord Comberley's house. Your father and I were present, and of course Lord Comberley. She is a pretty young woman, and worth £40,000 and an estate. Dear Creswell is to be much congratulated. . . .'

"I don't understand it," said Stephen, laying his letter down again. "I don't understand it at all."

Neither did Mr. Osborn. But he had less reason than Stephen to be astonished, never having heard that Creswell had planned a prank on a whore who passed as Lord Comberley's niece. And upon this subject Stephen did not think it would be judicious to enlighten him. Shaking his head, he returned again to his letter.

" 'You will not be so surprised to hear our Kitty is betrothed to Mr. Stafford. I hope they may be very happy. Pray write her a note of felicitation.'

"No, that doesn't surprise me particularly, though I confess I did wonder if Fan—oh, here's something about her now."

" 'We have no further news of Frances, and it is your father's wish and mine that she is not mentioned by any of you again. Of all the wicked, ungrateful girls—but I will say no more. I have known for a long time that she was unamiable and with a propensity to evil. . . .'

"Mamma was always hard on Fan. I used to be sorry for her. But she deserves recrimination now."

Stephen's pleasant face set for a moment in hard lines. What all the family minded more than Fan's personal abasement was the dishonour she had brought upon her house and name. Many things were forgivable, but the sin that they had every reason to suspect her of committing was not, in a female, forgivable.

" 'Barbara had a little girl Monday se'night, it is very pretty and fat. . . .' Barbara's babies are invariably pretty in Mamma's eyes, although she has never seen them when she remarks upon it. . . . 'She is to be called Augusta Mary, and her godparents . . .' um . . . um . . . um . . . that is not very interesting. 'We do hope Barbara and Mr. Fletcher will get to Gartonby this summer to pay us a visit, and the dear children. Your Papa has been a little troubled with the gout again in his left foot. . . .'

"That means poor Mamma will have been having a trying time," Stephen looked up, grinning. "This is very hard to read," he squinted at the edge of the paper. "Mamma has written across, and it is all in a muddle. 'Our J. and D. are well . . .' I think there are respects sent to you. '. . . something, Mr. Osborn.' That is all. Barney is not mentioned, so I suppose that means he is behaving himself. . . . But Creswell . . . !'"

He might have remained thinking of Creswell all night if Mr. Osborn had not picked up his candlestick and persuaded him to bed.

At the first light the coach which had been hired to take them to Hanover stood at the door, with another, smaller one waiting behind it, in which was to be carried the luggage. Four horses, fine, sleek, black Dutch horses, were harnessed to each, and these stamped impatiently, making the brasswork and the bits jingle to a happy tune; from out of their nostrils their breath came on the still air like puffs of smoke, as though they were eight angry dragons. The drivers of each team were grotesque, rotund figures swathed, it seemed, in a half-dozen caped duffle coats.

In the rawness of the morning, mist curled up from the canal, wreathing the dark, hurrying figures clip-clopping in their sabots over the cobbles. Only working people were yet abroad, and with no friend to wave them off, the coaches lurched forward, and with creak and jangle turned into the Lange Voorhout.

So began the long drive across the interminable flat, flat lands of Holland and north-west Germany. Straight roads for miles and miles, so that when one looked out from the coach window it was only to see, beyond the sweating horses, the road and the bare, neat trees lining it stretching away to a point where the sky came down to meet the earth. Flat fields, or rather, strips of land, waiting in the winter cold for birth of the crops already perhaps buried beneath the sullen ridges of the plough; flat as far as one could see. Here and there a farmhouse with its friendly huddle of outbuildings disturbed the bleak monotony; or a windmill, its sails idle, its very air derelict. The whole earth was holding its breath and waiting—waiting for the spring and the resurrection of every year.

Further on their way, beyond the Rhine, the scene changed to woods and ravines, and a hill might impede the steady pace of their lumbering progress.

The cold, though no snow lay on the ground, was biting and vicious. Stephen and Mr. Osborn were huddled in so many coats and fur rugs that they were but two bundles with faces peering out. Even so, they stamped their feet gently on the strawed floor of the coach, and with arms folded clutched at their ribs as though, by tight holding of themselves, they might find warmth. At least with the cold it was dry, and though the coaches rocked and quaked like a pair of ships in a turbulent sea, there was no fear of the wheels becomimg embedded in mud, and thus their journey being halted until another pair of horses could be found to help pull them from the morass.

Their way lay through Utrecht, Osnabruck, Minden: but they passed few big towns, and at the smaller ones where they changed horses or put up for the night, there were neither very good dinners nor good beds to be had. It was not the fashionable time of year for travel, and the hosts produced salt meats or old hens so newly killed that their flesh was scarcely to be torn by the strongest teeth.

It seemed to Stephen that each and every one of these small German towns was exactly the same as the one before it: so that they travelled weary miles all day only to arrive at night at the place they had left in the morning. And it was not only the inns and the round, red faces of the hosts that were the same; the pretty, crooked towns, with high fourteenth- or fifteenth-century timbered gables, cobbled streets and open market-places fronted by an ornate and stately *Rathaus* seemed all to have been designed by the same architect.

And every evening was a dull repetition of the evening before it. There appeared to be no travellers but themselves the whole length of the road to Hanover, unless it was a sombre-faced pastor who read in his Bible, or a rough fellow who was not worthy to set foot in the parlour with the milords (as English gentlemen were indiscriminately called), but must eat his supper in the kitchen as part of the host's family. So, after a meal and a walk through the dark town that he might stretch his legs, Stephen sat down by the tiled stove with Mr. Osborn (who did not care to walk out in the night air and said that the movements of the coach exercised his muscles quite sufficiently) and yawned over a bottle of wine that was inferior to any he was accustomed to from his father's cellar; or tried to read in one of the little calf-bound volumes from the small travelling book-case which had been Mrs. Jaspard's parting present to him. But whereas all day they froze, at night the heat from the tiled stove was overpowering and little conducive to intelligent enjoyment of even Mr. Pope's excellent translation of Homer's *Iliad*.

By day Mr. Osborn, from duty rather than inclination, tried to while away the jolting, inactive hours with disquisitions upon the Marlborough campaigns of the previous reign. He pointed vaguely into the flat distance, and said: here the armies met, there the French were in retreat; and Stephen listened and tried to appear interested when all the time he was wondering if he would ever again feel really warm out of doors or lose the dull ache from his shaken bones. The life he had lived before the journey began seemed remote as a dream, and beyond realization the hope that there would be again an existence other than comprised a jolting coach, a tedious evening by a hot stove, and a hard and sometimes bug-ridden bed with the gently snoring figure of Mr. Osborn beside him.

Osnabruck created a diversion in the wilderness of dreary days; for they held letters of introduction to a notable gentleman, and here for two nights were housed in a small palace and found comfort and comparative cleanliness again.

Upon the ninth day after leaving The Hague they arrived upon a sunny, gay afternoon in Hanover.

There were many English in Hanover, for it was something of the fashion now to seek out the so well-loved home of the English King, and insinuate oneself into the good graces of the fair boy with the blue, protruding eyes who one day or other might expect to be King in his grandfather's place. It was of course common property that his father the Prince of Wales was at loggerheads with the old King, and chose to keep his heir in Hanover rather than under that interfering grand-paternal eye in London. But what everyone did not know was that young Frederick was to follow in his father's footsteps and in his turn come to detest the tyranny of a Monarch-Father. Nor could they know that the homage and the adulation they gave to this thirteen-years-old lad was, in so far as it was directed at the shadow of the Crown, to be wasted; for death was churlishly to deprive him in middle age of his dear expectations.

It was upon his third evening in Hanover that Stephen turned his head in a ballroom and fell in love.

The object of his admiration, as he very quickly found out, was a

Miss Sarah Bayard, whose father, a baronet, held a minor post at the Electoral Court. Lady Bayard, it was whispered to Stephen, had been a Paddington dairymaid in her youth, and lucky indeed she was to find herself accepted by society. To be sure, went on the whisperers, it had been a hindrance to Sir William marrying so beneath his rank. He had, ever since his marriage, wandered over Europe, usually without point or purpose; very occasionally being used by his Government to negotiate some small matter, such as the raising of a mercenary troop or the loaning of a palace for a travelling dignitary. Only within the last month had he, through the interest of his relations in London, been given this Hanoverian appointment.

To do Lady Bayard justice it must be said that she had schooled herself far above her beginnings in the byre; and indeed it would now be hard to tell she had not been born to the distinction she occupied. To be sure, said the gossips, she was a handsome woman still, but did one not think her wide mouth a little common? And perhaps occasionally her laughter made the sensitive shudder; it was very well for bumpkins and young fools to laugh, but ladies and gentlemen of the highest rank should be content merely to smile their amusement. Miss Bayard, they agreed, was very pretty. Her mouth did not take after her mother's, but was small and of the neat shape of Sir William's. All her features were small, but—for these ladies could allow no one perfection—would she not have been improved if her stature was two or three inches more and (here they blushed and tittered) her bust a few inches broader?

Yes, she was small and slight, and merry as a fairy. To Stephen, who watched her as closely and as long as he dared, there was about her quickly changing expressions a likeness he could not place. It was as though he had known her before, or perhaps seen her somewhere. But careful questioning revealed that this was scarcely possible. So Stephen, romantically in love, believed she did not seem a stranger to him because she was the ideal of his heart, and that in his dreams which he could not remember he had often seen her. Are not all happy marriages made in Heaven, and might not Heaven direct dreams, and by these means enable one to recognize the pre-ordained mate?

Some long time was to pass before he learned a less fanciful, a hard, prosaic reason why that happy loveliness touched him with familiarity.

The second time that he spoke to her Stephen determined to make her his wife; though he could not of course tell her immediately of his intention. He was so grateful to Gertrude Dale for having broken her betrothal to him that he was able to think of her with a greater kindliness than ever before in his life. Certainly, had she not freed him, his difficulties would have been—not insurmountable, for he would, he felt, succeed in overcoming any dragons in the way to win such a prize—but

I

of so great magnitude that a break with his family, including the consequent poverty such insubordination must entail, would be inevitable.

Now he could not see that his father would have any valid objection were he to be successful in persuading Miss Bayard herself that there was none. Even if the family of Lady Bayard was of dubious origin—as apparently it was—Sir William could trace his lineage sufficiently far back to be accounted estimable. His rambling life was not perhaps one that brought him as much credit as had he sat, for instance, in the House of Commons, or taken, as a gentleman should, his place in his own county, yet his character was in every way respectable, and even the whisperers could cast no shadow across his morals. Which was less, Stephen said to himself, than it would be safe to predict of the General. Added to this, it would seem that his income was such that he could make suitable provision for his daughter. And that was a point that even the most lovesick suitor must take into consideration when endeavouring to see a match through his father's eyes.

Stephen's deliberations at last led him to the decision that it would not be in his best interest to make known at present to the General his attachment. Not only would he be bound to see it as a lonely traveller's sentimental inclination for a pretty fellow-countrywoman that would wither as soon as he moved to Paris and the charming object was out of his sight, but he must also consider it a slight upon his authority that his son should so much as contemplate engaging himself to a lady whose merits he, his father, had had no opportunity of assessing.

Stephen's wavering opinions on this grave matter had been brought to a conclusion on the day he learned that business was bringing Sir William—and therefore his wife and daughter—to London in the late summer, conveniently about the time of his own arrival home. Then, so he planned, the families could meet and mingle. The General could not fail to be won by Sarah's grace and daintiness, and he, Stephen, would confess his long and deep attachment. . . .

He had not overlooked the possibility of another bride being chosen for him before this happy London reunion could come about; but Creswell's marriage made him feel he was safe for this year from the General's match-making. Two weddings (with Kitty's) within a few months were surely enough for his purse if not his energies. Further— since he never willingly relinquished an idea—he probably cherished hopes that upon his return from the Continent, polished and erudite as a result of his travels, Gertrude Dale would look more favourably upon him.

Prudent as Stephen was, this quality deserted him on every occasion when he found himself face to face with Miss Bayard. He had not been in Hanover a month when he took the unconventional step of asking her—without recourse first to her father, as etiquette demanded—if she would be his wife. By this time he was tolerably sure of himself so far as Sarah herself was concerned. They had seen each other almost daily, and it needed no words from her to tell him that she reciprocated his affection. Indeed, as she was presently with confusion to confess, she too had felt the world change for her that night when he looked across the room.

It was not very easy for Stephen to see her alone; not only did she have to evade parental care, but Mr. Osborn's watchfulness, too, must be circumvented. He was by no means unaware of his ward's languishing gaze, and being highly conscious of his responsibility, soon felt it his duty to reprimand him. Stephen replied lightly that he must have some amusement, and what other young English lady was so agreeable a companion? and it was irksome to be talking French all the time to the German ladies. If he did not entirely deceive Mr. Osborn, the older man sighed and hoped for the best. After all, it was well known the Jaspards had philandering in the blood, and very likely the boy wasn't serious.

But when lovers are determined to meet free from spying eyes, it is a wonder if they do not upon occasions find their opportunities. So it was with Stephen and Sarah.

At a ball they had slipped away, and now stood in a draughty stone corridor at the foot of a back stone staircase. The gloom was lighted only by a small and smoky oil-lamp standing on a bracket; and the two of them, in their stiff, fine clothes, glimmering against the colourless background, might have been taken by any intruder for a pair of ghosts. Indeed, a more comfortless place on a March night it would be hard to find, but no dancers would come this way, and should a servant pass he would know better than to pause or stare.

When Stephen had kissed her (they had been privately betrothed three days), which he did with the disarming excuse that his holding her would help to keep her warm, he said, somewhat diffidently:

"I have been thinking everything over, and I believe it is better I should say nothing to my father till I see him. My father is—he is a very imperious man. He will not like receiving news in a letter of my having engaged myself. When I see him I may the better combat any arguments he may put forward."

"It would make it so much easier for us to meet if our engagement could be made public," said Sarah, twisting one of his coat buttons, and looking modestly down towards the cold paving-stones.

"I know, dearest. Don't think I haven't considered that. But—when you meet my father you will understand."

"Will he forbid you to marry me?"

She raised her big brown eyes, and it both hurt Stephen and made him delightfully proud to know that her doubt had faded the natural gaiety from her small, appealing face, seen dimly in the murky half-light, but with all its beauty remembered and imagined.

His first answer was to kiss her again. "I *shall* marry you, whatever he may say. But he will not forbid it. Oh, no! how can he? What is there against it? When he sees you, he will be charmed by you. There is that to be said for my father—he has a soft spot always for a pretty woman. And you are more than pretty. . . . Only, dear love, I do counsel patience."

"It is very well for you," said Sarah, pouting, "to be so secretive when your parents are far away, but how can I act a part all these months in front of mine? I—I must tell them, Mr. Jaspard—Stephen," she added as he mockingly frowned at her formal address.

Stephen was brought to agree to this on condition that Sir William and Lady Bayard were sworn to say nothing of the matter to anyone. Sarah was obviously disappointed at having to wait six months before she could wear the fine feathers of a suitable betrothal and receive the congratulations of her friends and the little Court; but Stephen's persuasiveness as well as the rather alarming idea he gave her of his father prevailed with her to be guided by his advice.

Both shivering slightly, they walked away from the stone passage and, at a discreet interval from each other, returned to the ball-room.

The elder Bayards received Stephen's offer of himself as a prospective son-in-law with quite as much caution as Stephen was showing in regard to his father. They had nothing against him, said Sir William kindly, indeed he seemed a worthy young man, but to rush into marriage without much thought and the full concurrence of parents on both sides was not seemly. Stephen pleaded that at least they were not rushing. It would be six months before he could see his father, and after that a month or two would be needed to make arrangements. But Sir William, who knew Mr. Jaspard by repute, was not to be cajoled. He was all for putting the matter before him then and there, but upon Stephen's promising to behave with decorum and in no way to mark Sarah out with his attentions in public, he agreed to do nothing for the time being.

But this love-affair of his daughter did bring him to a firm decision on a project he had been turning over in his mind for some weeks. Lady Bayard had been troubled with an aching in her bones, and the waters of Aix-la-Chapelle might, her physician said, effect a cure. Now he obtained leave from his unonerous duties, and ordered his family to

pack their trunks. By the time they returned, so he calculated, Stephen
would have left for Paris.

This departure of his beloved was a great blow to Stephen, but it
had the one virtue that it silenced gossip and quieted the fears of Mr.
Osborn who had seriously been considering whether it was not his duty
to inform Mr. Jaspard of his son's inclination.

Stephen spent an hour closeted with Sir William the evening before
the Bayards left, and between them it was arranged that Stephen would
speak to his father the moment he arrived in England, and at that date
Sir William would write to Mr. Jaspard and tell him that he was
agreeable to give his daughter's hand into his family if he himself had
no objections to the match; and inform him how much he was prepared, on the financial side, to do for her upon marriage. In the meantime he extracted a very reluctant promise from Stephen that he would
not write to his love, for, said Sir William sternly, they were in no sense
to consider themselves betrothed. Yes, no doubt Lady Bayard would
send him a few lines from time to time to keep him informed of Sarah's
health. . . .

With these, to them, very sad provisoes, the lovers took a distraught
farewell of each other. Tears were in Sarah's beautiful eyes, and
Stephen himself was not far from this outward sign of grief.

He went back to the house where he and Mr. Osborn lodged, locked
himself up in his bedroom, and wrote a poem to her.

But, how fruitless! when he could not send it. . . .

CHAPTER XIII

BARNEY PLAYS THE HIGHWAYMAN

WHEN spring came to London, throwing new green over the worn and
common swards of Marybone Fields, of Tothill Fields, of Southampton
Fields; over the royal swards in St. James's Park, sprinkling tight white
buds on the hawthorns and a green mist among all the trees, Barney's
heart was as heavy as though he remained alone in winter, a personal
winter with no hope of blossom.

Many weeks had gone by since he first met Lucy Brook, yet he had
not succeeded in his wooing. Now, indeed, she was openly smiling upon
the man Dick, whose glowering had changed to swaggering, and whose
waistcoats were now gaudier and his coats more tinselled than any of
the company.

That Barney knew the cause of his slow fall into disfavour did not help him. Lucy had intimated, with no crudity but beyond any possibility of being misunderstood, that she expected from those who were so presumptuous as to set up as her admirers both lavish entertainment and, from time to time, a gift worth the having. Put bluntly, Barney could not afford the luxury of being in love with Lucy. At this time his disappointed passion and his jealousy of the interloper were beginning to affect his health and his temper alike. He was quite certain that had he been able to lay at the feet of Lucy what she expected from him, she would very willingly become his mistress. So this lack of money seemed a needless, yet insuperable, frustration. If he thought the worse of her for her hard-headedness, it did not alleviate his misery. His desire to possess her was an obsession. Had he seen her commit murder, he would still have wanted her.

And Lucy laughed at him, and gave him just enough encouragement from her turning, naughty eyes that he continued to torture himself by seeing her two or three times in every week.

He had stayed away more than one Sunday from Hanover Square, and spent such money as he had in taking Lucy and her family to Vauxhall for the day. (Entertaining her was quadruply expensive, as Mrs. Brook and Mr. Raikes always came too, and he was lucky if Harry and a woman-friend did not join the party at his charge.) He told the family the following Sunday that he had not been well, and received at once from the General the disconcerting comment:

"Do not trouble to lie. Say rather you spent the day with a wench."

Barney had reddened, and caught Madam's eyes upon him with a look of even greater distaste than usual. Thereafter, he was not asked why he had not come home, though Mr. Jaspard, when he had missed a Sunday, was inclined to read him a lecture on—no, not on morality, but on the effects of immorality: a subject which, coming from the General, invariably filled Barney with confusion.

Fan's name was no longer heard in Hanover Square: she might never have been one of the family. By this time Barney had learned where Thomas Folkes's house was, but when he had called there he had found it let to strangers, and no one could tell him the whereabouts of the owner. At his place of business the clerks shook their heads and said they had no information to give him. He concluded he must have taken Fan abroad.

Otherwise, things went on much the same at home. Lord and Lady Manvington were usually there for Sunday dinner, and any number from one to six of their ladysheeps. Often, but not regularly, Creswell and his wife; a Creswell not so silent now, but with a hardness and worldliness behind his laughter that made him so much a stranger to Barney that it seemed unbelievable they had sat together in the gun-room, and he had confessed the beginnings of his marriage. Rosa, too, was more mature, but with no swelling of the breasts or thickening of the body, for which signs, upon her every visit, Mrs. Jaspard and Lady Manvington sought with raking eyes. Kitty was still untidy, but inclined to talk of stuffs and of clothes with the Ladies Louisa and Charlotte, subjects in which till now she had shown a deplorable lack of interest; Carlton Stafford beside her, attentive and complimentary whatever his private sentiments, as a man should be who in a month's time is to become a bridegroom. Delia unchanged, as perverse and morose as ever; and up in the nursery Jacky and Dorothy pining under Sunday restraints while he and Miss Finch talked of her father, or of how he himself should one day rise to a high position in the Office of Trade and Plantations—a flattering view of his prospects held exclusively by Miss Finch, and one that, though agreeable to hear, Barney could not believe in.

Though this family life, this Hanover Square atmosphere compounded for the most part of awe and good manners with a little free laughter thrown in, was very part of Barney's heart and mind, he did from one Sunday to another forget them absolutely.

Now, upon a May evening, he sat in the drawing-room of the Brooks' house alone with Harry, who was more resplendent even than usual in embroidery and gold lace. The rest of the family was out, and Harry, summoning from the black boy port and biscuits, apologized for their absence, and apologized more that in half an hour he must turn Barney out. He was expecting a lady: he would understand?

Barney did understand, and was filled with envy that Harry's lady, whoever she was, made and kept her assignations with him. It was seldom he saw Harry with no one else by, and it seemed the perfect opportunity to unburden his heart and perhaps get advice from the brother of his stony-hearted beloved.

When he had related something of his anguish over Lucy's growing coldness—and the very fact that she was now out increased the fires of his jealousy—Harry said forthrightly what Lucy, however clearly, had merely hinted.

"Give her a trinket, a piece of jewellery. Women always like that."

"Yes," said Barney doubtfully, and added, because he thought confession might elicit a helpful and sympathetic suggestion from Harry: "I have not, unfortunately, enough money to buy jewellery."

"No?" Harry gave him an interrogative look that with his twisted nose was almost sinister. "We were sadly disappointed in you," he went on, surprisingly. "I thought you were a man of means."

"I am sure I have never looked like a man of means," answered Barney, as one hastily disclaiming a charge of duplicity.

"Oh yes. That night I first met you. I observe small things. For instance, your hands were cleaner than ordinary, and your lace, though not profuse, was of a quality only worn by the wealthy. Then, your coat"—he fingered Barney's sleeve; he was indeed wearing the same coat as upon that evening—"though of broadcloth, is an expensive weave and not such as is worn by common men."

"That is why you spoke to me?" asked Barney in tones mildly indignant.

"Why else? However—you proved a good fellow in spite of it. But damn me! if you want Lucy, get the crap, and I'll say good luck to you." He brought his face nearer to Barney's. "Do you mean to marry her?"

Barney was discomposed. It is not easy to tell a lady's brother that such an idea has never seriously crossed one's mind. And Harry, even when he was benign, looked fierce.

"In truth, I—I am not in a position to marry. Er—I am entirely dependent on the goodwill of my relations, and——"

"And in short you must marry where they choose," finished Harry for him. "You'd not suit Lucy for a husband, anyway."

He filled his glass, pushed the bottle towards Barney and appeared to have finished the conversation. Barney, encouraged that he apparently thought none the worse of him for not having matrimonial intentions towards his sister, was emboldened to continue.

"You said just now: why do I not get the crap?" (He had already picked up this cant name for money.) "How *can* I get it? I have bought shares in lottery tickets whenever I had any money to spare, but my number never comes up. I have wanted to buy South Sea stock. If I had got it in January, when I first thought of it, I might have made a fine turnover. But it is still rising. If—if you know anyone who could lend me the money to invest, I could still make enough to—to buy jewels for Miss Brook."

What he really meant, as Harry well knew, was: would Harry lend him the money?

Harry, however, dismissed the whole idea with the sweeping and illogical statement that only fools trusted to win money by investment, or for that matter by lottery.

"How am I to get it then?" asked Barney sullenly, and not as though he expected an answer.

Harry drained his glass and replaced it on the table with a flourish. Starting his sentence with an extremely coarse oath, he said:

"Go out and get it."

"Go out and get it?" repeated Barney. "Where from?"

Again Harry swore. "From those who have it, to be sure."

Silence enveloped the room. Barney moved his chair a little, and the slight scraping on the floor sounded very loud.

"You mean—you can't mean—*steal* it?"

But he knew that Harry did mean just that. Now everything about this house became significant. The back door leading to a stairway on the river; the few servants, the dumb boy, the alert young men who paused and stiffened when a door banged, the plentiful money in the household. . . . It seemed to him that he had been very dense not to have deduced it before.

But though she might be in a den of thieves, might be—probably was—a thief herself, he still wanted Lucy Brook with all his heart and passion.

"Nimming is a genteeler word," said Harry, and passed his hand across his mouth, while his eyes above the crooked nose looked at Barney with something of the same amusedly obscene expression worn by a youth who relates to one more innocent than himself the process of reproduction.

Barney said feebly: "I don't know how to. It must be very difficult."

"It takes a man of parts and courage," agreed Harry complacently. He added, with what seemed complete irrelevance: "If you should ever see fit to relate to anyone the conversation we are now having, your body would be taken out of the Thames in a morning or two."

"Er—yes. I—I understand," said Barney a second or so later. So calmly, so indifferently had the words been spoken he had not immediately gathered their import.

"I must turn you out now," said Harry, rising. "Hire a horse and go out one of these dusks on any road beyond the town. Only don't poach on another horse-pad's preserves, that's all."

"How should I know if I was?"

It was fantastic, unbelievable. He was responding to Harry's outrageous suggestion as though he meant to follow it. To *steal*! He, Barney Jaspard, to go on the highway!

"*He'd* let you know fast enough," went on Harry, "and if you didn't heed him he'd put a bullet in your guts. Listen to me," he took Barney in a friendly manner by the arm. " 'Tis not so hard for a brave, lusty fellow. Get a good horse, that's important, and pistols you can rely upon. Wear a mask, choose a lonely stretch of road just as dusk is falling, and wait till you see a chaise or a chariot—leave the private coaches alone till you are handier at the lay. And Lucy will be looking for that pendant, b—— me! within a week."

Barney walked home very thoughtfully. It was a fine night, not yet dark, though colour had gone out of the buildings and, upon looking up, here and there a star could be seen shining in the deepening blue. He reflected that it was just such a time of evening as Harry had said was suitable. . . . The signposts of shops and inns, one affixed to almost every house, creaked in the fresh wind, and sometimes a householder came out and lit the lamp before his door. It was peaceful, comfortable, here in the familiar Strand. Hard to believe that so near at hand, down any alleyway, likely to pounce out like lions upon the passing deer, teemed thieves, pickpockets, highwaymen. Was he to join their number and become a candidate for Tyburn? No, it was unthinkable. Even for Lucy's charms it was unthinkable. . . .

But the thought nagged incessantly at the back of his mind. He could not rid himself of it; he caught himself planning: where he would hire his horse (a long way off so no suspicion could attach to him), where he would make his attack; the mask he had worn at the masquerade would do. . . . But, no, these were silly stories he was weaving. And he would return to a letter to a merchant in South Carolina with an effort at concentration.

A few days later he called on Lucy again. He was so fortunate as to find her alone with her mother. She greeted him with a sweeter smile, a more caressing glance, than she had bestowed upon him for a very long time. Presently Mrs. Brook, with some agreeable comment, got up and left them alone.

He at once seized Lucy's hand and kissed it, first on the back and then, turning it over, on the palm many times. Since she did not draw it away, but laughed in a soft, inviting manner, he was soon kissing her on the lips, on the eyes, on her neck, on her bosom.

At length she pushed at him. "Come, come, you disarray me altogether. A moment, if you please, sir. . . . Now, now, I mean it. Stop it!"

Barney, though he kept his hands upon her waist, did desist from kissing her. If he had disarrayed her, he had done the same for himself. His hair was rubbed from its neat powdered folds, and the lace ruffles of his shirt were crumpled. He was in a state of high excitement, and panting as if he had been running.

"My brother told me you had a pendant for me," said Lucy, in a charming voice that promised all delights.

"A pendant!" echoed Barney, taken aback. He endeavoured to kiss her again that he might distract her, but she dodged him, and indeed freed herself from his hold entirely.

"Do you not love me above what I can give you, love me here and now?" asked Barney, who was so deep in love himself that it did not seem possible to him that his ardour had not been communicated.

"You haven't got it?" was all that Lucy said, and her tone was degrees colder.

"No. But I love you. Lucy, dearest——"

"I see; it is that you are too afraid—too afraid to get me my pendant."

Her voice was cruel as well as contemptuous. It lashed Barney like a whip across his face. But already his love was making excuses for her. It was Harry's fault: he had told her she was to have the pendant; he had put it into her head that if it did not come it would be because he, Barney, was too lily-livered to go out in the way Harry had suggested and get the money that would buy it.

"You need not come here again," said Lucy. "I do not like— cowards . . . Oh, the weeks I have wasted on you!" she added with less dramatic irritation.

"Nobody has ever called me a coward before." He spoke with difficulty, temper and an overwhelming misery tending to get the better of him. "I shall bring you your pendant in two days' time."

"It is of no account," said Lucy airily, walking about the room.

"It is of great account to me. Lucy, when I—when I bring you this pendant——"

"It must have diamonds," she interrupted. "Not many, perhaps, but a few."

"Very well. When I bring you this pendant—with diamonds—will you—will you forgive me and—love me?"

Her face that might have been a mask in its lack of expression softened into gentleness. "Oh I shall indeed, dear Barney!" There was a hint of mockery in her voice, but he felt that it was kind.

"Let me kiss you, then, once more for a pledge."

"Oh no, sir," she said, curtseying. "Good night to you." She gave the bell-pull a tug. "When I wear my pendant, we shall both be happy."

He could say or do no more, for the black boy, extravagantly dressed in scarlet clothing, with a scarlet and gold turban on his head, came in and held the door open. Barney went out.

The black boy who could not speak smiled as he unbolted the street door, so that his white teeth showed brilliantly between his pinky-brown lips. Barney gave him a coin. He felt sorry for this dumb alien, a child and yet never seen to romp or play with children, a creature raised as a servant and chosen, one must conclude, solely so that he could repeat nothing of what he heard in the house where he served. . . .

Barney's determination to possess Lucy was now set hard as ice in a bitter winter. Have her he would, whatever the consequences. So, closing his mind to all doubts, all reason, all morality, with the single-heartedness of a drunken man, he set about making his plans.

He believed that he brought to these the thoroughness of an experienced criminal. An hour and a half's break was given to the Office clerks in the early afternoon for the purpose of eating their dinner. The day after he had seen Lucy he skimped his meal and crossed the river to a livery stable in Southwark where he was quite unknown. He chose a strong-looking, rangy beast (the best of a not very good selection), laid his money down, and ordered it to be waiting on the Thames Street side of London Bridge at seven o'clock that evening.

He had reckoned that riding through the city at an hour when the streets were still a-bustle he would pass as a mere merchant about his business, and so reach, without attracting any attention to himself or giving anyone a notion from whence he had come, the open land beyond the Tyburn Road. He wore a dark, inconspicuous coat, an unlaced hat, and in his pocket was the mask he had worn at the King's Theatre. Besides, in a holster at his belt was a pistol. He wished he had a pair, but even had he owned an extra weapon he had no means other than his open pocket for carrying it; for he had not cared to risk suspicion—as in the dubious neighbourhood of the livery stable he might have done—by insisting on holsters in the saddle.

It was a long way he had to go: past St. Paul's, along Fleet Street, through Lincoln's Inn Fields to High Holborn, turning north past Montague House and out into the fields beyond. From there he cantered slowly across to the Hampstead Road, above Tottenham Court Manor.

His timing had been perfect. Dusk was falling rapidly. The footpaths were empty. It was cold and very lonely. Occasionally a rider passed, and then Barney's hand held firm the butt of his pistol and his knees tensed ready to turn his horse aside, until the stranger had gone by and he was sure he was not one of those whose ranks he was joining and upon whose territory he might be trespassing.

After he had waited about a quarter of an hour, he saw down the road ahead of him two tiny, wavering, indistinct lights, and presently he was able to discern the looming grey shape of a vehicle, and hear the steady sound of hoofs, coming muffled on the earthy road, not clear and staccato as hoofs rang out over the cobbles and paving-stones of the town. He pulled his mask from his pocket and put it on. He noticed that his hands were shaking (from excitement, he said to himself), and although he was not warm he felt the sweat running in his armpits.

But the vehicle proved to be a great, lumbering coach, guarded by four outriders. Barney turned his back and rode his horse away.

He returned to the road a little higher up, further from the Manor. Another dreary ten minutes passed. If something did not come soon, it would be too dark to attack, or rather, too dark to risk flight on his horse at the speed he intended. Perhaps the Hampstead road was not a very good one to have chosen, and it must be true, what he had often heard said, that no one but a fool, unless he was under great necessity of doing so, travelled after dark beyond the confines of the town. It was little safe even in the heart of London, and highwaymen had penetrated into Pall Mall itself; but at least that took an exceptionally bold fellow, and there was a chance, though not necessarily a worthwhile one, of calling for the watch and rallying some stout passersby to one's assistance. . . . Only the thought of Lucy and the absolute necessity he was under of getting money kept Barney at his place.

Again lights were to be seen, twinkling, shaking, like the lights upon mastheads of ships riding at anchor very far away. Slowly, slowly, they came nearer. Barney fingered his mask to make sure it was in place, gripped his pistol comfortably, jerked up his horse's head and waited. Yes, it was a chariot, drawn by two horses and coming at a fair pace. Without stopping to think or plan—only summoning Lucy's image to give him courage—he stuck his spurs into his horse's sides and forced the animal to halt right in the way of the oncoming carriage.

"Stand!" he shouted, and in a peculiar voice enough. He had meant in any case to disguise it, but nervousness had added to it a high note he had not reckoned upon, and the result was a squeaking gruffness. The coachman, he saw, was whipping his horses and scheming either to run him down or make him, in terror of his life, give way. This last Barney, inexperienced as a highway robber, would almost certainly have done had not the pair of horses, as little eager as himself for a collision, pulled up short, neighing either a welcome or defiance to the saddle-horse before them.

Barney brandished his pistol in what he hoped was a terrifying manner, calling again in his strange voice, though it was firmer now, for excitement was gripping him:

"Stand and deliver!"

He approached the door of the chariot and had time to see that the occupants were two young gentlemen who would, in all probability, have enough money about them, or at least jewels, to satisfy Lucy's wants, when—just as he had noted this to his satisfaction—a pistol was fired. His horse reared up. The surprise and his own nervousness diminished his horsemanship, so that he was unable to keep his seat. His fall was soft and he suffered no harm, but his horse on whom he had relied to remove him rapidly from the scene of his robbery, with a shrill neigh of farewell to its new acquaintances, galloped away, and seemed little likely to stop before it reached its stable on the other side of the Thames.

He picked himself up quickly, but before he had even a moment in which to take stock of his new position a second shot rang singingly in his ears, and he felt an odd sensation, almost a bruise and yet with no further pain, in the upper part of his left arm. He twisted round, and with all the panic of a chased animal, ran across the fields.

"After him! after him!" he heard young, excited voices cry. "Forty pounds if we bring him 'fore the magistrate."

"And rid the world of a rogue!"

Glancing back over his shoulder, he saw that those he had hoped to make his victims were pursuing him with alarming agility. He was fortunate in knowing these fields and the Marybone ones adjoining them as well as he knew any part of London. If only he could keep his distance—or not be shot like a rabbit in flight—he could regain the streets and lose himself in the squares and alleys beyond the Tyburn Road. Recollecting now that he was still wearing a mask, and must therefore appear to any who might chance to see him as a villainous character, he tore it off, and dropped it from his hand. Increasing darkness was on his side, and he had that to thank, he felt, that the men behind wasted no further shots upon him. He circled round, crossed the road again, ran past the Saltpetre House and came into the Tyburn Road. Here he must steady his pace or, with cries of "Stop thief!" behind him (which he expected every moment to hear), he would immediately be seized by well-intentioned if interfering citizens. His hunters had been checked by the crossing of the paths near the Saltpetre House, and as Barney strode down Tyburn Road—an appropriate thoroughfare, he could not help grimly reflecting—he was nearly choking himself in his efforts to control his tearing breath, that the violence of it might not attract the suspicious attention of a curious passer-by.

He was surprised to find his pistol was still in his hand. He had supposed he must have dropped it when he fell, but he had no remembrance of that or of picking it up again. Now he tucked it back into the holster of his belt. . . . But he must stop and think where he was going. It was no good plunging on aimlessly as a bolting horse. A bolting horse? What of that animal he had hired? For sure it would make its way back to its stable, and no one could possibly connect it with him or with the night's escapade. . . .

At present he was heading in the opposite direction to his lodgings and safety. It was impossible to turn back, but he could work southward and down to the Strand.

"There he is, I swear!" cried a voice suddenly, behind him. "Hi! Stop thief! Stop!"

It might have been wiser for Barney to continue on his way as though he were a law-abiding pedestrian and knew nothing of any runaway desperado, but he was too flurried at the sound of that shout—

more terrible than hunting-horn to a stag—to weigh the wisdom of his actions. Fear drove his feet to a run as he turned down a side street, then down another, dodging, panting, desperate. Once somebody tried to stop him, but he pushed the man aside with violence and went on his way. Behind him he could hear the emphatic footfalls, pausing sometimes in perplexity, but then pounding on again, the emphatic footfalls of his pursuers.

Now he saw that he was at the back of Hanover Square. Was it chance? Or had he, unconsciously but with the instinct of a hunted animal, come to his home, his lair? But Hanover Square and the stern, just General who, whatever his transgressions, would never stoop to highway robbery, would offer him no sanctuary, no rest. Or would the house? His brain, as though lit up and quickened by his danger, told him rapidly that the area door would not be bolted yet. The servants would be at their supper. The back staircase. The dark of the landing. Aloneness. Hiding. Incoherently now, for that seeming light had gone out, he thought only in sharp sentences with no meaning or interpretation beyond them.

He turned another corner, ran a few yards and there was the area door. Not so strange a way in to him as to most of the family, for had he not been in the habit of using it when he wished to come and go without the General's questioning?

It was not locked. As he opened it very quietly, he heard the slight rattle of the watch-dog's chain, and he whispered the animal's name. As quietly he closed it. He did not wait to hear whether the footsteps, which still sounded in his head, went by, baffled. He passed, swift and quiet as a panther, the door of the servants' hall, from behind which came the clink of crockery and a hum of voices like bees about a hive on a summer day. So up the back stairs, silent, unlit.

On the landing he paused, listening, not now for any men in the street, but for the sounds of the house and the family in it. He had thought he would go into his old bedroom and wait. No one would be there, no one would come there. It was a small room down the corridor, beyond the nursery.

He was making his way there when he heard light, purposeful steps coming towards him. He lost his head, and slipped through the half open door into the dark quietness of the nursery. Then, as the steps came nearer, he saw that he was trapped. He had thought it was only a maid carrying, perhaps, a warming-pan to the big double bedroom; but now, from the authoritative, decisive sound of the steps, he was sure it was Mrs. Jaspard: she not infrequently came up last thing to look at Jacky and Dorothy in bed.

The nursery had two doors opening off it, one into the room in which the children slept, the other into Miss Finch's bedroom. He could see the glimmer of a light on the landing now. If Madam, who had never troubled to hide her dislike of him, found him here, lurking like the thief he so nearly was, she would drag him before the General, paint his case as black as she could, and what with the impossibility of his giving an account of himself—and for all he knew men were asking at the door already for a runaway highwayman—he would indeed be undone.

He looked round desperately for a cupboard, though he knew very well that this room had only the big shelved cupboard for toys and clothes running along one end: impossible to get himself into that. All this was through his mind in an instant. Also, the only means of escape open to him; and that a risky one, in all conscience.

Under the door to the left of him, Miss Finch's door, lay a streak of light. He opened it stealthily but very quickly, closed it behind him and slipped the bolt; saw an astounded Miss Finch in a loose grey wrapper, her eyes and her mouth wide. Without more ado he clapped his hand firmly over her mouth to prevent the scream that had so nearly split the silence.

They stood there, he tense, she shivering and wriggling in his grasp, the odd, muffled noises she was making moistening his palm, while steps crossed the nursery, a door could be heard opening; silence; then the shutting of it again; and now Barney stood more rigid than before, only his eyes were sizing up a cupboard to one side of Miss Finch's bed. But the footsteps crossed the nursery, another door closed, and all was quiet again except for Miss Finch's weak bleating, that was like a new-born lamb.

He released her. "I beg your pardon," he said, "I did not want Mrs. Jaspard to know I was here."

So mild a reason seemed even to himself hardly excuse enough for the rough treatment to which he had subjected Miss Finch.

"Mr. Barnabas! What——" Now the reaction of her terror over-came her. She sat down on the stool before her dressing-table and went so white that he thought she was going to faint.

But Miss Finch had the sea-captain's blood in her veins, and she did nothing so feeble. She said in a gasping voice, staring at him with eyes which fear still kept widened:

"What have you been doing? What has happened to you?"

He caught sight now of his reflection in the mirror. No wonder Miss Finch was gaping at him as if he were a man escaped from Bedlam. His coat was covered with mud, he had lost the ribbon that confined his hair, and this now lay in tangled confusion over his shoulders; his face had an expression, unfamiliar even to himself, of strain and furtiveness.

His left sleeve, he noticed, was torn in a rough hole, scorched about the edges: the passage of the first bullet that had so nearly hit him.

"I had an accident," he said shortly. "I apologize for my appearance." He began to push his hair back into position. "Can you give me a ribbon or a tape—anything to keep my hair in place?"

This concern to make his toilet seemed suddenly to bring home to Miss Finch what she had been both too frightened and curious to think of before: that it was ten o'clock at night, she had only a dressing-wrapper over her nightgown, and a man was in her bedroom; her own hair, too—though this was a small point beside the other enormities—lay loose without a cap upon it. Over a chair, in full view, were spread her rumpled calico chemise, her corsets, stiff still with their iron stays as a human body, as though a limbless female had been cast down. As her uneasy glance fell upon it, her white skin turned scarlet.

"Please leave my room this instant, Mr. Barnabas."

"Presently," he said calmly, "when I have tidied myself. I have begged pardon for my intrusion—or did I not?—and you must bear with me a few minutes. Thank you, I may have this?" He did not wait for permission, but picked up a narrow piece of dark-green ribbon lying on the dressing-table—a piece which, though he did not know this, had until recently been adorning Miss Finch's throat.

He was not thinking of what he was saying; and the impropriety of the situation, from Miss Finch's point of view, had not particularly occurred to him. His mind was too busy running on how to ensure Miss Finch's silence on to-night's episode. He remembered that he suspected she was more than a little partial to him: he must trade on that.

He smiled at her, and let his long lashes tremble over his eyes as consciously as Fan might have done. "Before I go, I must have your promise, your solemn oath, that you will tell no one I have been here—in the house at all, I mean."

"Please go. We can talk of that another time."

"We cannot. It has to be talked of now. And till you promise me, I will not go."

"What have you been doing?" she asked. And she was not the subordinate governess addressing one of the young masters of the house, nor yet even an outraged spinster reproving a man who has broken into her bedroom, but a representative of morality questioning a delinquent. Barney felt the implication of her tone far more forcefully than she could have suspected.

"I told you I had an accident. I don't wish Mr. Jaspard to know."

"You have been riding?" There was a surprised query in her tone because the Jaspard gentlemen were not in the habit of going about at night on horseback.

K

He looked down at his boots and spurs, and could not deny it. "Why shouldn't I be riding, in Heaven's name?"

"You have been fighting a duel?" Her eyes were on the tear in his coat.

"Yes," said Barney, thinking this was as convenient an explanation as any. But his answer came not quite confidently enough.

"I do not believe you," she said. "Or there is much more to it besides. If it had been only a duel you would not have come in such shame, nor been so frightened."

"Frightened!" he blustered. "What right have you to speak to me in this manner, to make these insulting and groundless implications——?"

Miss Finch had risen and stood facing him. She made a slightly ludicrous and altogether childish figure in her wrapper, with her straight red hair falling nearly to her waist: in her interruption she sounded more than ever a denouncing angel.

"I have the right, sir, because you force your way into my room late at night and treat me in the most rough and extraordinary manner, holding your hand across my mouth, and you refuse to go. What have you been doing, Mr. Barnabas? What have you got to hide? It will be my duty to tell Mr. Jaspard."

"I am not Jacky that you may come the governess over me," he said surlily, now seeing that his first plan of wooing Miss Finch to silence by prudent love-making was one little likely to have any practical effect. "If you tell Mr. Jaspard, ma'am, pray how do you intend to answer him when he asks what I am doing in your bedroom at this hour of night, and you in"—his eyes raked her insolently so that she blushed furiously —"in your undress?"

"I shall tell him, of course, that you forced your way in——"

"And if I deny that, and confess to an assignation with you, and intimate that we had a quarrel—no, hear me out, ma'am. There are many in this house who will uphold that it is not of all things the most improbable: it has not gone unobserved that I talk with you in the nursery many a Sunday evening."

Her colour spread right down her neck. It was not becoming, crossed Barney's mind.

"You would hardly—come to me in a muddy and torn coat, and with spurs and riding-boots." Her voice trembled both with rage and the tears that were near.

"While you are down informing Mr. Jaspard, what easier for me than to rid myself of my clothes, and be in your bed by the time you bring him back?"

"You brute! you brute!" Though there were undoubtedly answers with which she might have successfully countered Barney's proposal, Miss Finch was beyond continuing the unseemly, the indecent argument, and she sat down on her dressing-table stool, weeping.

This was capitulation enough to make Barney feel master of the situation. It was fortunate, he found time to reflect, that her room was an inner one, and that nobody passing along the corridor outside the nursery could possibly hear her.

"There is nothing to cry about," he said, with a mixture of gentleness and exasperation.

Miss Finch, however, paid him no heed, and her despairing sobs continued.

He began to feel that he was indeed the brute she had called him. Certainly, from her point of view, he had behaved inexcusably: stealing unawares into her room, using her roughly, and meeting her proper objections with threats the most unchivalrous that any man could offer. Suddenly it became very necessary that he should put himself in a less despicable light; and he knew that this was not merely because she must be cajoled into keeping silence about his presence here to-night. . . . He did not know why, but he did not like Miss Finch to hold a low opinion of him.

"If you will stop crying and listen, I will tell you why Mr. and Mrs. Jaspard must not know I have been here—no one must know. Ma'am—Carola, please stop crying."

At the use of her Christian name Miss Finch gulped, no doubt in renewed indignation, and looked up with red-rimmed eyes and blotched cheeks, a mild disfigurement which brought to Barney's mind the day he might be said to have made her acquaintance: when Jacky's money-box had been rifled by Fan.

"If you had—any gentlemanly feelings at all, sir, you would go at once."

"Yes, yes, I will go. I am not going to touch you or hurt you. I am truly sorry I have done and said to you the things I have. In a manner it was all forced on me. I—I have been in a bad scrape to-night." Barney, in spite of his earlier intention to play upon her feelings for him and desperately anxious as he was to make a more favourable impression, this time was not aware how appealingly he was looking at Miss Finch. "I—cannot tell you what it was. But it was bad. If anyone found out, I should be——" He broke off, and began again. "Mr. Jaspard would have nothing further to do with me."

"I understand," she said flatly. "Now you have told me, will you go?"

"When you promise me that you will never tell anyone that I have been here to-night."

She did not answer immediately. Then she said: "I will promise it, if you in your turn will make me a promise."

"What is that?' he asked, surprised.

"That, whatever this bad, and I am sure foolish, thing that you have done may be, you will never do it again."

"No," said Barney with fervency. "That I won't,. 'fore God! I won't."

He meant it. His fright had not been the normal fear of a man in a dangerous situation, which is a fear many can bear and overcome; but primordial, animal, naked fear, such as few above the lowest dregs in civilization ever experience.

Their eyes met for a moment, and she dropped hers hastily.

"Then I will promise," she said.

"Thank you. I shall not forget your kindness. . . . Mrs. Jaspard is not likely to come back to the children to-night?"

"Oh no, she never comes a second time. But why?"

"I must wait in the nursery till it is a little later and I may be certain everyone is in bed. I will go down and out by the area door. May I ask you if—you will be so good as to bolt it again after me, or when the servants find it open in the morning they will wonder, and questions will be asked."

"Oh no," she said with a little whimper. "If I were seen!"

"There will be no one to see you; that is why I am waiting. What time is it?"

She looked at her watch lying on her dressing-table. "Nearly eleven."

"In three quarters of an hour it should be safe enough. I'll knock at your door when I'm ready to go. You'll not fall asleep?"

"No . . . I shan't fall asleep."

He heard her slip the bolt home after she had closed the door upon him. Was she truly to be trusted? he wondered. Well, she held his secret, or a part of it, now. If she betrayed him he would be as good as his word, and brazen it out with a tale of a love-affair with the governess; which, though it would do him little credit, could not bring upon his head the shame and dishonour of the truth. But Carola Finch, he was certain, did not break her promises.

Then he forgot her. Sitting in the dark nursery, faintly lit by a white half-moon, with the night coolness gradually winning a battle over the lingering slight warmth from the dead fire, Barney, for the first time since his efforts at highway robbery had ended in disaster, had time to consider all that his failure implied. He could never see Lucy again. He had lost her for ever. She and Harry—and no doubt Mrs. Brook and Mr. Raikes—would look upon him as a poltroon. And even for Lucy— though with the extravagance of love he had believed that there was nothing he would not do for her sake—even for her he could not face again another attempt at playing the highwayman. Somewhere far back in his mind, too, he found the knowledge that intimacy with the Brooks' could but lead him, whether the road was long or short, to ruin, with Newgate and the gallows at the end of it. . . .

Nevertheless, he sat out the time of waiting, with his face in his hands, breaking his heart for the siren, Lucy.

At length, when he deemed it safe to go, he roused himself and scraped gently with his fingers at Miss Finch's door. She unbolted it at once, as though awaiting the summons—as indeed she evidently was. Even in his grief he was amused to see that she had dressed, and looked, except for the candlestick in her hand, like the Miss Finch of every day. She was taking no chances of being found wandering about the house in her night-clothes.

"Good night, Mr. Barnabas. I will come down and bolt the door after you have gone."

"Thank you. God bless you—Carola." He touched her hand.

To his surprise her fingers turned, and taking his, pressed them. She said:

"I trust you to keep your promise to me as I will mine to you."

"Why do you mind so much what I do?" he asked softly.

"I—should be sorry to see you get into trouble. Now go."

"Yes. I'll see you on Sunday."

"No, please." She blushed. "If—if it is true that—they are talking about—your coming so often to the nursery, please, please don't come."

"Oh—damn them! Well, I'll bring Kitty with me. . . . Good night."

On his way to the back door he met nobody, and the only sound he heard was the beating of the watch-dog's tail on the floor as the animal recognized his passing steps. He stood a minute or two in the deserted square. It looked spacious and noble in its emptiness, the moonlight picking out the cobblestones and making of them a miniature rough sea; the posts around the green in the centre, and those marking off the footway before the houses, each had its fine black slanting counterpart, more black, more rigid (it seemed) than the silvered posts themselves.

Behind him, in the area, he heard the rustling sound of bolts being slipped slowly home.

CHAPTER XIV

A HOUSE AT BLACKHEATH

WHEN Fan left the masquerade with Mr. Folkes, she had done so willingly and with her eyes open to all that it implied. For by that time she had decided there was no more agreeable alternative open to her than to place herself under Mr. Folkes's protection. If she had not known him to be a wealthy man, she would without doubt have subdued her inclination for his person. She was attracted by his big, well-built frame, by his gallant address, by the lingual force of his love-making, and all these attributes, mingled as they were with riches, made him irresistible.

She did not rush to embrace a life of concubinage without having reflected upon the matter as deeply as she was capable of doing. It had been clear to her for two or three years now that there were two things she needed from life: the one was money, and the other the admiration of men. It would have been preferable to have married first and had her adventures behind the concealing if flimsy cloak of wifehood; and that was the way she had planned it when she ran away from Hanover Square to become, as she believed, the wife of Carlton Stafford. When Stafford failed her she had, in her own opinion, no choice but to find some other man who would take care of her. Go home she would not— nor to Mrs. Fletcher in Northumberland—and she knew no eligible man from whom it was possible for her to seek marriage. She had been kept much in the background, and such suitable gentlemen whom she had met and who had professed themselves her devoted slaves, would not, she knew, stand by their fanciful compliments in the face of families who, unlikely to agree to an alliance with the dubious Miss Frances Jaspard while she lived at home, would certainly not do so when she was disgraced and dowerless.

Fan had been born without any sense of shame; unless one called by that name an emotion which made her fear to meet either the General or his wife now that she had declared herself a rebel against them and against convention. Upon her going to Mr. Folkes, therefore, she had no barrier of self-disgust over which to climb. Her situation she accepted, in the circumstances, as necessary. She wanted money, freedom of behaviour, and adulation. Here was the royal road. Only cowards boggled at the first step.

She held pitifully romantical ideas about the life she was choosing. No longer Fan Jaspard, but Dorinda Debonair, she would be the most sought-after courtesan in London. In her house in St. James's Square

—or some other equally fashionable quarter of the town—she would hold her salons; and every man of quality in town would be among the knockers at her door, the seekers of her company. At their hands she would receive jewels, valuable presents, sums of money; and her intimate favours should be given only to those who brought the most. It was an alluring prospect, and only a pity that the King of England was not now such a one as the attractive, amorous Second Charles. As it was, with the throne filled by an elderly German who could scarcely speak English, Fan did not aspire to become a royal mistress. A Duke would do her as well. . . .

One of the lesser but keen pleasures she looked forward to was the humiliation and rage of the General and Madam when they learned that she, the scorned and humbled Fan, was the toast of London, and her name on every man's lips. No, the General would not like it that one who was of his family and of his upbringing should become an exhibition and the talk of the town. In her thoughts Fan giggled. People would flock about her coach in the street—it was to be blue and silver and drawn by six grey horses in trappings of blue; at the playhouse everyone would stand up to see her enter, and she would smile upon them all exactly as if she were royalty, and the jewels would be flashing on her corsage, on her wrists and in her hair . . . yes, that would be like royalty too.

Of course, it would take a year or two before she was as famous as that. She would have to begin in a small way in Thomas Folkes's house in Golden Square. There she would hold small weekly assemblies, and gradually eliminate those of his acquaintance too nearly connected with trade. One might put in the *Whitehall Evening Post* a piquant advertisement addressed to the nobility in veiled but not unintelligible terms which conveyed to the reader that did he come to a certain numbered house in Golden Square on such-and-such an evening, he might expect a pleasurable and extraordinary entertainment . . . the precise wording would have to be considered.

But Fan's going away with Thomas Folkes did not lead to the realization of her dreams, or to anything resembling them.

She had mistaken her man. Fan was vain and inexperienced. These two qualities had prevented her from supposing for one moment that she could not handle any lover as she wished. When Thomas Folkes made her his mistress he made her his prisoner also.

This action, though it tallied with his thoroughly selfish nature, was in the beginning dictated by caution as much as by any desire to keep Fan confined. Though his acquaintance with the Hon. Robert Jaspard was of the slenderest, his reputation he knew very well. Were he to discover that he was Fan's seducer—and she had confessed to him that the tale of her marriage was a capricious lie—he would probably set the Law upon him and have him charged with rape. And the fact that Fan had come willingly would stand him in no good stead. Men as determined, influential and wealthy as Mr. Jaspard could tip the scales of justice when it suited them to do so. It crossed his mind more than once that Fan was a high price to pay for risking, possibly a capital sentence and certainly the loss of a name that, in spite of a self-indulgent even vicious life, he had managed to keep in fairly high repute. He was a fool, maybe, to have taken the girl; but when the loveliest creature he has ever seen offers herself, is it for a man to throw away his chance, and if he does shall he not be tormented for the rest of his life thinking of what he has missed?

He kept Fan in his house in Golden Square only one night, and after she had collected her things from her lodgings they drove away to another house he owned which, so he told her, was a little way out of London, and a safer haven for her for the present. She had supposed it might be in Chelsea or Kensington; and her surprise grew to annoyance when their way took them through the city, and beyond, until the houses thinned out and they were in the country. Fan, in the shrill tones her voice adopted when she was irritated or excited, protested that she had not bargained to live so far out of London as this.

He calmed her by dwelling upon the inconsolable state into which he would be thrown if now, after he had sipped at her beauty, Mr. Jaspard should find her and wrest her from him before he had drunk deep of the lovely cup. This was language Fan understood and enjoyed . . . the rest of the drive passed very agreeably.

This house at Blackheath was a modern brick building, graceful in its proportions, but forbidding because of the high wall which surrounded its garden and, as Fan was to discover, cut it off completely from the outside world.

Even Fan, with her vanity and her inexperience, could not fail to understand that Mr. Folkes—that respectable head of a leather manufactory who collected subscriptions for a charity for bastard children—kept this house at Blackheath for just such adventures as this one. Obviously another woman—probably many other women—had stayed here before her. The bedroom, at one glance, was not a single gentleman's bedroom: it waited, with its sumptuous hangings, its frilled dressing-table, to receive a lady. And the bed, with blue velvet curtains descending from a gilt dome ornamented with huge gilt feathers, was so extravagant a piece of furniture, even allowing that it was the fashion for beds to be luxurious, that it seemed to invite no respectable couple to repose beneath its canopy.

It was not a large house, yet the staff seemed to Fan unreasonably scant. All the work indoors was done by two sisters: tall, plain, long-nosed women dressed in sober colours, and in their speech and expression sober also. Fan announced that she must have a maid, but Mr. Folkes told her that he did not like a covey of servants, and the younger woman, Grace, could do as much for her as she would require. He added, kissing her ear, that he himself would be her maid. To give Mr. Folkes his due, he appeared to be willing to forgo also the ministrations of a personal attendant. Certainly he brought no valet with him from London; though Fan learned later that the one man employed about the garden and stables was occasionally called in to perform small services of the toilet for his master.

The day after their arrival Mr. Folkes found that it was absolutely necessary for him to go to London on urgent business. It would not take above two days, and then he could return untrammelled to Blackheath, and forget for a while the cares of the world. He did not tell Fan —expecting that she would object, or at least suspect that her stay in Blackheath was to be longer than she anticipated—that his principal business in London was the letting of his house in Golden Square. He had recently speculated unluckily, and here was an opportunity to recover something of what he had lost. Before he left, he instructed Fan not to go beyond the garden; for who knew if they had been tracked from London? It was foolish to take risks when Mr. Jaspard must have all the town agog for her. This, in the circumstances, seemed to Fan no peculiar command, and she little guessed that not for months, except for an occasional drive with Mr. Folkes, would she pass beyond the high pink wall.

During these two days that she was left alone she learned that the gates in the walls, one for carriages and a smaller one for walking in and out, were kept always locked, the keys being in the possession of Mr. Folkes. The back door of the house gave egress onto a lane, and it was here that the tradesmen delivered their goods. This door, too, was constantly locked, and the key held by the elder of the guardian sisters.

These women Fan from the beginning disliked. Their manner as they waited on her, though it did not allow of complaint, yet successfully conveyed that they held her in small esteem, and supposed that her stay here would be no more permanent than that of others before her. To any questions she put to them, either then or in the future, they replied in mere monosyllables, or with the unvarying rejoinder: "If you wish to know, you must ask the master."

His house disposed of and his stock-broker consulted, Mr. Folkes remained at Blackheath; once in a week or a fortnight, however, it was necessary for him to go for one day to London to keep an eye upon his leather-works. Fan still accepted her seclusion without demur, seeing the wisdom of remaining out of reach of Mr. Jaspard until such time had elapsed when even he was bound to recognize that it was too late for him to interfere with the life she had chosen to lead. That Mr. Folkes would bring her back to London within a few weeks she did not doubt. The novelty of her situation and the constant companionship of Mr. Folkes were enough to amuse her at this time. Once she had accustomed herself to her lover's peculiarities she was quite happy.

Mr. Folkes's sensual character need not be enlarged upon. It is enough to say it was his pleasure to drape black velvet over a couch and to lay Fan's naked body upon it, and adorn this with a collection of necklaces, bracelets, pendants. The rubies, the sapphires, the diamonds flickered and winked upon her white flesh thrown into relief against the black velvet. . . .

But Fan never handled these jewels at any other time, nor could she discover where he kept them.

For a few weeks this life of voluptuous dalliance filled the hours of both to the exclusion of any other desires. But the day came when Fan began to rate him that he kept her still at Blackheath, and had as yet given her no presents or arranged an allowance for her. He stopped her complaints with kisses; and the following morning set out for London. Thereafter, he began to go more often until soon it might rather be said that he was living there and spending only occasional nights at Blackheath. No, he told her, she could not come to his house in Golden Square, for it was let until Michaelmas. As for himself, he slept in a room above the manufactory . . . there was a deal of business to be attended to at this time of the year.

Even so, it was a little while longer before Fan could bring herself to accept the fact that she had given herself up to the power of a man for literally nothing more than a home—and a home neither so comfortable nor so free as that she had run away from. When she lived in Hanover Square she could walk out among the shops when she pleased, she did go occasionally to entertainments and, in the visitors who came to the house, found her chances of meeting people. Since she had been confined at Blackheath, she had seen no one besides Mr. Folkes and the servants: her exercise and amusement were limited to what she could find to do inside the high brick wall that surrounded the garden.

The loneliness, the imprisonment—so unbelievably different from what she had planned—Fan might have borne with a degree of patience had Mr. Folkes been generous. Then she could have consoled herself by saving up for those days when Dorinda Debonair would be the toast of London. As it was, she reflected bitterly, no woman had ever sold herself for less. He gave her nothing. Nothing at all. Her wardrobe consisted, it will be remembered, of only those dresses she had bought

in expectation of becoming Mrs. Carlton Stafford. Thomas Folkes told
her they were enough, and for his part he preferred to see her without
any clothes. As for jewels, did she not wear them every night, and often
by day as well? And it was safer for him to keep such valuable stones
under lock and key rather than leave them in her careless keeping.
What did she need with money? She had all she required, and he did
not choose for her to go shopping. Neither did he choose for her to go
beyond the garden. Why? Could she not guess? She was too pretty, too
precious, to be seen by other eyes. Now he could feel that for his delight
alone had she been created.

Fan, who a few weeks ago might have been impressed by this
compliment, raged at him. She did not accept this mean tyranny without fierce fighting. Her abuse was wordy and spiteful, and he laughed
at it. Then she tried to withold herself from him, but he was a powerful
man . . . and he seemed to enjoy this combative love-making as much
as any more sentimental that they had indulged in. Fan began to hate
him, and to be afraid of him; yet, because of his virility and his pro-
ficiency as a lover, she remained fascinated by him also.

From vituperation she turned to pleading: a woman expected gifts
from her lover; it was his tribute to her beauty and the pleasure that she
gave him. Thomas Folkes still laughed, and whispered in her ear that
he gave her tributes of another nature. . . .

Through the many days that she was alone she plotted to escape,
though rather as a pastime and to annoy the women who dogged her
than because she had serious thoughts of carrying it out. If she did
succeed in getting beyond Mr. Folkes's wall, what then? She had only
the few shillings that had been in her purse when she went to the
masquerade. Ah! if she could but find where he kept the jewels! Many
hours she spent wandering from room to room, feeling the panels in
hopes of pressing a secret spring, searching behind pictures for a
concealed cupboard, turning over all his possessions: and every search
was as fruitless as the one before it.

A good deal later, and after Fan had discovered that she was going to
have a child, the jewels were no longer brought out to be played with.
And when she mentioned them Mr. Folkes stopped smiling, and he
answered shortly that he was tired of them, he preferred to see her
unadorned. . . .

CHAPTER XV

ROSA IS INOCULATED

CRESWELL was in his dressing-room. He had just dismissed his valet, and was standing before the mirror, not noticing his reflection but absorbed in wondering—as he so often did—whether he would be able to leave the house unobserved by either his wife or her uncle.

He was not dressed for the Court, nor indeed for the card-party which he knew was being held that evening downstairs. Creswell, like his father, was always something of a dandy; that is to say, he was never seen without long lace ruffles to his shirt-sleeves, or a thick bunch of lace beneath his chin, or in a waistcoat that was not heavily embroidered. But this evening he was, for him, sombrely attired in a sapphire-blue coat edged only with narrow silver galloon; yet his wig was newly curled and powdered, and his lace-edged handkerchief freshly sprinkled with scent.

A knock sounded on his door. As he turned round, his handsome face assumed an expression of querulity.

"Who is that?" he asked in a manner that must have daunted anyone. There was a pause, as though whoever waited beyond the door considered what to do next.

"May I come in?" said Rosa's low, rather hesitant voice.

Creswell looked even crosser, but he gave a grudging assent.

She came in and stood quite still with her back against the door. At once she took in that he was about to go out, perhaps more by the defensive manner in which he looked at her than deducing it from his hat waiting on the stool beside him. She herself was evidently dressed for company, in her excessively wide embroidered petticoat, the elaborate lace cap upon her fair curled hair; lace frills, deeper than Creswell's own, finished her sleeves at the elbow and caressed her arms in a fine foam. Below these, a pair of emerald bracelets sparkled on her wrists.

"You are not going out?" she said, in the tone of voice people use when they know very well that the person addressed has the intention of doing what they have just announced he will not do.

"Yes," answered Creswell shortly, "I have an engagement."

"But you knew there was to be a party here to-night. Lord and Lady Clair are coming, and Mrs. Valentine and——"

"I heard it mentioned for the first time only this morning, and my engagement was already made."

"It was decided upon only yesterday, when Uncle and I were

drinking tea with the Clairs, and Uncle said that he knew you were not in waiting to-night."

"And therefore I should be free to do exactly as he pleases," said Creswell, coldly angry. "No, thank you, ma'am. If you and your uncle choose to make arrangements for me without consulting me, you must not be surprised if I do not fall in with them. And now, please let me pass, I shall be late."

"You are not to go, I shan't let you go," she announced, with the childish imperiousness that was very much a part of her temper. "You—you are only going out to gamble and drink with those—rakes at your club."

He did not contradict her for, though he was not in fact going to meet his club, it was better that she should think he was than guess the true nature of his appointment.

She went on, working herself up as nagging women do: "You come in late every night now. I cannot sleep for wondering when you will be disturbing me. It is too bad I should be kept awake night after night. 'Tis nuisance enough when you have to be in waiting till midnight or later—even then you do not come directly home . . ."

"I suppose you will allow I must eat some supper," he interrupted her. "That will do, ma'am. We have talked of this often enough. I intend going out to-night, and there's an end on't."

"What shall I say to my guests?"

"Tell them, if you will, that I am drinking myself insensible with the rascalliest scallywags in town—I don't care what you say to them. Now stand aside, Rosa. I don't wish to remove you by force, but I am not going to be kept in my room like this as if I were a child, while you vent your spleen upon me."

Sulkily she stood aside.

He said to her then, quite gently: "I pray you consider, Rosalind, that it is your fault, and your fault alone, that I cannot abide to spend my evenings here in what should be my home. If you cannot mend your ways to me, I will leave you here with your uncle, whom you so dearly love, and set up my own house by myself."

"You cannot! The scandal! You could not stay at Court if you——"

But Creswell, with a slight bow, had left her, and she was talking to herself.

This had been but one of many such scenes since their marriage, four months before: but not until to-night had he ever threatened to leave her.

Creswell felt that he had honestly done his best to be a good and a loving husband. Indeed, he could not yet bear to contemplate the first few weeks following their wedding-day. He had been deeply in love with her, and as much as his spirit his vanity had suffered at his failure to infect her with his own passion. She had never repulsed him, and indeed upon occasions nature had triumphed over what he believed to be her planned frigidity, and then he had been, till he fell asleep, gay and hopeful; but the next morning she was again the Empress and he the criminal slave. For she made him always feel that, because he had behaved to her once as a brute, he was depraved in his character beyond redemption.

It was perhaps that same rigid sense of honour that had made her insist upon marrying him whom she despised, which now prevented her from admitting that he could ever sufficiently rise in her estimation to be treated with the respect, if not the affection, due to a husband.

Her behaviour to him in public, when she adopted a manner coldly gracious and always excessively polite, while it probably served to hide the worst of their differences, seemed to Creswell to emphasize the contempt she felt for him when it was no longer necessary, for society's sake, to play a part.

This treatment over weeks brought with it at last swift reaction. Creswell fell out of love with his wife, and so cruelly had she lacerated all his most intimate feelings that he now endowed her with a malevolence and a cunning greater than, at sixteen years old, she could possibly deserve. He thought of her in the Biblical term of a whited sepulchre, and this simile came perhaps particularly to his mind, because he could still, against his will, be sometimes moved by the pure loveliness of her face, or the outline of her bosom if she were standing by a window where the light etched it out.

This spring smallpox was creeping about the town, not (as in the previous year) scattering its evils lavishly like a man in a fury with a whip beating at all about him, but rather picking out with his lash one here, one there. And it had come unsought into Creswell's mind that were Rosa to get the disease and die of it, he would be a free man again. In justice to him it must be said that he was as horrified by this unwarrantable thought as though he had caught himself planning to murder his wife. He pushed it away from him, appalled by his new knowledge of the Satanic suggestions to which the human mind may all unawares be open.

Lord Comberley aggravated the many difficulties which lay in Creswell's path. The latter was prepared to agree that the older man had every reason to condemn him, even to find unpardonable his behaviour to the innocent Rosa; but surely, as a man of the world and one more experienced than the young couple, it had been his plain duty, once the marriage was effected, to assist Creswell to the dignity and esteem of a husband.

Instead, he had continued to allow his displeasure, his contempt, to lie like a fog in every room where he and his nephew-in-law met; so that, Creswell supposed, even the very servants must be aware of it. He upheld Rosa in all her whims and wishes, he joined with her in nagging at him because he had begun going again to White's Coffee-House of an evening and spending convivial hours with his club, which included, among its members, Tom Brabazon and Lord Penge. It was not perhaps surprising that these last-named companions were looked upon with especial disfavour by uncle and niece. For, though Creswell had taken care to keep silence on the matter, Rosa, who naturally met them when she went to the royal Drawing Room, to her confusion and shame recognized them, and so told Lord Comberley of their having been present at the *Green Periwig* that night.

Lord Comberley, however, did not succeed in getting them dismissed from Court. To do so, he must put before the King a valid excuse, and as the only excuse he could offer meant extending even further the knowledge of Rosa's dishonour, he did not choose to give it. Fortunately for their own prospects, Brabazon, Penge, and Creswell himself, though wild and often stupid in the gaieties of their free time, were yet at Court models of correct and decorous behaviour.

The threat of having him removed from his position as Gentleman-in-Waiting was a sword that Lord Comberley had kept poised over Creswell's head, lowering it with, as it were, a rattle in the scabbard every time Creswell more than usually displeased him. But one night, only a month ago now, when he had been upbraiding him for keeping late hours and once again used this means in an endeavour to subdue him, Creswell both astonished him and won a victory by saying:

"Very good, my lord. You carry your complaints to the proper quarter, and I am ready to relinquish my post to-morrow. 'Twill be a vast relief to hear no more that it is about to happen to me. . . '. Besides, I am a sufficiently wealthy man—or will be in a year or two, and on that I may get what credit I will—that I do not need to consider whether or no I draw a salary."

Lord Comberley spoke no more of dismissal. It was better far that Creswell should have some occupation than that all his hours be left free to spend in rakish companionship. And, he was bound to reflect, the Hon. Robert Jaspard would be unlikely to submit meekly to any insult to his heir. In short, Lord Comberley was a blusterer, and now that Creswell had learned to call his bluff, he had freed himself to some extent from one tyranny.

He had wished to leave Cleveland Court and set up house alone with Rosa, in which circumstances, he had then believed, he could still mend his marriage. But Rosa, who was less contemptuous of this than most of the ideas he put forward, represented to him how lonely her uncle would be. Creswell pointed out that he had been alone for many years before she came. That was true, agreed Rosa, but he had come now to rely upon her company. Besides, a house of their own at present was very unnecessary, and certainly one could not be found more convenient to St. James's Palace. Lord Comberley, as might be expected, opposed the suggestion vigorously, intimating—without actually putting it into words—that it would be a bad day for Rosa when she was deprived of his protection. As he held Rosa's purse-strings till Creswell's twenty-fifth birthday, Creswell was not in a position to argue very forcibly.

At the same time he could well afford, with his allowance from his father, his salary as a Gentleman-in-Waiting, and a sinecure position he held besides, to establish himself in a modest house of his own in a neighbourhood less fashionable than St. James's.

This house he had already leased and furnished, and it was thither he was going on this evening when Rosa wished him to stay behind and play cards. It had been his plaything and his possession for just three weeks, and the object of those nocturnal outings of late when Lord Comberley and Rosa supposed him to be gaming at White's. Brabazon and Penge, who missed his company, had an idea of what was in the wind, and when they met him they nudged him with friendly significance, and to outsiders held their tongues.

Creswell, as he jogged in a hired chair to Covent Garden, in the vicinity of which his house stood, felt his bad temper and the constraint in which he lived in Cleveland Court ebbing out of him. He felt refreshed, happy; a smile, without his being conscious of it, came to his face.

In a few minutes he would be told, as Rosa never told him, how fine he looked, how handsome he was, and love, simple and unpretentious—too simple indeed to mask itself—would wrap him about like a warm cloak in winter, like clean pure linen felt against the skin in summer.

He had first met Alice two months before. She was crying in the Piazza at Covent Garden, while two apprentices jeered at her grief and suggested to her, with unrepeatable obscenity, an alleviation of her troubles. Creswell was walking with two friends, and with them smirking over a list of whores, containing a detailed description of their persons and the direction of the rooms where they might be found—this informative piece of literature having just cost them twopence from an importunate vendor. The sound of sobbing had made him look up, and he was struck into seriousness by the utter abandonment to grief of this woman with her face buried in her hands. His companions, not wanting a brawl with a couple of common louts, and in a district where they might call many more to their assistance, tried to dissuade him from interfering: she was only a bawd, for sure, they said, and not to be seen as a female in distress. Creswell, however, by the magnificence of his presence, and the haughty manner of his father which he could at times assume, routed the apprentices without any voiced resentment on their part. The woman looked up to thank him, and he saw that she was very young and that her eyes, though blurred and magnified by tears, were soft and golden as a deer's.

He signalled to his friends to leave him, and escorted his new acquaintance to the none too reputable King's Coffee-House just over the way.

That had been the beginning. At first he had merely been kind to her: she was hungry and he fed her; she had a sorrow and she unburdened herself of it; he gave her money and comfort. Her words of gratitude were gentle as the touch of kind fingers on his sore heart, and so he saw her again . . . and a second time . . . and a third.

He did not make her his mistress without a struggle with his conscience—not on her behalf, for she was, as he had surmised, fallen already—but he had not been married so long that he did not feel an inclination to be a faithful husband.

As soon as he had succumbed and found that Alice was all that Rosa was not, and brought him in overflowing measure love, comfort and satisfaction, he made his resolve of setting her up in a house where he might visit her freely and feel himself to have a real home. And now every day the temptation grew stronger to leave Cleveland Court, as he had threatened to-night, and reside permanently with his mistress.

Certainly, Alice had not the characteristics of an ordinary whore: she demanded of him neither money nor jewels, and what presents he gave her she demurred at taking; with the little house in the purlieu of Covent Garden she was as enraptured as if it had been a palace. More important, far, than these assets, she adored him, and in her eyes he could do no wrong. This, for a man who had been treated as Creswell had, gave her a hold over him stronger than she knew. She was a simple creature, a country girl of no education at all; but her simplicity was native and honest, so that it did not irritate, as stupidity may. Even so, had Creswell's circumstances permitted him to spend days in her company instead of snatched hours devoted to love-making, it is probable he would soon have found that by her very limitations she must fail in companionship. Each had been brought up, not only with so different a background, but the one highly educated and with ideas poured into his ears since he was four years old, and the other knowing nothing save of the caring of stock and butter-making, that they must have found it as difficult to sustain for long a conversation as though they had been inhabitants of opposite ends of the earth.

L

How did Alice, this girl from the plains of Wiltshire, come to London? She told Creswell all her story that first night. It was no unusual one. She had had a lover in Salisbury, a young journeyman cabinet-maker who, under promise of marriage, had persuaded her to lie with him. He had gone to seek his fortune in London, and she heard from him no more. Finding herself to be with child, she had managed to learn from his brother, casually as it were in conversation, the London address of her lover. She had left home and come to London with her little bit of money and a change of linen tied up in a neckerchief, expecting to find the capital only a little bigger and as friendly as Salisbury. The thronged, the endless streets, the thousands of houses, perhaps even more than these the incessant noise, the shouting, the din, bemused her. She had gone this way and that with her piece of paper (for she had paid a man a penny in Salisbury to write the address down while it was fresh in her mind), but when she could get anyone to read it, he only shook his head and said he didn't know those parts at all; one man cheerlessly remarked that it was "a long way from here", and then asked her to come home with him instead. She had got frightened, and begun to run. After that she did not remember very much: she believed she was knocked down by a dray. Anyway, she woke up in a dirty bed, and found that she was losing her child. . . .

She was ill many days, and the old woman who had taken her in at the time of the accident and was kind to her in a rough fashion, took all her money from her in payment, as well as her change of linen in the little bundle she had carried from Salisbury; and as soon as she could walk had told her she must go, she had mouths enough of her own to feed.

By this time the piece of paper with her lover's address written on it was lost: all she remembered of it was Crown Court, and the old woman told her there wasn't a parish in London but had its Crown Court. "Fifty of 'em if there's one," she had said.

She had looked for work all that day, but no one would take her without a character. Towards evening a shopman, watching her loitering while she tried to pluck up courage to ask if he needed a servant, told her she looked hungry, and supper was waiting on the table within. In truth, she was ravenous, and so tired she could go no further; in weakness and despair, though guessing what it meant, she accepted his invitation. He was good to her, and she had lived with him for a month. Then, his wife who had been away nursing her sick mother, returned home unexpectedly, and turned her out neck and crop. . . .

When Creswell found her she was crying because she had nowhere to go, and with the mocking of the apprentices she saw herself having to take every night whoever would give her the price of her supper and a bed. . . .

On this night, knowing that the card-party at Cleveland Court would mean the family there keeping late hours, Creswell spent longer than usual with Alice. Even so, upon his return, as he saw from the light shining beneath the bedroom door, Rosa unfortunately was not asleep. Presently he heard her maid leaving her, but though he dawdled over his undressing, the pale gold line remained obstinately there.

She was sitting up in bed. The flames from a double-branched candelabra on the table beside her shed wavering pretty lights on the golden curls falling beneath her cap.

"I heard you in your room," she said, "so I did not blow the candles out." She added, with her candour that so often amounted to sheer tactlessness: "I thought, when I saw you had not come to bed, that you would be very drunk when you came in."

"I trust, then, that you are agreeably surprised."

But he was not ill-humoured, and made an effort to be pleasant. This was due as much to his sense of guilt (a feeling which, while blaming Rosa entirely for his transgression, he was not yet hardened enough to suppress) as to the soothed state of mind in which he always left Alice, and which took some hours to wear off.

"Your friends stayed late," he suggested amiably.

"Yes," said Rosa. "I won nine guineas. We did not play deep."

"I hope you never will. What were you playing?"

"Pam. I was dealt Pam twice." Her tone was absent.

"What is this?" Creswell's eye had been caught by a sealed letter which lay on the dressing-table.

"Oh yes, I forgot, that was brought for you about nine o'clock . . . Mr. Jaspard—Creswell . . ."

This was the first time he had heard his Christian name on her lips since their marriage service, and he knew by the tension that had come into her voice that she was forcing herself to say something she must have been deciding upon while lying waiting for him to come in.

"Well?" His finger was about to rip open the seal.

"You—you did not mean what you said this evening—that you might set up your own house and leave me?"

He looked at her, and his face hardened.

Rosa went on flounderingly: "If you would try to be different, I would try, too."

Although she put forward improvement in his behaviour as condition of improvement in her own, it was the first time she had, whether tacitly or openly, conceded that there might be faults on her side.

He understood, while standing there very still, with the unread note in his fingers, that his threat had thoroughly frightened her; and if it had been only an empty threat with no intent behind it, he might have exulted. But with all his heart he wished to leave Rosa—though seeing it as a step that could not be taken without very grave consideration of every aspect—and more even than Rosa, the hostile atmosphere of Cleveland Court: every portion of a night he spent with Alice it became harder to turn himself out. . . .

"I am not going to discuss this with you now," he said. "I will say only this: that I certainly did mean it."

With a rustling, decisive sound he ripped open the letter, and carried it over to the bedhead that he might see to read it.

Rosa watched him. . . . He had not moved, though she could see the letter was only a few lines, and he had had time to read it many times.

"What is the matter?" she said. "Is something wrong?"

He straightened himself. "Yes. My sister Kitty—she has the smallpox."

"O-oh! I am sorry. . . . Oh! we were there last Sunday. I remember she did not feel well."

Her face twisted, and he saw that she was terrified. But instead of rousing in him pity, her fear exasperated him. He controlled the sharp retort that was leaping to his tongue; he said only:

"Her wedding will have to be postponed."

"That letter, I have touched it, it—it may carry the infection. They should not have sent it."

He was so angry, because of his distress for Kitty, that he threw the flimsy piece of paper on to the bed beside her. Then, recollecting that unspeakably evil thought that earlier had crossed his mind, he was as shocked as though he had cast the smallpox itself at her.

Rosa indeed cowered back as if the piece of paper was a veritable instrument of death. "I can't help it," she said, whimpering. "I have always been terrified of smallpox. When I was a very little girl I saw a woman whose face was black from it, pits all over, nowhere it hadn't touched. I see her face in nightmares still."

He swore at her. "You like to make it worse for me, I suppose, that my sister should be ill. While you, you selfish jade, think only of your own skin."

"I am sorry," she said, in a voice he could hardly hear. "I—did not mean to—to grieve you. I was not thinking of what I was saying. I am sorry for Kitty, truly I am."

He picked the letter up off the bed and, holding it by one corner, let the candle flame catch it. It flared up. He dropped the last corner on the floor, and trod on it.

"How many of your family have had it? You have, have you not?"

"Yes. Delia and myself—when I was about five years old. My mother had it at the same time, very lightly. The brother next to me in age died of it." He knew he was being unnecessarily cruel in mentioning this fact, but he could not prevent himself.

"How terrible!" said Rosa.

"But it is the marking that alarms you most, is it not?" he asked her, with a slight smile. "I remember that we had our hands tied to the bed-posts, so that we could not scratch our faces, Delia and I and Gilbert."

"Wasn't that dreadful to bear?" asked Rosa, interested in spite of herself.

"It was not pleasant. It was a damnable torment. But you see we—Delia and I—have no scars on our faces—oh, I have two small ones on my temple you may have noticed"—his fingers went up to the indentations. "I succeeded in rubbing those on the edge of the pillow."

"But with your hands tied to the bed-posts, you could not have turned over or lain on your side?"

"No."

"Oh, I could not bear it. . . . Were Mrs. Jaspard's hands tied too?" The subject seemed to fascinate her.

"I suppose so. I do not know. In any event, she had it very lightly, and perhaps she had the will we children had not, to refrain from scratching."

"Will they tie Kitty's hands?"

"I hope so," he said abruptly.

He was remembering, as he had not remembered for years, the insufferable agony of that illness: the fever, the dry, aching heat, the interminable, insupportable itching, the foul stench of the broken pustules, and through all these the constant racked discomfort of lying perpetually upon one's back, with hands (and wrists so sore) tied above one's head. Poor Kitty! God help her! At five years old one bore those things better, or so it seemed now.

"I wonder you did not all get it," pursued Rosa. "So many children, and your mother must have been with every one of you."

"There were not so many of us then. Only Stephen and Barbara, who did not get it; they were away staying with my grandmother at the time, and my father too."

"It is very catching, isn't it?" asked Rosa, gulping.

"Some people, I believe, are naturally immune. However, if you had troubled yourself to read my letter you would have seen that you are frightening yourself unnecessarily. My father is going to have all the family who have not had the smallpox and who were there on Sunday inoculated. The physician is coming to-morrow morning—that is, this morning—and I am to take you to be done."

"Inoculated?" she repeated, in tones so far from comforted that they were more horror-stricken than she had yet used. "But—but that gives you the smallpox, doesn't it?"

"In a very mild form. You will scarce notice it."

"No, no, I couldn't! I couldn't! You shan't make me. It—it is a loathsome idea. I know, they cut your vein open and put—put infection into it. I shan't be done!"

"You are a contemptible little coward, and you shall be done, for your own good. Do you imagine that the Princess of Wales would have consented—as she has—to have her children inoculated if there was any danger?"

"But it is so new. The doctors do not know enough about it."

"I think you may rely upon my father having chosen an able physician. And now, if you please, we will talk no more to-night; I wish to go to sleep."

He blew out the candles, climbed into his side of the bed, then pulled the cords that drew the bed curtains close about them.

After a longish silence, during which he had nearly fallen asleep, Rosa said, in a humble diffident voice, such as he had not heard from her before:

"I am sorry I was so—so stupid about the smallpox. As you had it when you were young, you cannot understand how I feel. I—can't help being frightened."

Creswell only grunted. Evidently Rosa, in pain of his leaving her, a scorned and deserted wife, was doing her best to placate him.

She moved a little nearer to him. He sensed that she was still in dread of the coming inoculation, and in her dread was lonely, and wanted to be taken into his arms and comforted. Let her want it. He had wanted comfort often enough and she had denied him. Her hand came out, as if by accident, and touched him. He pretended to be asleep.

Did Rosa think it strange, he wondered, that it was seldom now—indeed only when he came in a little drunk and had not been with Alice —that he behaved as a husband to her? Or was she still so unversed in the ways of life that she assumed it a natural condition between a married pair who disagreed together, even though they still shared the same bed? There was no answering these questions.

The next day Rosa was very subdued. She rose earlier than usual, and visitors, whether acquaintances or tradesmen who called at the dressing-hour, as was the custom, were told she was not at home. But, how sincere soever may have been her intentions a few hours since, it was not possible for her to reform herself overnight. No sooner was she downstairs than she irritated Creswell exceedingly by asking her uncle whether or no he advised her to be inoculated. This dependence upon his opinion—whether the matter were trifling or, as in the present case, momentous—was one of her traits that exasperated him more than any other. A man should be lord over his wife: it is for him to say what she must or must not do. He went out of the room in a huff, saying:

"Damn you! if you *want* to get the smallpox and become an ugly crone, pray do so. The chariot will be at the door at eleven, and *I* am going to Hanover Square."

"How dare you swear at your wife, sir?" said Lord Comberley.

Creswell, already in the doorway, turned round. "If you, my lord, had been arguing with a silly child as I have, to do the only possible and sensible thing in the circumstances, perhaps you would swear too."

Whatever the ensuing discussion of uncle and niece may have been, at a minute or two past eleven Rosa came downstairs dressed to go out. Creswell had half expected that if she came at all she would have insisted upon Lord Comberley's accompanying them, that she might have the benefit of his support; but he recollected that he was engaged at the Palace, and besides, not having been himself to Hanover Square for three weeks, he would be incurring needless risk by entering the infected house.

As Rosa drove in the chariot beside Creswell she was white as ashes, except for two absurd spots painted upon her cheeks, which now appeared as fantastic blobs; though indeed they never looked natural, for undetectable improvement of one's face was considered the prerogative of whores. Creswell, in a very impersonal way, remarked:

"I liked your face better as it was before you were married, when you had not begun to paint it."

"But—everybody paints," objected Rosa, who, upon finding herself suddenly let out upon the world, had adopted with surprising enthusiasm the foibles and habits of her contemporaries.

"Yes," agreed Creswell, quite uninterested.

Her low spirits had sunk even lower at his criticism; for, like all women and particularly pretty women, her self-esteem was largely dependant upon her satisfaction in her appearance.

In Hanover Square they found Mr. Jaspard in the library with the physician, whose instruments and bottle lay upon the table beside him. The General appeared in good spirits and had, Creswell suspected, enjoyed rounding up such of the servants as had not had the smallpox and insisting upon their undergoing inoculation. They were all done now, he announced. Only two, a kitchenmaid and the youngest footman, had withstood threats and persuasions alike; and all, it was intimated, had come forward in varying degrees of unwillingness and fear. Oh yes, the two recalcitrants had been dismissed immediately. . . .

"This prejudice the lower orders have against anything new is extraordinary, quite extraordinary. 'Pon honour! I believe they would sooner go marked all their lives than submit to a little cut."

"The prejudice is very general, sir. I dare say many of the people fear there is witchcraft in it." The physician, who was now speaking, was a lugubrious figure in his black clothes, with a long yellow face beneath an iron-grey full-bottomed wig. His mournful aspect did nothing to reassure Rosa.

"Even many of my profession," continued the doctor, "look upon it with the greatest disfavour. Mankind has a natural tendency to dislike progress. You and I, sir"—he bowed slightly towards Mr. Jaspard—"are privileged to understand that this new discovery will be of inestimable benefit."

"But—does it not—sometimes fail, sir?" asked Rosa. "I mean—do people not sometimes get the disease very badly—just as if they had caught it in the ordinary way?"

The doctor gave her a professional scrutiny. "It is nearly three years now, madam, since Lady Mary Wortley Montagu discovered this inoculation in the East; and though it is true we in England have begun the practise only a matter of weeks, I assure you Lady Mary has convinced the more enlightened members of our fraternity that not above one in a thousand take any ill effects from the operation. . . . You are in a highly nervous condition, madam. Is this one of my patients, sir?"

"Yes," answered Creswell. "My wife is very nervous. She had better be done immediately, if that is convenient. I hope you are as pleased as may be with the condition of my sister?"

"We have every hope it will be a light attack. It is, though, rather early to say." The doctor, under the fascinated and horrified gaze of Rosa, was stirring the nasty mixture in his small bottle, and balancing a blob on the end of his instrument.

"Gertrude Dale, as soon as she heard," said Mr. Jaspard, "was so good as to call here, and begged your mother to let her assist in nursing Kitty—she has had the disease herself. Hm! I took it very kindly of her in the circumstances. I have been a little hard on her. Perhaps, when your brother comes home——" He left his sentence unfinished.

The doctor then asked: "How many more patients, sir, am I to attend to?"

"My daughter-in-law here, and the children in the nursery and their governess."

"Now, ma'am, let me pull your sleeve up a little. . . . If you would be so good as to hold the lace out of the way, sir? The lady is not quite in a state to do it for herself."

Creswell did as he was bidden. Rosa shuddered, and an odd dry sound came out of her throat.

"I—do not think I can. I want to change my mind," she said.

"Don't be silly," chided Creswell, quite kindly. He was standing behind her, holding her by both her arms, with his fingers round the uplifted flounces of her left sleeve.

"Pray, ma'am," said Mr. Jaspard with a contempt devoid of all sympathy, "do not let me see my daughter-in-law behaving like a foolish kitchen-wench. I have undergone it, and it does not hurt in the least degree—a mere prick."

"It is not the hurting," mumbled poor Rosa.

The doctor's fingers gripped the flesh of her upper arm. The needle held in his other hand pierced the vein a little above the inner side of the elbow, and was dragged down to make a small cut. Blood came in a slow trickle, brilliant against her white skin. With deft movements he placed a piece of cotton wool to arrest the slight stream while he brought forward the instrument upon which was the infected matter. . . . Creswell felt Rosa sag. She had become like a body without bones. Only by an effort did he prevent her from falling to the floor.

"She has fainted," he announced unnecessarily.

"A highly nervous constitution, as I remarked," commented the physician, unconcernedly finishing his operation; dabbing the matter well into the cut, and then placing a half-nutshell over it, and binding the whole tight with a bandage. "She will soon come round if you will burn a feather under her nose—then give her a little brandy to restore the vitality."

"She is not breeding, is she?" asked Mr. Jaspard with blunt interest.

"No," said Creswell, a little confused, for he knew his father was looking for him to have a son. "She is just frightened."

"She will be perfectly well presently," said the doctor. "On the eighth day she will have a little fever. Keep her in bed till it is over, and there is no more to it than that."

While Rosa lay upon the sofa, having by the uses of a burning feather and a glass of brandy recovered her senses, Creswell said to his father:

"Barney has never had the smallpox, has he? I presume he is to be inoculated, too."

"Barney?" Mr. Jaspard glanced at the doctor whose attention had been momentarily caught by a paragraph in yesterday's *Whitehall Evening Post* lying on the table. He went on in a low voice: "I sent a footman to his lodgings last night, and the man came back with the information that though he has not given up his rooms he has not slept there the last two nights, and from what the landlady says he does not intend to sleep there in the future. He had been in an hour before and collected his clothes."

"Indeed," said Creswell, musing that it was hardly possible that Barney could have, like himself, set up his own establishment. That was a rich man's luxury.

"Impertinent puppy not to tell me what is he doing!" said the General. "If he takes the smallpox it is his own fault."

Creswell looked across at his father with a slight smile. "Whatever it may be that Barney is up to, it hardly sounds on the face of it as if it would be of a nature that he would care to confide it to you, sir."

The presence of the physician prevented them pursuing this conversation.

CHAPTER · XVI

CORYDON SEEKS PHILLIS

WHEN Barney at length returned to his lodgings from his abortive attempt to become a highwayman, he was both too wretched and wrought-up to get to sleep. Even dawn did not bring him repose, and having had all night only a few fitful dozes he rose earlier than usual, unable to bear any longer his hot and tumbled bed. The house was always early astir, since the master of it was engaged in a tannery across the river in Southwark. It was, therefore, not difficult for Barney to call for his breakfast at this unaccustomed hour. In spite of his grief—a grief which was mingled with a certain degree of self-contempt for his ignominious failure to procure for Lucy the present she desired—he found himself hungry, and remembered that he had supped but lightly the evening before.

Having finished his meal, he was too restless to stay indoors. He had no purpose or plan, and his feet carried him from habit, since he did not think where he was going, in the direction of the Customs House. He would, no doubt, have wandered along the Embankment until the hour came for him to go to the Office—and for once he was actually anxious to begin work that he might drive the devils of disappointment and chagrin from his mind—but a heavy shower descending at that moment, he was forced, unless he chose to be drenched, to take shelter.

Thus it was that he came to the room where he worked a half-hour before his usual time. Indeed, he had hardly expected to find it unlocked, and when the door gave to his turning of the handle, he supposed he would see a cleaner as the only inmate.

It was a long and dreary room, devoid of any surplus ornamentation, except on the ceiling which was, unexpectedly, coved and decorated in plaster with a lozenge pattern. Wooden desks ran down the length, beneath the three tall arched windows which looked out, not on the pleasant nautical bustle of the river, but on the meaner buildings that lay to the back of Thames Street.

Though no cleaner was in the room as he had anticipated, it was with only mild surprise that Barney saw one of the senior clerks had arrived and was seated at his desk at the further end of the room; so absorbed was he in some writing that he had not heard the door open.

"Good morning, Mr. Fielden," said Barney.

Then he did become greatly surprised, for Mr. Fielden started with as much appearance of terror as if one he knew to be his assassin had entered. He hastily rustled his papers together and, having evidently made an effort to recover himself, said:

"You are in very early this morning, Mr. Jaspard."

"And you earlier still," answered Barney who, roused by the odd behaviour of his fellow clerk, had walked rapidly up to him. "Writing letters to the plantations already? Is it the matter of the refusal of that company in Maryland to pay the excise on tobacco that is troubling you?" He leaned forward as though interested in the papers.

"No, no," said Mr. Fielden with obvious agitation. "It is no concern of yours, Mr. Jaspard. A—a strictly private business I am doing for—for Mr. Bluetot." (Mr. Bluetot was the Chief of their Department.)

Mr. Fielden's pallor, his trembling fingers, excited Barney's curiosity further.

"Yes. Mr. Bluetot, though he did not tell me the nature of the business, instructed me to get here early this morning that I might assist you in the copying of the letter." It was an invention at random, but it certainly increased Mr. Fielden's disquiet. He glanced at Barney with astonishment and suspicion in his eyes. His fingers fidgeted ceaselessly.

"Let me see," said Barney, and reached out for the papers.

"No. I forbid it," almost shouted Mr. Fielden. "I must remind you I am your senior, Mr. Jaspard, and you are to obey me. Unless I had received Mr. Bluetot's specific word that you were—you were to—er—assist me with the—the business I spoke of, I could not allow it."

Barney was now in no doubt at all that Mr. Fielden had something to hide. His eyes narrowed, and he said grimly: "Perhaps you would like me to bring this subject up before Mr. Bluetot as soon as he arrives. I will, I promise you, if you do not show me what papers those are."

Though he expected this threat to have some effect on Mr. Fielden, he was not prepared to see him break down completely.

He was a man of about forty years old, and in the crumpling up of his face beneath the grey wig, as a child's crumples before it cries, there was something more ludicrous than pathetic. He laid his arms defensively over the papers, and sobbed. Barney pulled them away from beneath his elbows and examined them. His eyebrows went up.

"Spare me, in Heaven's name! Don't tell anyone, I beseech you. I'll never do it again, never! Mr. Jaspard, I am a married man, with five children. If I'm disgraced, I'll starve, we'll all starve. Have mercy! Have mercy, as you must hope to have it yourself at the Judgment Seat. I am not a wicked man. I'll give you my word I'll do it no more. I would not have stolen, I would have given it back. Yes, in two days' time I would have given it back. I was told of some new stock, it will double itself by Thursday . . ."

This rigmarole, delivered between gulps and sniffs, went on while Barney looked at the papers and learned that the hitherto respected Mr. Fielden, a clerk of many years' service in the Office, had been forging the signature on a draft-form of the Office of Trade and Plantations which would enable him to draw money from Mr. Hoare's bank. That it was forgery there was no doubt whatever. A piece of paper with practice specimens of the signature was among the incriminating evidence.

Many thoughts went through Barney's head; and it must be admitted that the first of them was whether he should not himself take advantage of Mr. Fielden's evident skill in copying a signature: they might go shares. But this possibly alluring prospect was soon dispelled by his conviction—brought home to him so recently—that he had not the temperament, indeed perhaps not the nerve, for a life of crime.

"Why did you not do this at home, where no one could discover you?" he asked, both from a desire to know and to gain time while he considered how best to handle the affair for his own benefit.

Mr. Fielden, who was now endeavouring to compose himself, blew his nose, and stared into his handkerchief at the snuff-brown mucus he had discharged.

"It was not easy for me to take the draft-form away unobserved. Besides, if my wife had seen me—and the children are always crawling about at home. Only consider, Mr. Jaspard! five innocent mouths—six innocent mouths, my wife, dear heart! is the soul of probity. I am in your hands——"

"Pray stop whining," said Barney with some irritation. "You should have considered these innocent mouths before. 'Tis a bit late now. What is the stock you were thinking of buying?"

"It is a company promoted for the improving of malt liquors. They say the whole town is taking it up. The shares must double in two days, treble in a week, and I could have paid the money back at the end of the two days and then bought more, and so have made a competence for my children. It would not have been *stealing*, Mr. Jaspard. When a poor man hears of fortunes being made overnight, simply by the buying and selling of stock, and he has five sweet souls—six—dependent upon him, why then——"

"And how would you have put the money back?" interrupted Barney.

"I should have taken it in my hand and paid it in—they know my face at Hoare's. I should have said it was a cash payment for the Office's account. . . . Mr. Jaspard, the rest of the clerks will be in presently. May I have your word as a gentleman this will go no further? My prayers shall be for you, sir, till the end of my life, and I shall teach my little ones to pray for you——"

Barney, unconcerned by these promises of assistance towards his salvation, cut him short.

"You were willing to do the Office out of £50—and your stock *might* have failed to fulfil your hopes of it; very well, you give me £50 instead, and you shall have my oath I'll keep silent."

"Give you £50!" Mr. Fielden's tear-smeared face assumed an expression of righteous indignation. "Give you £50!" he repeated. "C-certainly not." Under Barney's menacing stare, his firm tone had wavered. "I—haven't got £50. If I had, would I have been raising it by these means? I am a poor man——"

"I am aware of that. And also that you have five innocent mouths to feed, or is it six? If I did not know you were a poor man, Mr. Fielden, believe me, you should not escape for so paltry a sum."

"But I haven't got it," he groaned, and the tears came out of his eyes again. " 'Pon my oath, I haven't!"

"Then you must find it, I care not how." Barney carefully folded up the forged draft and the piece of paper with the copies of the signature, and put them in his pocket.

With a dignity in contrast to his former outburst, Mr. Fielden rose from his desk, and said: "I am in your power, sir. You are very young. You may yet learn what it is to be defeated and shamed. May God forgive you! You must do as you will, but I have not £50, and to give it you I must steal it from another." His lips began to tremble. "My children—if you were a father——"

"Sink your children! Well, I will compound with you for twenty guineas. That is my last word. You old hypocrite! You have something at home you could sell, I dare say. Why, that is a little diamond in your stock pin."

Mr. Fielden's fingers went up to his small ornament. "I—my wife would miss it. And it would not raise the sum you require."

"No doubt you have a relative who will advance you the balance— or your friend who is doing so well in the malt-liquor shares. It is not for me to suggest means to you. You should consider yourself fortunate, Mr. Fielden. What I ask is a trifle compared to—you do know that the penalty for forgery is Death? Even with extenuating circumstances you could hardly hope for less than—shall we say?—fourteen years' transportation. . . . I—happen to need money very badly myself, or I would not be harsh on you. I see you, indeed, Mr. Fielden, as an instrument sent to me by Providence. . . . Somebody is coming. You shall have till dinner-time to give me your answer, and I advise you to make it a favourable one. May I remind you, that in the event of your refusal to comply with my conditions, I shall likely be granted by a grateful Office at least the same sum of money for informing against you as a felon?"

He moved away to his own desk as two other clerks came in.

.   .   .   .   .

When Barney found himself with the unfortunate Mr. Fielden's twenty guineas in his pocket, which happened two days later—during which time he had not ceased to remind Mr. Fielden whenever opportunity offered of his pressing debt—he went, the moment his work was over, to a jeweller in the Strand in order to purchase for Lucy the pendant he had promised her. He was a long time choosing one, because, though he wished to give his love a present worthy both of her beauty and his devotion, he was also tormented by a desire to put some of his money into the stock Mr. Fielden had been so certain would bring him a handsome profit within two days. And, as he had ascertained, it was still rising. Everyone drank ale: it must continue to be an attractive concern, and so increase in price.

To be sure, the town was full of projects this summer: the children, as it were, of that opulent and fat parent, South Sea stock. It was still this latter he hankered after; but five guineas, which was the most he could spare were he to give Lucy diamonds in her pendant, was a mean sum for so vast a company. A smaller concern might serve him better as a stepping-stone.

South Sea stock stood now at 700 per cent and had consequently risen 550 per cent since he had first had ideas of buying it some four months ago; yet it was rising still, and showed no sign at all of a decline. It had had a setback a month earlier when the Act was passed in Parliament for the South Sea Company to take over the entire national debt, but public alarm had not lasted long. Already fortunes had been made. Thousands of pounds' profit within the space of a few weeks—if not days. One bought and one sold. Then, maybe, one bought again, and sold again. It was the simplest thing in the world to become a rich man, to set oneself up for life, if one had but the money in hand to start with. It was too bad it was only a clerk, one not much richer than himself, that he had caught in a felonious act. Had it been, say, Mr. Bluetot himself, he might have called for a few hundreds. . . .

Barney had known a momentary shame when Mr. Fielden (his diamond pin missing), with a certain cold hauteur and refraining from mentioning his little ones, had handed over the gold; but he wanted the money too much, and the pleasure he expected to purchase with it, to allow consideration of Mr. Fielden's straits to trouble his mind.

Pendants with diamonds were not to be had for a trifling sum: besides, he needed a little money over to give her a supper suitable to the night before them. . . . Regretfully, he had to decide that stock-buying must be postponed.

He choose, after much bargaining, an amethyst shaped as a heart, surrounded by small diamonds, and this he persuaded the shopman to part with for seventeen guineas.

Exultantly, he made his way to Lucy's house. His difficulties had been surmounted. When he had failed as a highwayman, Mr. Fielden's forgery had been thrown in his way. Fate must be upon his side, and Lucy was to be his.

It was a clear, lovely evening: still full daylight, but the sky paling, and the wind that caught one round the corners of the streets chillier than an hour before. The earlier rain of the afternoon still trickled, though now soiled with every sort of filth, down the kennels, and puddles shone like pieces of mirror strewn among the cobblestones. Women went by on their high pattens, their skirts lifted to show blue or green stockings; and the drays and carts splashed dirty water as regularly as playing fountains to the accompaniment of the curses and abuse of those who happened to be splashed.

The shouting and the incessant noise that was part of the very life of the London streets was, however, subdued in comparison with the midday uproar. Few went by calling out wares, and the shopkeepers had tired of shouting by their doors of the excellencies of the goods within. It might seem to the imaginative as though London herself, like the individuals who made up her population, was tired at the end of the day's work; and the lessening traffic in her streets was the slowing of her sleepy pulse, and the diminished shouting and all the daytime hubbub the lowering of her vitality. Yet, presently, she would stir in nightmare when the villains—the footpads, the housebreakers, the highwaymen, the whores and the procurers—were spewed from the tumbledown alleys, the crooked, sour-smelling streets, and came creeping evilly in the darkness to be about their marauding, their murder and their lechery . . .

The dumb black boy opened the front door to Barney. Standing in a shadowed corner of the hall, where one did not notice him unless one knew, as regular visitors did, that he was there, was the burly, improbable footman. Showing his teeth, the boy smiled, but accompanied this with a vigorous shaking of the head.

Before Barney, who had asked for Miss Brook, had time to say anything further, Harry, dressed to go out, came down the stairs.

"You!" he said in some surprise. "I am sorry, Jaspard, that we cannot entertain you this evening, I have a previous engagement."

"It is Miss Lucy I have come to see. I have—for her what I promised to get her. She is at home?" He spoke eagerly, and with a boyishness unusual in him.

Harry took him by the arm, and made as if to go out by the street door.

"She is at home, but you would be well-advised not to press to see her. I'm confoundedly sorry, Jaspard, 'tis none of my doing. But the women will have their way, and if they won't receive us, that is all there is to it."

"What do you mean? I don't understand you." His voice was rough.

"I thought I made myself plain. As a friend, I gave you a hint. I repeat it. Do not try to see Lucy. I know she does not wish to receive you—or any visitor."

"Is she not well?"

"Do you deliberately misunderstand me? She is perfectly well."

"Then I must hear it from her own lips that she does not want to see me. I'll not believe it else. I must insist upon seeing her."

The large footman had come a step or two forward. Harry waved him back.

"If you want to be a fool," he said to Barney with an oath, "go and be one, and a pox on you! I believe you will find her in there." He nodded towards the living-room where Barney had always seen her before. "A good night to you. . . . The door, boy."

Barney was left in the hall. He felt the eyes of the black boy and the footman upon him in curiosity. He said angrily to the negro:

"Show me to your mistress."

The ridiculous, gaudy scarlet-and-gold little figure walked ahead of him and threw open the door. There was a rustling of material and exclamations as of people taken by surprise.

Barney stood and stared. The lady of his heart was dishevelled in appearance, and her cheeks were very red. By her side, fumbling at his lace jabot and looking also somewhat disconcerted, stood a gentleman in the magnificence of evening dress. He was as foppish as Harry himself, and the salient points of fashion about his clothing as exaggerated. The skirts of his coat stuck out; there was no space upon his waistcoat unembroidered, and the cuffs of his coat were heavy with encrustations of gold lace; from his right shoulder depended a knot of gaily coloured ribbon reaching to his elbow. He was a stranger to Barney, a man perhaps ten years older than himself, therefore considerably older than the restless, lean young men whom Barney was accustomed to see about this house.

"You!" exclaimed Lucy, exactly as her brother had done. "Where is that blackamore? I shall beat the hide off him. I told him I was at home to no one." She looked about her, as though to lay hands on a whip then and there.

"It was not the boy's fault," said Barney slowly. "Harry told me you were in, and I insisted on seeing you."

"Did you indeed! That was insolence, Mr. Jaspard. Oh—Sir Peter Heath, this is Mr. Jaspard."

The two men inclined their heads at each other with the utmost coldness of manner. Barney was thinking that he would take an oath the bedizened figure in front of him had come by his title neither by inheritance nor accolade.

"Now that you have seen me, and seen that I do not wish to see you, perhaps you will go," continued Lucy.

Barney, who had been slow to collect his wits and was even yet too shattered by disappointment to consider the situation at all carefully, said: "Before I go, I must see you alone. It is very urgent. I have something for you."

"Something for me! How dare you be so free? There is nothing, sir, you can have to say to me in private."

"Is there not?" burst out Barney, in an anger now thoroughly whipped up. "You made a promise to me. I have done my share and brought you what you wanted and, 'fore God! I don't intend to be played with. Sir," he turned to Lucy's visitor, addressing him, in spite of the polite appellation, in the tones he might have used to a servant, "I must ask you to leave this lady and me. I have that to say to her which is not for you to hear."

"I leave at her command only," replied in a vicious voice he who

M

had been called Sir Peter, while his right hand fiddled with his sword-hilt.

"I shall *never* command you to leave me," cooed Lucy. Then, with a distinct change of tone she added: "We shall soon be rid of this intruder. Pull the bell-cord for me, sir." To Barney she said, tossing up her head: "I trust you will understand, Mr. Jaspard, that I mean it when I say that I never wish to see you again, and that my servants shall have orders not to let you in. So you will be wasting your time do you call here."

"But what have I done?" asked Barney desperately, his anger giving way to overwhelming misery. "Lucy! Lucy! What I have gone through, what I have been about, to get this for you, the pendant you wanted! You must at least tell me how I have offended . . ."

The door had opened, and the thickset footman waited for orders.

"Your presence here offends me, it will always offend me. I want no company now," she had raised her voice, "but dear Sir Peter's. Is that perfectly clear to you?"

"I cannot believe it," said Barney, still appealingly. "You must be playing with me. I have known you so long."

"And been so mean and tedious. I assure you I am not playing with you. Sir Peter I have known but a few days, and yet"—her laughter tinkled out—"*there* is a man for you to emulate, Mr. Jaspard. If you did but know of his courage, his exploits, his gallantry. . . . Charlie, show this gentleman out, and never let him in again."

"Very good, madam," answered the man in a cockney voice which offered no pretentions to gentility, as did most footmen's. "This way, if you please."

Barney noticed the insolent absence of any "sir", and guessed that if he lingered he would find himself in a moment being forcibly ejected.

His last words to Lucy were a curse; and as he spoke them the man Charlie moved a step nearer to him. He went out. The negro boy did not smile at him, and he heard the bolts rattling to against him.

He waited outside the house for a long time, nearly an hour. He did not know why: perhaps he wished to see if she and her flashy companion were going out, or to keep the lighted but curtained window in his sight. When, finally, he left, the lights had gone from the downstairs room, and a window on the first floor that had been in darkness now showed a dull glow behind the curtains. . . .

Swearing, half-crying, he turned away, walked up the street into the Strand, and went into the first tavern he came to. It was a low place, ill-lit and smelling disagreeably of stale smoke and liquor; ordinarily he would not have dreamed of entering it. A man near to him, seated at one of the unscrubbed wooden tables, was laughing very heartily, and it did not seem that he had much to laugh about. He had sores on his face, there were rents in his clothes, and it might be doubted whether he wore a shirt beneath his coat . . . but he was laughing. And the drink in front of him was gin.

Barney had tasted this spirit only once in his life, and then from curiosity and bravado. He remembered the occasion now. He and Stephen, when they were no more than fifteen years old, had stolen out one holidays (the General was from home) and gone to a brothel. They had come away at last with the girls' gibes in their ears, having been no more vicious in this adventure than drinking too much gin which, in combination with their youth, had rendered them incapable of enjoying the pleasure that, in the safety of their playroom, they had planned.

Now he found it glowing, but it did not bring him the comfort he had expected. He had no idea how many hours had passed, or of the number of times he had signalled to the drawer to refill his glass. Once or twice somebody spoke to him, but he only stared at him, and the man had shrugged his shoulders and turned away.

Then a woman sat down beside him, and at her affectionate suggestions a degree of clarity and great anger came to him. He did not want a whore—and she was a bedraggled and unattractive one—and he told her so in round terms and with oaths. Frightened, she left him alone. . . .

But he did want someone . . . someone to whom he could carry his grief, his humiliation . . . someone who would care. . . . He remembered Phillis: the only woman who had ever said to him: "I love you." She had said more, too. She had made him promise that if he were in trouble or distress, it mattered not when, he would come to her. . . . What matter if she were oldish?—she was attractive still, and she loved him. She had sincerity and truth. She loved him . . . loved him. . . .

He got up, paid his reckoning (at the insistence of the watchful drawer, who knew that patrons grew absent-minded rather than were wilfully dishonest), and lurched out. It was quite dark now, and as he stood in the doorway of the tavern with the cool air striking on his hot cheeks, he tried to pull himself together. It was just such an hour of night, and he in just such a fuddled condition, as a footpad would choose to knock him on the head and search his pockets. And hard in his pocket he felt the pendant that Lucy would not wear. . . .

He bawled for a chair, but this was not a part of the town where chair-men waited after the shops were shut. A ragged boy, however, quickly appeared, and offered to find him one.

"What time is it?" Barney asked him in thick accents.

"St. Clement's told eleven several minutes gone, your honour."

" 'Leven. Huh! Get me a chair, damn you! and make haste."

Phillis's house showed two lighted windows upstairs, but he had to hammer for what seemed to him an inordinately unreasonable time before anyone came. With the desperate frustration of the drunk when their wishes are not at once fulfilled, he banged the knocker up and down like a child in a temper. A passing watchman eyed him with both inquisitiveness and suspicion; the latter evidently taking the uppermost hand, he decided that discretion was wiser than courage, and continued his beat around the corner.

At length there was a clanking of bolts, the door opened a couple of inches, and Barney saw in the dim light from the oil standard above his head the glint on the muzzle of a blunderbuss. A male voice demanded who he was and why did he disturb respectable folk at this hour.

"My name is Jaspard. Your mistress will see me. Go and tell her."

But the handler of the blunderbuss was evidently not so certain of this assurance.

"My mistress did not tell me she was expecting anyone, your honour. I believe she has retired." The voice had changed its menacing tones to the respectful yet firm ones of a well-trained servant. But the door opened no wider, and the blunderbuss, though its muzzle now slanted less aggressively, remained on guard.

"She will see me," answered Barney, loudly angry. "Go and ask her. And a pox on you, keeping me standing in the street like a tradesman or a villain! Let me in, I say, let me in!"

Heedless of this outburst, the man behind the door slammed it to, and a bolt was drawn across. Barney began to knock again. The fury of the sound must have been heard by many good citizens in the houses near at hand.

Very soon the door reopened, and in the darkness of the hall he heard voices whispering. A lamp was held up near his face, dazzling him. He blinked, and drew his head back.

"What the devil——!"

"It is you, Mr. Jaspard. You must forgive our precautions at this time of night. But pray, what has happened? Have you been in an accident?"

It was Phillis's voice speaking.

She said more words to the footman in an undertone, and then, touching Barney on the arm, said: "Come upstairs and take a glass of wine. 'Tis not so very late, and you will be refreshed to go on your way again."

He followed her up to the same room where they had supped.

"Wait," she said. "Don't tell me anything yet. The man will be in in a minute or two with the wine. . . . Won't you sit down?"

But he continued to stand there, in the middle of the room, swaying a little, with bloodshot eyes; his clothes were rumpled, and twisted on his body.

Presently the footman carried in a tray of bottles and glasses and, having spoken a few words to his mistress, withdrew.

"Corydon! Corydon, dear, what is the matter?" said Phillis, and took him by the hand.

CHAPTER XVII

BARNEY IS BETROTHED

MR. JASPARD, as may be supposed, did not allow Barney to vanish from his lodgings unheeded. He sent a peremptory note to him, addressed to the Customs House, commanding that he present himself at the physician's house for inoculation that evening, and then come immediately to Hanover Square.

This secretive removal of his natural son from the house where he had placed him had been something of a shock to Mr. Jaspard. It was not that he was uneasy about his physical welfare, or indeed that he feared him to be in a deal of mischief. No, it was that these illegitimate offspring of his, Barney and Fan, had the seeds of rebellion in their hearts. Fan had escaped him entirely. Discreet questioning through the town had not brought to light a single clue as to her whereabouts. That she had not been the unwilling victim of some man's wickedness he was certain: by her removing such jewellery and valuable lace as she owned, it was evident her flight was premeditated.

Mr. Jaspard disliked mysteries that he could not solve, and particularly when they occurred within his own family. It was odd, he thought —remembering Delia as a young girl—that one's daughters might kick over the traces with more abandon than one's sons; and the consequences when they did so were permanent and shameful. But Barney must not get out of hand yet—damn him for a knave!

His musings were here led to Creswell. It was only by confounded good fortune that his heir, who certainly did not deserve his luck, had married so well in the world. But already he had heard a rumour that Creswell kept a mistress somewhere towards Covent Garden. Well, those things happened, but he prayed he'd be discreet, for it was a shade scandalous to desert your wife before half a year of matrimony was over. In any case, Creswell should have done his duty first, and got an heir. Time enough for philandering when the nursery was full. . . .

The General was in a bad temper upon three accounts. His gout, that was increasing in his left foot, may be reckoned one of them. But, to give him his due, the first was perhaps his anxiety over Kitty; the next that his sister-in-law, Lady Manvington, also lay ill with the small-pox. Now, though Mr. Jaspard had no warmer feeling for this relative than has many another man, her life was of the utmost importance to him. Were she to die, who knew but Manvington might not marry again and raise up an heir to the Earldom? For many years Mr. Jaspard had considered the Earldom as good as his; at any rate, Creswell's, and as a certain amount of his public credit was also built upon this assumption, it would be plaguily hard to relinquish it. Manvington, though older than himself, was still a vigorous man. . . .

As for Barney, though looking forward only with trepidation to the interview ahead of him, he did not think of disobeying either of the General's injunctions: he feared the smallpox more than he did the means of prevention, and he knew he must, sooner or later, offer some explanation of his conduct. He had by this time also read the first note left at his lodgings, for he had returned there to collect the rest of his belongings and to close his account with his landlady.

He consulted Phillis as to what he should say to the General; but there was little she could suggest. His uncle—as she naturally called him—must find out eventually that he was living in her house, and whether he would accept the implication that he was there simply as a lodger, or on a protracted visit, it was impossible to forecast.

Barney remembered nothing of that first night he had spent in Phillis's house, the night he had gone to her with Lucy's pendant in his pocket, and his heart sore and broken, his mind dazed with gin.

He had been awoken next morning by Phillis, fully dressed, shaking him by the shoulder and telling him to make haste or he would be late for his work. At the breakfast-table, a half-hour or so later, he had felt very shamed, and would not meet her eyes; for indeed it is not a pleasant situation to be ignorant of whether or not one lay with one's hostess the night before. . . . On the whole, he thought he could not have done so. . . .

Phillis, as she poured his coffee for him, was brisk and kind, and refused, in answer to his mumbled apologies—for he did remember that he had been very drunk, and his throbbing head served in any case to remind him—to discuss at all his unconventional coming or what had followed it. If he would return this evening, they would talk it over then. He had better, on his way to Thames Street, call at his lodgings and reassure his landlady that he had not been murdered during the night, and perhaps bring with him anything he might require. She feared her husband's old razor was somewhat blunt. . . .

When evening came, she dealt but lightly with his questions concerning the previous night. He gathered that he must have behaved like a maudlin fool, and cried, and that she had held him and comforted him. He had muttered about a pendant and a woman of whom, whatever he may have thought of her in the past, he now appeared to hold a very low opinion . . . never mind, they would forget that and all to do with it. A woman who had scorned Corydon, she implied, had neither taste nor discernment. . . . And Barney, to his surprise, discovered that the thought of Lucy now brought with it, not the aching agony in which he had waited outside her house, in which he had drunk himself into boorishness; but a hard, bitter rage that pounded his heart with a greater violence than love itself had done. He had risked the very gallows for her, and she had cast him out—for whom? A popinjay with ill-gotten money and a spurious title to his name. Bitch! blowse! whore! Every word of abuse for females that he had ever heard came into his mind. . . .

But by Phillis he was loved, cosseted, made to feel that his very presence was a delight. With her, if he did not find rapture, he found content, peace of mind and the strange excitement of being beloved. He was like a man—if such can be imagined—who has bread for the first time: a natural, kindly food which all the rest of his countrymen (except a pitiful few in like or worse case than himself) have accepted all their lives as a birthright. Barney's half-brothers and sisters were fond of him in a casual manner as one of the family, while seeing him, too, as an outsider; but never, even as children, had they been demonstrative in their affection. Since the day Mrs. Jaspard had laid her unwilling lips on his baby cheek, he had not been kissed except, occasionally, by a kind nursemaid, or by a wench who expected to be paid for the service.

Phillis understood his loneliness and his need with a remarkable insight that Barney perhaps never fully appreciated. Her position was not an easy one. He had come to her wounded and angry in default of having the woman he really wanted. It was unlikely he would fall in love with her, and she, loving foolishly this man so much younger than herself, had to fill with all her resources of tact, sympathy and good-humour the exacting role he expected of her as both mother and lover.

.   .   .   .   .

When Barney arrived at the front door in Hanover Square, he took care to slip from his finger the ruby ring that Phillis, on the second night he had spent in her house, had given him. The explanations he had to make were difficult enough without his letting the General see him in possession of a jewel it might reasonably be supposed he was not in a position to purchase.

"Oh, so you have come," Mr. Jaspard greeted him. He was sitting by a fire in the library, with his painful foot upon a stool in front of him. "What the devil have you been at, sir?"

"I have been to Mr. Drake as you bid me, and have been inoculated."

"You know well I didn't mean that. Sit down, sit down!"

"May I ask, how is Kitty?" Barney, who really wanted to know, also hoped this inquiry might deflect questions about himself.

"It must run its course. She has a high fever, but no worse than to be expected. The rash is on her thick now. By the grace of Heaven, Mr. Drake thinks 'tis not the worst sort of smallpox. If we take care of her, she should not be marked."

"I am very glad to hear that, sir."

"Miss Dale is helping us to nurse her—I need hardly say she has had the illness. It is very good of her, however." His tone forbade any comment from Barney on this somewhat surprising news that the woman who had jilted Stephen and been banished the house was now back on terms of so great intimacy.

"As soon as she is well enough," continued Mr. Jaspard, "we intend taking Kitty to Gartonby, and spending the rest of the summer there. There can, of course, be no question of her being married before the autumn. A complete clearance of the face may take several weeks to effect, not to mention that she will be in a greatly weakened condition."

"Mr. Stafford must be much disappointed," murmured Barney politely.

"I suppose so. He has fortunately had it himself as a child, so we do not have to worry over his taking it—though I have no doubt he would have agreed to inoculation. . . . And now, pray tell me why you were not to be found when I sent a note to Beckford Court?" Mr. Jaspard's tone had changed.

"I am—staying with friends," said Barney, and did not succeed in sounding anything but confused.

"At least you should always leave a message where notes are to be redirected. What, for example, if I had been dying, and wished to see you?"

Barney could find no adequate answer to his somewhat improbable supposition.

"Strange friends indeed," went on the General, drawing down his grey brows, "when you cannot divulge to your own landlady where you are, how long you are gone for, or when you intend to return. May I ask the name of your friends?"

"It is—nobody you are acquainted with, sir."

"How can you be sure I do not at least know *of* them. I am acquainted, i' faith! with most of the respectable families in London."

Barney said at a tangent, touching his arm as though an itch had reminded him of it: "The inoculation hurt less than I expected, but it is uncomfortable. I think he has bandaged me too tight."

"Tcha!" exclaimed the General in scorn, "don't lay a side trail for me. To be sure, Barnabas, you are a man now and must go a man's way. But in one matter at all events I still have a right to control you, and that is to see that you do not run into debt. If you are keeping a woman, as by your shuffling, evasive answers, your hang-dog air, one must assume you are; pray, how on your emolument from Trade and Plantations and the little I allow you, pray, how do you keep two establishments going?"

"I am not—keeping a woman, sir," said Barney, blushing with shame that he spoke the truth and, in fact, the circumstances were exactly the reverse.

"Indeed. Then why is it so difficult for you to tell your rightful guardian where you are staying? . . . Come, Barney, I shall begin to think you are out on bail from Newgate."

You would not jest, thought Barney, if you knew how near I came to making your words true—but there would have been no bail for me.

"I am staying with a widow, sir. I met her some time ago, and she has since invited me to her house. She is—a woman considerably older than myself, and—and very respectable."

Mr. Jaspard stared at him in a disconcerting manner. He said, with a great deal of contempt: "I think I begin to see the truth. It is your affair, but when I was a young man, I'd have thought shame to batten on an older woman. Lord! what fools they can make of themselves over a young fellow! . . . At least, since she does you the honour to be favourable to so callow a youth as yourself, I trust you treat her with decency and consideration."

Barney, whose confusion was now overwhelming, plucked at the edge of his cuff as though all his interest lay in this trivial occupation. "You misunderstand the matter, sir," he mumbled, though so indistinctly it may be doubted whether Mr. Jaspard heard him.

The General went on: "I must warn you that you will be hurting yourself and—what is far more important—other people, if you become too deeply involved in any affair you may have on hand. I wish you to marry soon."

"Marry!" repeated Barney, astonished into immediately stopping his fiddling with his cuff, and looking up at Mr. Jaspard.

"Yes, marry." The General adjusted his gouty foot, then took a slow and deliberate pinch of snuff before saying anything further. "I have been talking it over with Lord Manvington, and we are both agreed it will be a suitable match for you to marry Lady Charlotte. . . . Do not interrupt me, please. Her mother, you may not have heard, has the smallpox, and we do not intend to declare a betrothal between you until she is recovered. However, it is as well you should know of the matter. Now, what is it you have to say?"

"Why this, sir. I do not want to marry Lady Charlotte."

"Do not want to! Sink you! You shall marry where I think best. Lady Manvington is anxious to see another of her daughters wedded, my brother has no objections, and I have none either. I shall make suitable provision for you, though not precisely"—he paused and tapped his snuff-box—"as though you were one of my sons. Lord Manvington understands this, and he for his part will do what he thinks proper for Charlotte. So, in short, you may consider yourself a very fortunate young man."

Barney's anger was rising. Since the General had so airily denied his paternity, he had been staring at him in a manner hardly respectful. It was as well the General did not look up from his snuff.

"I can only repeat, sir, I do not wish to marry Lady Charlotte, and I have no reason to suppose she wishes to marry me."

"On the contrary, she has no particular objections. She does not know, perhaps I should say, that anything definite has been arranged. But Lady Manvington sounded her as to whether, *if* the matter should come about, she would be filial and comply. . . . Come now," the General was speaking with apparent good-humour; but this, Barney well knew, was a mere mask to an unswervable determination. "Come now, you are over-modest. We will be straight with one another. Charlotte will be thankful to have a husband, and she might do a lot worse than a randy young fellow like you."

"She is older than I am, much."

"I should not have supposed, from our recent conversation, that that should be an insuperable objection." (Barney looked down at his cuff again.) "Four years older, is she not? What is that? In a few years' time you will not notice it. You shall not have a chance to marry any other Earl's daughter, you know."

"I do not care about marrying an Earl's daughter. Then, besides, she is my cousin."

Mr. Jaspard frowned slightly, but since Barney was supposed, according to the never-uttered theory, to be the son of some fictitious brother of his, he could hardly deny the fact.

"What of that? There is nothing in the rubric that I know of against cousins marrying."

"Why is it to be me? If Lady Charlotte wants to be married, why should she not marry Stephen?—he is near a year older than I am."

"I do not choose for Stephen to marry her." Mr. Jaspard's tone had become very cold. "Stephen will, I should not be surprised, finish by marrying Miss Dale, as we intended."

"I am sorry, sir, but I must refuse to marry her," said Barney, getting to his feet, and immediately feeling he had an advantage over the seated and lame Mr. Jaspard. "And you cannot make me," he added.

"If you mean that only by bringing you bound to the altar and forcing you by torture to make the responses, then I cannot. But let me remind you of this, sir——" Mr. Jaspard, feeling his inferior position, rose too, and limped one step nearer to Barney. "Let me remind you that I have taken you into my family, brought you up since you were an infant, found you the means of livelihood you enjoy, ay! paid for the very coat that is on your back, paid for the lace of your shirt, for every garment on your body. But for me, boy, you would be a pauper."

"And why should you not do all that?" retorted Barney, breathing fast and in a temper that had far outdistanced discretion. "Yes, sir, I owe you all those things, but you forget to mention one thing I owe you. My life itself! And is it not a father's——"

He got no further. Mr. Jaspard, as he had done sixteen years before when the little Barney had called him Papa, slapped him hard across the face.

"How dare you!" he said. "You insolent, good-for-nothing bastard! Get out of my sight, sir, get out of my sight!"

Barney, with a red mark vivid across his jaw, stared at his father, stupefied for a moment by the suddenness and shock of the blow. Then he bowed slightly.

"I shall be glad to do that, sir."

"No. Wait. Come here!"

Barney, who had reached the door, turned.

"Come here, I said. Don't stand by the door like a footman."

Though he would have liked to escape, Barney had obeyed the General for too many years to shatter all his chains in one evening. He came back into the room and waited, his expression, though he was not aware of this, one of both anger and contempt. For indeed, he despised his father for upbraiding him with his bastardy. The shame was his father's and not his. Or it should be—though in the world it did not work out that way.

Mr. Jaspard was himself a little ashamed of his outburst, though his anger towards Barney for his disrespectful, impudent behaviour was not lessened.

"I wish to tell you that this display of temper on your part makes no difference at all to my plan that you shall marry Lady Charlotte. As I have informed you, no betrothal will be announced at present, so you will have time to grow used to the idea. If you defy me in this matter I shall find means to bring you to heel. . . . Before you go, you will apologize to me."

"I do not see—why I should apologize—for speaking the truth."

Barney did not feel so bold as he sounded. He only dared to argue with the General because he believed that if he could push their present quarrel to a break, it might save him much trouble and unpleasantness in the future. The General might—certainly would—dock him of his meagre allowance, but he could hardly, for a whim, get him turned out of the Office of Trade and Plantations. And behind him, with her full and far more generous purse, stood Phillis. . . .

"It evidently does not occur to you," said Mr. Jaspard, speaking calmly now, but with a cutting contempt, "that it is not upon my own account I have taught you to look upon me as your uncle. Were you to bandy freely another relationship between us, you at once offer Mrs. Jaspard a humiliation that I cannot allow from you. That is why—and I leave aside your unbecomingly insolent manner to me—I demand an apology of you. You owe Mrs. Jaspard much, whether you care to admit it or not."

Barney had an impulse to answer that he owed Mrs. Jaspard nothing, but a moment's reflection made him hold his tongue. The assertion was at least arguable, for, though she had always disliked him, in material considerations he had in his boyhood shared equally with her own children.

He capitulated, and said ungraciously: "I am sorry, sir."

Mr. Jaspard inclined his head in acknowledgement that he had heard; then, shaking out the lace of his cuffs, he reseated himself.

Barney turned to go, but before he could reach the door, it opened and Mrs. Jaspard came in.

"Oh—I did not know you were here, Barnabas."

"Barney is on the point of leaving, I believe. I have been telling him of our plans for him and Lady Charlotte, and he has upset himself a little over the matter."

"You will certainly make no better match," said Mrs. Jaspard to Barney in a tone that suggested he would have difficulty in getting any lady of breeding to marry him. To her husband she added: "I have told Thomas to bring your madeira in here, and my tea also. I did not think you would wish to trouble yourself to move into the drawing-room with Delia and me. Is the pain easier?"

Mr. Jaspard did not reply to her inquiry as at that moment the footman came in with a tray containing his master's usual evening madeira and biscuits, and a pot of tea with a plate of bread and butter for his mistress.

"You will take a glass before you go, Barney," said Mr. Jaspard. "Thomas has provided for you." His tone could not be said to be friendly, but it was the polite one of a host to a guest.

"No thank you, sir," said Barney.

"Sulkiness is the attribute of a child, Barnabas. It is high time you outgrew it." Mrs. Jaspard poured her tea while she delivered this rebuke.

"I beg your pardon, madam. I was on my way out when you came in and, with your leave, I will go."

"As you wish. Good night."

"We will see you on Sunday," said Mr. Jaspard, making a statement and not asking a question.

Barney hesitated for a moment. "No, sir, I cannot come on Sunday."

"Cannot!" said Mrs. Jaspard. "You will do what Mr. Jaspard tells you."

"Mr. Jaspard, madam, has been reminding me that I am a poor man. And, since I ceased to live under your roof, your footmen now expect vails from me when I come to dine, and the truth is I cannot afford it every week."

Although this was, both to Mr. Jaspard and his wife, an obvious excuse, it was also true that to Barney it was a long-standing grievance he had never before this dared to air. Sometimes, because he could so ill spare it, he failed—or pretended that he failed—to see the hands greedily curved by the footmen's sides as they ranged up to let him out upon a Sunday evening. It mattered not whether one was son or foster-son, upon leaving home one was expected to pay for those services that formerly the footmen rendered freely as to a member of the household. To his surprise Mr. Jaspard laughed. "Well! well! here's a guinea for you, so poor as you are!"

"I will take it," said Barney coolly, "for another time. But this Sunday I have an engagement."

"You are an impudent dog," said Mr. Jaspard, repocketing his guinea. But he sounded less ferocious than might have been expected.

"Impudent and ungrateful," Mrs. Jaspard corroborated as Barney left the room.

When the door had closed, Mr. Jaspard said: "He is the most difficult of all my brood to manage. Indeed, there's a great deal of my own spirit in him, but a streak I do not like so well which I suspect he gets from the other side of the family."

"Mr. Jaspard," said his wife, in an indignant, tremulous voice, "I must ask you not to mention that boy's parentage in my presence. I always said there was bad blood. His sister——"

"Silence, Melissa! I will not hear her name spoken."

Mrs. Jaspard, with a high colour, drank her tea. She made no attempt to disobey her husband.

He said, in a cruel, teasing way that he only occasionally adopted towards her now: "Are you not proud of the young gentleman who is to be the Lady Charlotte's husband? If it had not been for *you*, my dear, he would no doubt now be a journeyman in some trade or other, if he were not carting hay in a dairy in Paddington."

"His mother was a common woman, then?" Mrs. Jaspard had as much curiosity as any of her children as to the type of person this unknown female had been.

"I did not say so," answered Mr. Jaspard suavely. "She wished to desert her children, and they would, consequently, have been brought up at the expense of the parish and set to earning a livelihood at thirteen. Hrrm!" he sneezed over a pinch of snuff. "That reminds me, I saw the notice of your—your lover's death in the news-sheet a week or so ago."

"He was not my lover." Mrs. Jaspard stared into her tea-cup. She could feel no emotion now for the man who had excited her so many years ago. She was thinking, with some bitterness: If Robert had loved me as he ought, I should never have wanted or needed the admiration of another man.

"But you would have liked him to have been," said Mr. Jaspard.

The tears came into her eyes. "Why are you so unkind to me? It was only your neglect——"

"Egad!" he interrupted good-humouredly, "it is late in the day for us to be quarrelling over that old history. . . . Pour me out another glass, if you please, my dear. It is irksome for me to move. Confound this foot!"

In the hall Barney paused and looked at his watch. Half past ten. It was too late to go and talk to Miss Finch; very probably she was going to bed. He had not seen her alone since the night he had burst into her room. The next Sunday, as he had said he would do, he had taken Kitty with him to the nursery, but as they had ostensibly come to see the children, and Kitty, he felt, was watching him with unusual interest, he had not been able to address any words to Miss Finch—at least, none that had not to do with her charges. As he was leaving, however, he had contrived to give her a significant smile. Miss Finch's white skin had turned pink, and she had lowered her eyes.

He wondered whether he should have a word with Delia, who must be alone in the drawing-room with her unending embroidery, or a book. But he decided against this. She would not particularly wish to see him, and would probably make some such sour remark as that it would purify his character were he to take the smallpox and endure the pain and the fear that were inseparable from the illness. No, he had had enough for one evening of Jaspards looking down their noses at him.

When he got back to Bond Street he gave Phillis an uncandid account of his conversation with Mr. Jaspard. He admitted that the General assumed him to be living with her in no state of innocency, but he forebore to reveal the more derogatory remarks he had made upon the matter. Of the quarrel he had had with his father when the latter had struck him and called him a bastard, he made no mention at all. For Phillis, he was sure, did not as yet suspect his illegitimacy, and he was in no hurry to enlighten her. It was only on the subject of his coming betrothal to Lady Charlotte that he was perfectly frank. At first Phillis looked grave and sad, but upon his declaring that never, never would he marry his long-faced, stupid cousin, she smiled again, and told him—what indeed he had hoped to hear—that if he suffered financially through defiance of his uncles, she would assist him to the utmost of her power.

This seemed a good opening to a subject Barney had been wanting to bring forward ever since he had renewed his association with her; but one that must wait upon the right moment and not be rushed into with indecent haste or indiscretion.

In short, it was the subject of South Sea shares. Barney, with unusual eloquence, sketched out the reasons why this stock must continue rising, and foretold that had he but a few hundreds to invest he could make himself independent of Mr. Jaspard for the rest of his days. It was a chance that came to a man but once in a lifetime—and a woman too; for Phillis should reap in this rich harvest also. It *could* not fail. He cited to her tales he had heard: how this one had cleared £1,000 in five days; how that one had made since January a fortune of £130,000. . . . Phillis, who heard him out until he had exhausted his persuasions, and very nearly his breath, said rather sadly:

"I know little of money, Corydon; that is, how it comes, how it grows. But I could not help you if I would. All the money I have, the jointure from my late husband and a small fortune I inherited from my father, is in the care of trustees. I am not allowed to draw out of the Funds in which it is invested any large sum of money. Indeed, unless I go before my trustees and explain the reason of my need for it, I can draw no extraordinary sum. I have money enough for everyday uses, Corydon, and to give you presents and to save you all expenses, but hundreds of pounds to put in the stocks I cannot give you."

"I understand," said Barney somewhat surlily. "Well, but ont hundred pounds. That is not so extraordinary a sum."

"No, Corydon. I am sorry. But you will appreciate surely that I am not too anxious to have my trustees questioning me closely as to why, suddenly, I am spending quite a lot more money than I have been doing in recent months. They will think nothing of it in the ordinary way: suppose I have increased my household—as indeed I have," she smiled at him, "but if I start asking for sums of money over and above my income, they must begin inquiring into my way of living—need I say more, Corydon?"

"But you could say you wanted the money to buy shares for yourself," he urged, still loth to relinquish his dream of easy riches.

"They certainly would not allow me to do that. I told you, I may not touch the investments. Corydon, dear, does it mean so very much to you?"

He swallowed his very bitter disappointment and assured Phillis it did not matter a thing in the world; it was an idea that had occurred to him, he would think no more of it. Since it was not true that he cared for Phillis only because of her money, he was very anxious that she should not believe it to be so. He began to talk to her of more agreeable matters.

Thus it was that when the South Sea Bubble broke four months later, Barney had in it only a small sum saved from his salary, and Phillis was untouched by the calamity that overwhelmed hundreds of homes.